# THE
# WALLS
# OF
# JOLO

# Alan Caillou

# THE WALLS OF JOLO

*Appleton-Century-Crofts, Inc.*
*New York*

Copyright © 1960 by Ted Loeff

PRINTED IN THE UNITED STATES OF AMERICA

# THE
# WALLS
# OF
# JOLO

It was a war which need never have been fought at all. It began in hysteria, and it ended in bewilderment; and it accomplished practically nothing.

But when it should have been over, it was then that the fighting really started—against a different and unexpected enemy. The casualties, which had been negligible, began to mount alarmingly. The fighting went on, and on, and on. It seemed that it would never stop.

The struggle for the control of the Philippines began at 5:41 A.M. on May 1, 1898, when Commodore George Dewey, from the bridge of his flagship Olympia in Manila Bay, gave the terse order, "You may fire when you are ready, Gridley." Thus began the assault on the pitiful Spanish vessels of Admiral Montojo. It ended, a few hours later, with the complete destruction of the Armada.

It was a pathetic little farce that put an end to Spanish presumptions of Empire in the Pacific. The press had their heroes, and the war was over.

But was it?

In the huge masses of the Islands, so far removed from insular American ken that even the President admitted he did not know, until he searched his globe, where they were, the Filipinos promptly took advantage of their overlords' defeat and declared their independence.

Washington was astonished, indignant, and angry too. When the occupying Army landed to preach, hopefully, its gospel of happiness under a distant sovereign, the native temper was ripe for hostility. Overnight, the ludicrous Spanish-American war, the objects of which were at least clearly definable, had drifted into a series of skirmishes which were prompted by nebulous misunderstandings and indeterminable hatreds.

The skirmishes grew into battles. The Army met force with force, until the whole population was in armed revolt against the new exarchy.

The list of hostile tribes seemed inexhaustible: Ibanag, Ilokano, Pangasinan, Tagalog, Visayan—these, it seemed, were all Christians of a sort; there were the Ilongots, Negritos, Kalingas, Kankanais, and Bontoks, who were all pagans with their own separate beliefs rooted in the depths of prehistory; and there were the Moros, the Mohammedans whom the Spanish had contemptuously branded (as they locked themselves in terror of them behind their stone walls) as Moors. These were the pirates who came from the southwest, many centuries ago, and who sprang, it seemed, from the roots of a bamboo. The Moros had brought to the archipelago which they had conquered a heritage of violence, of rapine, and of unbridled ferocity.

They had no cohesion, these varied peoples, because never in their history had they been anything more than heterogeneous and mutually warring tribes; but one thing brought them together—the occupation of their country by a bewildered American Army which could not understand why the seed of its benevolence brought forth nothing but hatred. Happiness, peace, and prosperity could only be thrust upon the tribes by force of arms, and after two years of guerrilla activity, General Arthur MacArthur, who had taken over the Philippines as Governor-General, was constrained to insist that forty-five thousand troops were needed for the pacification *of the Islands. Even this was not enough; when the strength of the garrison grew to seventy thousand men, some of them could reflect that the number originally considered sufficient for the reduction of Spain in the Pacific had been less than twelve thousand effectives.*

*The fighting continued.*

*This was the background against which a Captain of the Twenty-third Infantry, stationed on the Moro island of Sulu at the southern extremity of the Territory, played out his fatal drama.*

*He was a career officer who was highly regarded by his superiors. His home was in Richmond, Virginia, and he had come to the Islands with Brigadier-General Greene's expedition on the transport Zealandia in the summer of 1898. This was his third year of combat against the Moros.*

*He was tall, awkwardly built, and—except in the heat of battle —slow-moving and cautious. He was well liked by his brother officers, but he always held himself a little aloof from them.*

*He was in his late thirties, and he was a man of competence, of integrity, and of courage.*

*His name was Shay Sullivan.*

# 1.

THERE WAS SOMETHING AWESOME IN THE SILENCE THAT SURROUNDED them.

Shay Sullivan could feel the damp of the sweat in the palm of his hand, and he rubbed it along the polished red stock of his lance. When he shifted his position and cleared his throat to break the oppression of the silence, the Brigadier looked across at him with an impatient, sidelong glance that clearly implied his distaste.

Sullivan bit his lip and said nothing. They sat in the shadows without motion, the others, as though they were part of the forest on whose fringes they had found relief from the rising heat of the new sun while they waited for the native beaters to come through. They looked like the twisted knots of mangrove stump which they had left far behind them on the long haul up from the coastal slopes below, like gnarled clumps of deadwood, shaded by the mottled foliage, that somehow had taken the weird shapes of crouching men. It was as if the forest itself had spewed them up out of the ground. Watching them, he could feel the strange pain that writhed deep down inside him, low in his loins. He knew that it was excitement; but he feared, as he always feared, that it might be fear itself.

It was often like this, the moment before the final climax of danger came upon him. When the silence of the waiting became unbearable, then it was always into his loins that the knife of apprehension struck, twisting itself and tearing his bowels open until the borderline of fear had passed. And then, there was nothing to do but break the spell by breaking the silence.

Close by them, the tall trees seemed to support a stifling blanket of dark green high in the air above them, providing a pleasant shade that turned, a little deeper among the thorns, to a somber darkness in which the long lianas still dripped with the slime of the night, although the sun had been up for more than two hours.

Had it? Sullivan took the heavy gold watch from the pocket under his military belt and stared at it, wondering about the work that was waiting for him back at the camp, wondering if he'd ever get to it. There was the casualty report to send in. There was the letter from the Adjutant-General in Washington about the men of the Fourteenth Regiment who had married Filipino women. There was the cable from General Kobbe about the "important" surrender of the guerrillas on Mindanao . . .

One Colonel, three Lieutenant-Colonels, one Major, five Captains, twelve Lieutenants, 245 men, 223 rifles . . . surrender unconditional . . . believe this surrender will influence hostile forces other sections of province to surrender . . .

He thought bitterly about the General's hopeful assumption of mass surrenders, and about the guerrillas' arrogant presumption of military rank; Colonels in bare feet and Majors in gaudy turbans. Almost subconsciously, he brushed at the top of his highly polished boot, feeling his scorn for them. He thought angrily: *Some other hostile forces may surrender, but not here. The lucky ones in the north will soon be on the transports back to San Francisco, but here . . . here we'll stay till the end of history.* Kobbe was fighting the northern islanders, but here on Sulu they were fighting, instead, against an anachronistically primitive race, against the Moros. They were fighting, instead, against fearless, violent men who respected no authority, not even that of their own Sultan; men to whom the arts of war were second nature, men to whom the final exultation lay only in the swift precise slicing of flesh and in the

[ 6 ]

free red flow of human blood; for this moment in their history, it was American blood, because the Americans were there and were easy to kill, but any blood would do.

He hated them, and he hated himself because he knew that he too was competent only in war.

The Brigadier was frowning at him across the dry grass, and he looked away toward Colonel Ericsson, who was standing quietly by the horses tethered to bamboo clumps and champing at the cogon grasses under their hoofs. They were Filipino ponies, much smaller than American horses, and wiry, with tight, gleaming muscles; they could gallop on a mountain trail where not even a mule could find its way.

Beyond, he could see the huge pile of volcanic lava that was Mount Tumangtanis, the Shedder of Tears, twenty-five hundred feet high, cold and bare at its purple top, but warm with bright rich greens on its lower slopes.

Then the call came to them out of the forest, a high-pitched sound like the note of a horn, repeated twice. The others clambered to their feet and turned their heads in the direction of the sound. It came again, and the Colonel looked over to him and raised his eyebrows. He shook his head, waiting, holding his hand up for silence. The call was repeated, three short whoops this time, then taken up again on their flank to the south. He pointed to the north and said quickly, "That's it, gentlemen. Over here. First heat to the north by the gully, second heat to the east of the first."

They ran to their horses then, all except the Brigadier who had to be helped up on his mount because of his great weight. The ponies, well-balanced back on their hocks, pranced excitedly while the riders set their lances, knowing the sound of the call, knowing the feel of the lance-boot, knowing that the pig hunt was about to begin and enjoying it almost as much as the men.

The Colonel looked across at the Brigadier, who nodded, and then turned to him and said briefly, "Captain Sullivan."

He looked back at the Colonel. "Better get the first heat at the edge of the forest, sir. The boar will come out about . . . about there." He pointed with his lance, feeling the perfect balance of it, testing it lightly with a delicate twist of the wrist.

[ 7 ]

"All right," the Colonel said, accepting the courtesy of command from the acknowledged expert. "You take the first heat, I'll take the second. Four horses each. I'll back you up." Lowering his voice, he added: "Of course, the Brigadier will take the first run."

Sullivan smiled, a little sourly. "Of course."

He swung round in the saddle as the Brigadier came cantering over, a lumpish porpoise of a man, shiny-faced, squatting awkwardly on his McLellan saddle with his pudgy legs sticking ludicrously out at the sides, his belt loosened under the flaccid corpulence of his paunch. The sweat was dripping down to the end of his nose. The Brigadier said, pointing to Sullivan's long spear, "I want to see this, Sullivan. You're not sticking pegs, you know."

Sullivan was thinking: *You'll see, porpoise.* He said, "The Bombay spear . . . It's very efficient."

The Brigadier said, "I know that. I know a Bombay spear when I see one. It's good for pegs, for sport, for a static target. If the boar's charging, he'll unhorse you."

Sullivan shrugged, smiling. "Depends how well you sit a horse, doesn't it? Catch him low down, it's easy enough."

"He'll throw you."

"No, sir."

The Brigadier's pony, a light chestnut, was prancing impatiently. Sullivan said maliciously, "If you'd like to try it, sir?" It was almost a challenge.

The others all carried the conventional jobbing spear, only five feet long. He saw the Brigadier's pig eyes, almost lost in the puffy red flesh of his cheeks, staring narrowly at the Bombay lance, weighing its values. The Colonel said, "Hadn't we better get into position, Sullivan?"

"Waiting for the final signal, Jed."

"I see."

"I was just suggesting to the Brigadier that he might like to try my spear. It's the only one of its kind in the Garrison."

"Too dangerous," the Colonel said affably. "We'll stick to the tools we know best. Leave the experiments to the experts."

The last signal came from the beaters then, three long whoops from the darkness of the forest; the sound of them had moved a little to the south. Sullivan dug in his heels and shouted, "To me . . . first heat!"

They wheeled into position, charging across the flat ground close to the trees, the dust and the sand and the dead twigs flying up under their hoofs. It was a moment of elation after the long wait in the silence, and even the ponies felt it. They reached a point where Sullivan guessed the boar would come out of cover, then reined sharply round in answer to his signal and pulled in their horses sharply, feeling the sure-footedness of them as they jinked round into position and sidestepped to a distance of twenty paces.

There were four, side by side, watching.

There was Shay Sullivan, Captain, Twenty-third Infantry, detached from Headquarters at Manila and assigned to the Garrison on Sulu (Jolo) Island. He was tall, powerfully muscled, with long legs loosely jointed; it made him walk awkwardly so that his limbs seemed to have the uncoordinated volition of stilts. Astride his light-gray stallion, his feet seemed almost to brush the ground. His face was leathery, and the somber set of his mouth made him appear older than his thirty-odd years.

There was Withers, a journalist, one of six at the camp who were always under the feet and in the hair of the military. He was a silent, uncouth man, suffering his cold association with the gentlemanly officers of the garrison because of his urgent need to tell his readers back home that the Spanish-American War was not yet over in spite of the Spanish surrender and in spite of the Treaty of Paris. American boys were still being killed in the Philippines, and he had joined the pig hunt because he wanted to tell his readers what the officers of the Army were doing while the boys were roughing it in camp and facing the nightly terror of the Moros. As he sat his horse awkwardly, envying the easy competence of the others, he was framing scornful phrases in his mind because his editor liked a little anger in his dispatches.

There was Baroni, Lieutenant of the Battalion of Engineers, an ardent Catholic who had been transferred to Sulu to supervise the construction of the tiny blockhouses which the missionaries had prevailed upon the Army to build along the southern shores of Sulu from Tu'tu Bay to the Sultan's town of Maymbung. He was young, impetuous, naive, and full of priestly zeal.

And lastly, there was the Brigadier, a short, fat, bad-tempered career officer who knew that one day he would command the whole Archipelago. His temper was not improved by his forced association with the journalist Withers, but Adjutant-General Corbin, in Washington, had had some harsh words to say about the offhand treatment the press was getting in the Islands; he knew very well, and he knew that Corbin knew it too, that this was a lot of nonsense. He felt that the press was doing its damndest to keep the spectacle of the war going because wars made heroes and heroes sold newspapers, but he had resigned himself to the necessity of treating them, even a wretched fellow like Withers, as a fellow officer. He sat his horse like a pink dumpling balanced precariously atop an impatiently dancing cat.

They all stared at the forest and waited, watching for the sudden flurry of ill-temper that would be the boar coming out and at them.

Behind them, the gully widened out into a broad river bed, quite dry at this time of the year, where the white pebbles lay bleaching in the sun. There, the second heat of four horses waited, with the bamboo flowering lacily above their heads, four men standing by to take over when the first heat had failed, not moving till then, in strict accord with the rules of the game. There was Colonel Jed Ericsson, a mild, good-natured, efficient man from the Fourth U.S. Cavalry, which had not been brigaded, detached, like Sullivan, to serve with the Headquarters Staff on Sulu; and Major Pattman, a small, nervous man who could never be sure that he was doing the right thing, and therefore spoiled his accustomed easiness with sudden uneasy smiles. There was Major Wentworth, a stoop-shouldered giant who never spoke unless he had to, and then only in monosyllables. And there was Lieutenant Stiles, a young blond boy from Minnesota, who believed fiercely that the Army was the only possible life for a man, and who wanted, one day, to be a Scout. He was young and he was eager, full of the bright innocence of youth. They sat their ponies close together, bunching up under the shade and watching the first heat, holding their lances upright, watching too for the sudden onrush of the boar and feeling the vicarious excitement as the others waited, listening for the angry sound of the charge and hoping that they would get a chance to go in for the kill.

It was Captain Sullivan who heard it first. It was a rustling in the shrubbery a hundred and fifty yards away from them, and then the big boar charged out, snorting, his porcine eyes aflame even at this distance, ears pricked back, huge tusks gleaming, and his cuneiform head lowered so that the wet underside of his snout brushed the dead leaves under the trees. He was a big one, standing three good feet at the shoulder, and weighing, no doubt, more than two hundred and fifty pounds, a *sus cristatus* which some of the servants called a Soor . . . the crested killer that could rip a man wide open with one quick slash of its foot-long tusks. It pawed at the ground for an instant, and then took off across their front at incredible speed; its hoofs pounded the hard ground.

Sullivan resisted the temptation to drive his heels into his pony's flanks. Instead, he said to the Brigadier, quite calmly now that the hunt was on, "Your boar, sir."

The Brigadier swung his pony round. There was a bright light in his eyes that was partly, Sullivan thought, pure malice. Holding up his short jobbing spear, he shouted, "Catch, Sullivan. Give me yours."

The spear came at him before he was ready for it, but he leaned far over in his saddle and fumbled with the left hand, catching it before it hit the ground. As he dropped the reins, the Brigadier said impatiently, "Come on, man, give me your lance. The long one."

There was a brief moment in which he saw that the journalist Withers was watching him closely, and then he swung his arm up and over and sent the long Bombay spear, leaded haft foremost, over to where the Brigadier was waiting to catch it. He was momentarily surprised as the pudgy arm came up and caught it expertly, and then the plump pink dumpling wobbled for a moment and took off after the boar.

He had time to shout an urgent warning. "Underarm, sir. Underarm!"

"I know that, you fool!"

He was gone. Scornful of the weight on its back, the tiny horse was charging forward, ears back, nostrils dilated, its mane flying and the muscles on its flank catching the sunlight. The Brigadier was tucking the long lance under his armpit, its point close to the ground and the colored ribbons of the haft waving behind him and above his head, too high above. Withers closed in until his horse was touching Sullivan's flank. Not taking his eyes off the Brigadier, Sullivan murmured, "If he lowers that point another inch, he's in trouble."

"Isn't that what you want?"

Sullivan turned to him in surprise. "How's that?"

"I said: Isn't that what you want? I saw the look on your face when you offered to let him try it."

"So?"

"He knew you were taunting him. It was as clear as daylight."

"You're a fool, Withers. He's stuck more pigs than you or I will ever see. In spite of his bulk."

"Yes. With a jobbing spear."

"How come you know about lances?"

"It's my job to know."

"It's your job to make trouble."

"Like the trouble the Brigadier's going to be in if he lowers that point?"

"He didn't have to accept."

"No. But you knew he would."

"Go to hell, Withers."

Withers scowled at him, thinking up the right phrase for his dispatch.

Sullivan said coolly, "You're next. Give the Brigadier two passes and then ride in. Baroni follows you, I follow Baroni."

"The expert."

"If one of us doesn't get him, the second heat will. The Colonel's better than any of us."

The sun was already beating its fierceness at them, even though they were in shade. It seemed to search out and find the brighter patches of the yellow grass and bounce its heat back up at them. The purple top of Tumangtanis had lost its shadows to the red glare of the lava, and there was a solitary cloud poised above it like a tuft of kapok in the blinding blue of the sky.

The Brigadier had overtaken the boar now and was wheeling his pony round to face the charge. As they watched, they knew that he was showing off his expertise, taking the quarry from the fore instead of the side. Sullivan, suddenly worried, shook his head and waited.

They were fifty yards apart now, the pig still moving fast to the cover he had selected, and they heard the hunting-cry as the Brigadier dug in his heels and the pony burst forward, scarcely checking its gait as it jinked round on its hind legs.

Then the two of them met, head-on. The tip of the long lance dropped, the pink dumpling swayed, and the boar swerved with quick cunning, ripping at the pony's hoofs. There was an instant of astonishment, and then Sullivan lunged forward, shouting to the others to stay clear, as he saw the Brigadier, thrown from the perch of his saddle, seeming to dangle high in the air like a pole-vaulter, with the long lance bedded into the ground below him as the haft went on and over. The sound as the plump body smacked into the hard earth beside the wounded pony was unbearable, and Sullivan knew that he could not recover in time to meet the second charge of the angered boar. He swung into action.

He saw the pig check itself on short, stubby legs, driving its forefeet into the sand, then turn quickly in a flurry of dust, turn to face the unhorsed Brigadier. He galloped forward with the short lance raised, yelling as he went: "Stay where you are, sir!" He saw the Brigadier stumble to his feet and cursed him as he reared up his horse to clear, jabbing downward at the black swift movement below him in the same split second of time. This was a wise pig, and one that had been hunted many times before. It slipped under the pony's belly, and with a sick spasm of revulsion Sullivan felt his mount stumble and fall.

As he threw himself sideways, he saw the Brigadier's violently angry face, heard him screaming, "Get back, you fool, he's mine!"

Then he was falling, and the Brigadier was on the ground underneath him, pushing him clear, and from the corner of his eye he could see the pig coming at them. He fancied he could see the malevolence in its tiny eyes. His lance had struck it a glancing blow among the bristles that stood up along the spine. He had felt the shock as it had struck and turned on the shoulder blade, and he could see the shiny patch of blood on the dirty gray flank. He leaped to the side as it went past him, gathering up the fallen short lance in a continuation of the same movement, seeing that his stallion's leg was broken, seeing that the Brigadier was still on the ground beside him.

The boar was whirling on him again, and there was a moment of panic when he saw the awesome size of it and knew that he was standing, unhorsed, at close range, to face it. And then the skill came back to him and he spread his legs and waited, the lance held overarm with its point steady and motionless three feet in front of him.

As the pig came in he leaned forward and out, and placed the steel tip almost delicately at the edge of the hairy neck, throwing his weight onto the haft, swinging sideways as he felt it go in, deep into the chest. He swung to the side, losing the lance, feeling the breath of the animal as he sidestepped the tusk that came ripping at him. The pig was dying now, but it was not yet dead. It whirled and came at him again, the lance sticking forward out of its chest, spurting blood. He took his own long lance quickly, the Bombay spear which had thrown the Brigadier, and lugged it out of the ground, then sidestepped again because there was not room to use it. As the pig went by him, he turned, blinded by a rising anger now, and thrust it with all the strength of his shoulder deep into the black matted hair of the animal's flank, throwing his weight back and pulling the spear free again.

The others were riding up now, Withers and Baroni, yelling and swinging out to draw the pig off him. He saw Withers foolishly getting off his pony, and he shouted angrily, "Get back on your horse!"

The boar came at him for the last time, the blood pumping in little short spurts onto the sand. He raised the lance to the overarm position and thrust it forward and down, its sharp steel point ten feet in front of him. There was a fierce jubilation inside him as he felt the soft quelching when the blade struck home, missing the broad shoulder blade and burying itself deep into the fleshy part of the chest. He felt the sudden softness when it reached the loins, and the weight of the charge sent him sprawling off his feet, clutching the haft of his spear and fighting the violent motion of it, feeling the edge of the blade slicing through the intestines. He was up again in a reflex instant, hauling his weapon out and thrusting it again and again, savagely, into the bleeding, trembling carcass, conscious of the struggles of the stallion that lay beside him, conscious of the blood that was smeared over his clothes, conscious of the puffy-faced Brigadier who lay still and silent and close to the bloodied side of his horse.

He saw that the Colonel had come riding in and was dismounted. He wondered what had happened to make the second heat interfere, and then someone took him by the arm and shook him, and he saw that Withers was bending down over the Brigadier, ripping a piece off his own shirt. He knew that his mouth was open, and he closed it with an effort.

Baroni pushed past him and crouched down by the Brigadier. He knew then that something terrible had happened, and he said blankly, trying to shake the fog out of his mind, "But . . . but . . . is he all right?"

Baroni looked up grimly. "Right in the belly."

For a moment, he thought that it must be his own lance that Baroni was talking about. Then Withers said angrily, "While you were busy changing lances. Didn't you see it? A tusk in the belly— ripped wide open."

The Brigadier's face was the dirty gray of Army flour. Sullivan knew he was trembling. He said furiously, "But—but I *had* to ride in. He lost his horse. He wasn't used to the long lance. He could have— I thought he'd be killed if I didn't come after him."

Withers looked at him, saying nothing. He could feel the angry accusation that was in his eyes. The others were milling about them, slipping out of their saddles and pushing forward over the flanks of the two wounded horses, looking at the Brigadier and at the pig that had opened his stomach. The Colonel was down on one knee beside the soft and silent body, pulling open the bloodied trousers and speaking quickly. He said, "We must get him back as fast as we can. Get the men together, Sullivan. Let them cut staves and

[ 15 ]

we'll make a stretcher. Two of you ride on ahead and have the medico come out to meet us. There's nothing we can do here except make him as comfortable as possible and pray that he doesn't recover consciousness. Get the bearers to work, quickly."

Looking up at Sullivan, he said clearly, "And it wasn't your fault. I saw what happened. You were right to ride in when you did. If you hadn't, I'd have done so myself."

"Thank you, Colonel. I was trying to—"

"I know. Get the bearers."

"Yes, sir."

Sullivan knew that the Colonel wanted him away from the silent reproach of the others. He moved a little to one side, gratefully, and cupped his hands to his mouth. In the direction of the forest, he shouted for the bearers.

"Suleiman! Mahasari! Jamalul!"

He waited for their answering call, wondering at the silence, then raised his voice and called again.

"Jamalul! Mahasari! Aliyud!"

There was no reply. He walked to the edge of the forest and shouted again, and then went back to the others and said, "I don't know what's happened to them. Will you lend me a horse, Stiles?"

The Colonel looked up from the work he was doing. A white pad of cloth in one hand and a strip of shirting in the other, he said testily, "What do you mean, you don't know what's happened to them? They were at the edge of the forest a moment ago."

"I called them, Jed, but—"

"Well, call them again, dammit. They should be here, with us. No damned discipline any more. They're probably squatting under the trees getting drunk. Go and find them."

Sullivan looked at his stallion. He said, "The horses, Jed."

"Yes, of course."

He took his rifle from the boot beside the saddle and put one round into each of the two hurt animals. Baroni came over and said, staring at them, "Pity. That was a nice pony of yours."

Sullivan nodded, saying nothing. He swung himself up into Stiles' saddle and rode over to the edge of the trees. He cantered up and down the whole length of the clearing, calling to the bearers

[ 16 ]

repeatedly, and then, worried, rode back to the others. He said grimly, feeling the excitement beginning to build up inside him again, "They've gone. There's not a bearer in sight."

The Colonel was staring at him. After a moment he said lightly, "I see. Well, that can mean only one thing, can't it? How many rifles do we have?"

Looking round at the others, Sullivan made a quick count. He said, "Stiles and I have rifles. Major Wentworth, pistol and saber. Major Pattman, pistol. Baroni?"

Baroni's face was set. "Rifle."

Sullivan looked at the journalist. "Withers?"

Withers spread his hands wide, hopelessly. "I wish someone would tell me what this is all about."

Sullivan said angrily, "Are you armed?"

"No, of course I'm not. I'm a civilian, not a soldier. What's it all about? Where have the Filipinos gone?"

Sullivan turned to the Colonel. He said briefly, "Three rifles, three revolvers, and your own shotgun. One saber, and our lances."

Withers was spluttering at him again, "But the Filipinos—they were here a moment ago. I saw them. We can't carry the Brigadier in without them."

He broke off and stared towards the hill that lay to the south. There was a note of personal triumph in his voice.

"Over there," he said, pointing. "There they are. One of them, anyway."

They stood and watched together, a little group of seven officers, one of them badly hurt, and one civilian. On the crest of the hill, two hundred yards away, a small, slight figure was silhouetted against the brightness of the sun. With the light in their eyes they could not see very much. The Colonel said quickly, "Sullivan! Get him!"

Sullivan flung up his rifle, flipping up the sights at the same time, but before he could get a bead on the target it was gone. He thrust the rifle back into the boot and swung the horse around, preparing to gallop off to the hill. The Colonel said sharply, "No! Better stay with us. There may be a hundred of them up there."

Withers' voice was strained and his face was white. He said hoarsely, "Moros? You mean the Moros?"

Sullivan slid from his mount. He said brusquely, "Well, that's what you came here to write about. You and your colleagues. The war."

Withers swallowed hard. "The war?"

Sullivan said clearly, trying to keep the venom out of his voice, "A raiding party of Moros. They've scared the bearers off, and now they'll come after us. As you've been trying to prove to your damned readers ever since you came here, the war's not over yet."

"But here? We're only a few miles from Jolo."

The Colonel said gently, "If you'd been on the Islands longer, Mr. Withers, you'd know that the Moros have no respect for our Garrison, even within gunshot of it."

Withers said harshly, "Yes—yes, I know that. I didn't expect to meet them here, that's all."

Sullivan said suspiciously, "Oh? What's that meant to indicate?"

Withers had the grace to feel uncomfortable. He said hesitantly, "I—well, I talked to some of the natives in the market. They seemed to think that—that there were none of their raiders around here."

Colonel Ericsson said quietly, "It's not very wise to discuss prospective military movements with the sea-Moros, Mr. Withers, even when it's only an innocent pig hunt. You should know better than that."

"But the sea-Moros—they hate the Moros as much as we do."

"We don't hate them, Mr. Withers. We defend ourselves against them while we try to impress them with our way of life. I think you have been very foolish."

Withers said angrily, "I didn't say I told them where we'd be."

"No, you didn't," Sullivan said unpleasantly. "You forgot to mention that."

The Colonel turned away. He said to Sullivan, "Better get some staves cut for a stretcher. Perhaps Major Wentworth will lend you his saber."

He took the saber and cut some long poles from the bamboo clump where the rest of the horses were tethered. Withers came over to him while he was hacking the ends off them. He said awkwardly, "Look, Captain, you can't hold me responsible for this. I didn't tell anyone we'd be here, and in any case it's the Army's responsibility to see that it keeps out of trouble, not mine."

"We'll need your jacket for the litter, Withers."

"Yes—yes, of course."

The journalist stripped off his coat and began removing the stuff from the pockets: a rolled-up sheaf of papers, some pencils, a wallet of money, his identity card. He said slowly, "Of course, this might be a false alarm, don't you think?"

"No. I don't."

"The Filipinos could have just lit out."

"It's their payday tomorrow."

"Well then—"

"Yes?"

Withers raised his hands. "I—I just don't know."

Sullivan hacked savagely at the ends of the bamboo poles, wondering why the devil Wentworth didn't keep his saber properly sharpened. He said angrily, "Well I do. The bearers have seen something they don't like. They're scared stiff of the Moros. They've had God knows how many years of their raids. They've seen a prahu down on the beach, or they've seen some footprints in the forest, or—your guess is as good as mine. But they've been scared off one way or the other, and that means only one thing. It means they're all around us, Withers, waiting for the right moment to hit us. And when they do that we'll be fighting for our goddam lives. It'll give you a good story, anyway."

He knew that Withers would seize upon the implication, which he had not intended to make, that they would, somehow, come through it all alive. Before he could correct the impression, Withers said quickly, appealing for comfort, "When we get back to Jolo?"

Sullivan said somberly, "We may not, Withers. We may not."

He knew that he ought to be giving comfort, but he knew also that the same fear that was in Withers was in him too, even if it were not so easily visible. He hated himself for it, knowing that he would be frightened until the final moment. He knew that when the fighting started he would fight better than any of them, better even

[ 19 ]

than the coolly efficient Colonel, because all the waiting that went before would build up inside him a determination to stifle his cowardice, and that this would blind him to anything except the overpowering need to lash out with whatever weapon he could lay his hands on, with his feet and his fists if need be, to fight like a madman, to fight like one of the Moros' own juramentados, within whom the urge to kill was so strong that they went on fighting even after their hearts had been bayonetted out of their bodies.

It was this that disturbed him so deeply; the knowledge that he would fight with a desperate, savage abandon after a long and painful period of terror, the kind of terror that gnawed at your vitals all the more painfully because you had to hide it. It had happened before, and it would happen again. It always happened.

And he did not know which he despised the more, his cowardice or his bravery.

They had cut two long poles from the giant yellow bamboo and had lashed them, one on either side, to the saddles of the two best ponies, Pattman's little sorrel and the mare that Stiles had been riding. Between the poles, a horse's breadth apart, a cord of bejuco vine had been woven into a crude webbing, and this had been padded with the men's jackets. The solid plump body of the Brigadier, its rosy pink changed now to a parchment pallidity, had been carefully placed dead center in the slung hammock where the irregular motion of the two animals would be felt the least; and Stiles had been detailed to lead them.

The tiny column moved slowly along the ridge of the long-dead cone that a million years ago had bubbled out of this boiling rock and then frozen into immobility so that a million years later an Army detail, consisting of eight men and six horses, could thread its hesitant way over the cold gray cinders. The forest folded back as they moved, giving way to open bush where the clumps of yellow gorse were spiked with dark green thorns. It closed in on them again as they moved in uneasy silence, looking over their shoulders into the darkness of the bushes, watching for a betraying movement from the Moros who, they knew, were watching them closely; and knowing too that there would be no betraying movement, that all would be stillness and silence until the last pain-filled moment when the air would suddenly be rent with a thousand terrible shrieks.

The Colonel was out in front; tall, erect, cool, secure in the knowledge that even now he was in complete control, knowing that every second of respite was another second of life for the men under his command, knowing that they were trained, and skilled, and fearless men of his own Second Division of whom he could be justly proud. Behind him, on his left and right flank respectively, Wentworth and Baroni followed, each deeply preoccupied with his own thoughts, their sturdy ponies, lightly reined, picking their way with delicate feet. Stiles walked behind them, leading the two horses between which the litter was slung; the reins were slack in the crook of his arm, and his rifle was loosely held in his right hand, his campaign hat pushed to the back of his blond head and the traces of sun-blisters scarring the snub scoop of his nose.

Then came Withers, on foot, angry because they had taken his horse and made him walk, knowing they had done this because he was just another civilian in an Army world and therefore not entitled to any consideration. He bit his lip as he limped along, worrying about the expensive shoes he wore, which he had bought on his last trip to San Francisco. Across from him, on the right flank, Major Pattman walked, loping along in the peculiar gait that distinguished him so comically from the others, and behind, in the center, on the other horse, Sullivan rode rear-guard, keeping his distance, letting the column get ahead and then cantering quickly forward to prance from side to side as the distance between them grew slowly once more and he could close it again with a quick spurt forward. Once, he drew his rifle from its boot and rode into the forest after a sudden bright flash of red silk that he was sure could be nothing but a Moro's turban. But the gaudy splash of color rose with a whirr from the bushes and made off on the wing, just one of the thousand unnamed birds that displayed their brilliant feathers against the trees. Once, he was sure he heard them calling to each other, and he rode forward quickly and told the Colonel; but Colonel Ericsson, who had been fighting Moros for a long time now, merely smiled at him and nodded, and, rebuffed, he dropped back into position to ruminate on the fact that when they came out of hiding there would be a shriek of defiance, and that this would be the only noise they would hear; until that moment, there would be no sound of them, no sight of them, and no smell of them. Even though they lurked in their bright clothes among the variegated greens and moved solidly in a body as the column itself moved, keeping up with them, watching them, and hating them.

Withers, panting now with the exertion, stumbled over to walk beside him. He said reproachfully, "I'm not used to this sort of thing. They should have let me keep the pony."

Sullivan knew there was a fight building up inside him. He said, trying to keep his temper under control, "We're two horses short, Withers. If there's a fight you'll be glad the soldiers are mounted. Fighting Moros is just like sticking pigs."

Determined to fight, Withers said angrily, "And all this started with a gleam of malice."

"How's that?"

"A gleam in your eye. I told you I'd seen it."

Sullivan was shocked into anger. "You're trying to blame this on me? Is that it?"

"If he'd used his own lance he wouldn't have fallen. And if you'd let him tackle the pig alone who knows? But no, you had to charge in there like an excited schoolboy and throw your weight about."

"God blast you, Withers, you know damn well that's not true. If I hadn't ridden in—"

"How the hell do you know, Sullivan? You trying to tell me you knew what you were doing?"

It hit him like the smack of a bullet. *Is this true?* he asked himself, knowing that he could only ask it because he had himself suspected it. *Is it true that in the heat of battle I lose control to the extent that . . .*

He said harshly, "There's not much time to stop and think when you're fighting, Withers. Whether it's a pig or a savage, you don't have that much time."

Withers, screwing up his eyes and squinting at him, had won his point. He said softly, "That's exactly what I mean. It's a reflex, isn't it? Hit out hard at whatever's in the way."

"Is that so inexcusable?"

"Yes, Captain. It's inexcusable. Stop and think about it some time."

The menace of the forest was too strong. He said slowly, "I won't fight with you, Withers. I will if we ever get out of this alive, which I doubt, but I won't fight you now. You may be right, at that."

Withers was swallowing his fear. "I am right, Sullivan. Think about it and you'll know damn well I'm right."

"So get back into position. The left rear flank, remember?"

The tension that was between them lost its tautness as Withers, mumbling to himself, stumbled back to the edge of the convoy. Sullivan, pushing the thought to the back of his mind, took a long drink from his canteen, and then, seeing the sweat on Withers' face and knowing that it was not all fear, called out gently, "Better take a drink, Withers. You're sweating too much."

The journalist looked at him and said nothing. He was thinking: *A good soldier. One of the best. Is this why I hate his guts? But I'm right. A man should fight because he knows it's right to fight; but that one fights because it comes as naturally to him as it does to a goddam Moro. And he hasn't the sense to know it. Now he's telling me to take a drink because he knows I'm right and he wants to make it up to me. Let him rot in hell.*

He turned away again and unscrewed the metal cap of his canteen; the water tasted sour and salty in his mouth.

There was a sudden scream in the forest close beside him, a sharp piercing yell like the shriek of a madwoman. Withers squealed with fright as the sound of it went to his heart and twisted it into a ball of sudden terror. He dropped the shotgun he was carrying and swung round in apprehension, expecting to see the bright uplifted blade of a barong. Instead, there was only silence again, and the gentle movement of a bush a few yards away. He stared at it, fascinated by his own terror, and he heard Sullivan say, without reproach, "A monkey, Withers, just a monkey."

He picked up his shotgun and wiped the back of his hand across his chin, feeling the cold wetness of his own saliva.

The column moved slowly on. The cogon gave way to a greener grass, and the red lava remained with them only as boulders atop high needle-peaks of granite where the surrounding sandstone had been washed away. They crossed a small stream and stumbled up the muddy bank on the other side, and the Colonel called a halt to let the horses drink. They crouched at the edge of the gently flowing rivulet and refilled their canteens, and Stiles, the practical one, sliced up a lemon he had been carrying and handed them all a piece to squeeze into the water to kill off any pestilence. They spoke little, and when they did it was in subdued tones, as though they were in church. The beauty was still in the forest, but now it had been crudely thrust aside by the naked claw of fear that was poised above them.

The soft body of the Brigadier was motionless and silent. The Colonel felt the pulse at the plump wrist and shook his head, and then they all mounted once more and continued the long trek back to Jolo. From all sides, a hundred pairs of eyes were watching them. Knowing this, they knew also that there was nothing they could do but wait, and keep moving, and hope that a miracle would come to save them.

The column moved slowly on.

# 2.

THE BARRACKS IN THE MILITARY TOWN OF JOLO, OR, AS THE SPAN-
iards used to call it, Xolo, lay to the north in the old walled portion
of the port known as Tiyangi Sug, or "the shops of Sulu." It was a
stone-walled building put up by the Spaniards, overlooking the fishing village of Busbus to the northeast, and the entrance to the roadstead on the other side of the lighthouse. Headquarters was housed
in the Fortress of Alfonso XII, once known as Daniel's Fort, which
occupied the strongest defensive position on the island, on a slight
eminence which gave a commanding view of the roadstead on the
one side and of the widely-spaced blockhouses which partly encircled the town on the other. The two buildings were connected
by the paved esplanades of the Plaza de la Marina and the Calle
del Commercio which led down to the beach where the fisherfolk
worked at their nets.

Further east, beyond the last of the redoubts, the river called
Tubig Hasa'an crossed the old haciendas on its way from the twin
volcanic slopes of Bud Datu and Bud Agad, before draining itself
in the marshes of the little bay. It was not a stream of much con-
sequence, barely big enough to provide water for the old grind-
stone, or hasa'an, that in years past had been set up at the springs

[ 25 ]

which were its source, but in later times some ambitious farmer had deepened its natural bed so that it could supply some sort of irrigation for his crops. A second stream, called Subig Ligayan, showed itself for a mile or so before disappearing underground, and a few miles further south, the craters of the extinct volcanoes lay in a long line of cruel sores, pointing their broken flesh up to the bright blue sky: Tambang, Pula, Datu, Agad, and the greatest of them all, Tumangtangis.

On the lower slopes of this mountain range, the hard backbone of the island, the timber was tall and luxuriant, and the soil was rich and firm, cut here and there with fast-moving streams which had carved their way through the softer earth and left only the harsh outcrops of granite and lava to jut out sharply against the brilliant blue of the sky and the lush greens of the uncontrolled vegetation. There were bright patches here, where orchids splashed their crimson colors, and tall yellow ferns sprayed their delicate leaves. Vivid-feathered birds moved in the treetops, and sometimes a mouse-deer would skelter away from the water's edge at the approach of a civet cat. On the higher slopes of the mountains, the huge furry bats would scuttle in odious fluttering, deep in the recesses of the dark caves and the fissures between the red and yellow rocks.

From the crater of Bud Datu a man could look out across the whole forty-mile length of the island, across the broad western bulge and the smaller eastern one, and across the narrow neck of land that joined the two together; and then he might think that there could be no other place in the world that was more beautiful, with the trees and the vines crowding each other for space in the hot bright sun, with the wide sweeps of the well-tilled haciendas spread out like gorgeous carpets below, and with the curves of the white beaches framing the whole rich Eden of the island. Tiny islets were dotted in the blue of the sea, and sometimes he might see the whirling rush of water as it changed its course into the Sug, or as it was rendered in Magindanao, Sulug, which gave the Archipelago its name—sea current.

The great craters were extinct now, their open sores no longer pulsating, but remaining there like dead gray cones, solidifying just as they had ceased their heated bubbling, and giving shelter only to the rats and the shrews and to the men who sometimes came to hunt the fur-bats for their skins and for their meat.

But where the forest closed in upon itself and became jungle, where the creepers no longer sought only the sun but also the life that was in the trees, then the towering mahogany slowly decayed under the encroach of the sucking vines that bled its sap away until it slowly died and tumbled, rotten, to the dank humus that was the jungle floor. And here, the vegetation fed upon itself and upon the dampness, and here a thousand fetid crawling things bred and lived and died among the rotting mush.

And here, too, the Moros hid out, safe among the secret tracks which only they could discover.

The column moved slowly in the grasses at the edge of the forest, stumbling down the slopes to the lower levels.

The Colonel called a halt, dismounted, and looked at his watch. He summoned Major Pattman to him and said, "We're moving too slowly, Major. We'll never make it before dark. I'm going on ahead to get help."

Pattman wiped at the sweat on the back of his neck. He said slowly, "Might be better—might be a wiser thing to send one of the Lieutenants."

"I can't do that. If anybody's going to get through . . ."

"And there's been not a sound or sight of them."

"I know."

He went over to the stretcher and stood looking at the Brigadier. Pattman, following him, said anxiously, "He'll be dead by the time we get him there."

"Not if I can get a doctor back here. Should have gone ahead right at the beginning."

"Jed, you'll never make it. One man alone! God knows why they're waiting now, but a single man . . ."

"On a fast horse, I've got a good chance."

The others were cantering up, waiting for instructions. The Colonel said to Wentworth, "These goddam mountains. Five hours, and we haven't covered more than two miles."

"It took us all night to get here."

It was the first time that Wentworth had spoken since the accident. Irreverently, the Colonel wondered if he could prompt him to speak again. He said, "Yes, but we were taking our own good time. Now, we're supposed to be hurrying."

Wentworth nodded silently and turned away. Sullivan came riding up from the rear, his long legs awkwardly close to the ground. He said, pulling in, "Not a sign of them, Colonel, but they're out there somewhere. They must be." He could have said, instead: *Nothing there but silence and shadows and terror*. He said again, "Not even a whisper. Nothing. Could we be wrong?"

The Colonel shook his head. "I wish we were. But we're not. I'm going on ahead to bring help. Major Pattman will take command here."

Sullivan felt the sudden clutch of fear at his heart. He said hesitantly, "With due respect, Colonel . . ."

"Yes?"

"If there's only a handful of them, together we'll get back, but alone you won't stand a chance."

"It's a risk I must take, Sullivan. The Brigadier won't last out much longer."

"Suppose I go, Jed?"

He did not know why he offered. He only knew that the fear was a tight knot of anguish in him and that he had to subdue it. The Colonel shook his head.

"No. Thank you. Keep your formation, your weapons ready. I'll bring out a doctor, some Medical Corps men, and a strong detail of Infantry. When you get to the bridge, you'll probably find it's been cut. That's where the danger will be."

He swung up again into the saddle and gathered up the reins. He said again, "The bridge. It's a couple of miles further on, and that's where the trouble will be."

Pattman said urgently, "Then why don't you wait, Jed. Ride on ahead after we cross the bridge."

"There's not that much time."

"Jed, wait till we pass the bridge."

"You heard me, Major."

[ 28 ]

He wheeled his horse around, dug in his spurs, and was gone.

They stared after him for a moment, and then Pattman, asserting his authority, said brusquely, "All right, let's get moving. Dismount. We'll save the horses."

They all clambered down, then, and started moving forward again. At the rear, Withers waited for the others to get ahead before falling into step with Sullivan. Feeling the need to talk, he held out the Remington they had given him.

"A shotgun," he said disgustedly.

"You know how to use it?"

"If I have to. I'm more use with a pen."

"That's the conventional attitude."

"But you don't believe it."

"No, I don't. Too many damn correspondents putting their imaginations to work. I spend half my time cleaning up the dirty pictures you send home. You think I've nothing better to do than straighten out your reports?"

"So this isn't war any more? When you even have to arm your journalists?"

"If they move in on us, you'll be glad of that shotgun."

Withers was silent. He said at last, uneasily, "You're sure they will?"

"Quite sure."

"How many of them?"

"Your guess. Could be half a dozen. Could be a couple of hundred."

"They have rifles?"

"They don't need them. You've seen the way they fight. Or have you?"

Withers turned away, embarrassed. "Well," he said. "Not exactly. I've talked to the soldiers."

"No combat?

"No."

"And you're the man who tells Secwar in Washington just how to finish off this campaign. Listen."

They halted, then, the two of them. Sullivan stood close by the trunk of a teak tree, his head thrown back. Beside him, Withers looked over his shoulder nervously. They could hear only the sound of the horses up front.

Seeing the alarm on Sullivan's face, Withers said anxiously, "You hear something?"

"I don't know. Maybe it was just a bird. But I think we'd better close up a little. Don't let the others get too far ahead of us."

They moved forward, keeping fifty paces behind the main party, staring into the forest as it dropped behind them, listening and hearing only the padfalls of their own feet. The silence was uncanny. It seemed as if even the animals had fled so that they would not be trapped in the fury that was about to descend on the green floor of the clearing. Withers, his voice low, said uncomfortably, "I know—I know that you don't think too much of me, Captain. Well, maybe I'm not a soldier like the rest of you, but you don't have to worry about me when the fighting starts. I can keep my end up."

"I'm sure you can, Withers."

"When it's a matter of my own life, I can fight as well as the next man."

"But you've had no combat."

"Not this sort."

"Oh? Then where?"

"Chicago. New York. San Francisco. Any place where there's a gutter."

Sullivan turned to look at him. He said slowly, "It's easy to take too much for granted, but—this isn't exactly the kind of fight kids get into on street corners."

"You'd be surprised. A broken bottle can hurt just as much as a barong. Leastways, it can scare you just as much. You never noticed it among your own men? The best soldiers are the tough kids from the tough quarters who've had a tough life."

"The best soldiers are the ones who've listened to the lectures the Army gives them."

"It's your whole life, isn't it? The Army."

"You know of a better one?"

"If that's what you want."

"That's all I want. It's enough for any man."

Withers sighed. "Every man to his own trade."

He was wishing he'd had some training, too.

They came to the bridge, or what was left of it, an hour later.

It was a crude affair of stout logs that had been laboriously hauled across the narrowest point of a deep crevasse that split the slope of the mountain in two. At its widest, the gash in the earth was half a mile across, but here it funneled into a near-joining of two opposing bluffs, and forty-foot-long tree trunks had been laid across the gap and covered, crosswise, with smaller logs which, in turn, had been heavily laced with bamboo twigs that had taken root in the earth on either side of the bridge. It had been there a long time, so long that none of the islanders could remember when it had not been there. Creepers had crawled across it, and it had been as solid as part of the ground itself.

But now, the creepers had been slashed away, the logs forced apart and scattered, and the tree trunks had been toppled down into the bottom of the canyon a hundred and fifty feet below.

Pattman shouted an order, and the others slid quickly to the ground. Their weapons at the ready, they formed a tight semicircle and waited. When Sullivan came up, Pattman said briefly, "Better scout around, Captain. See what there is to see."

It did not take him long to find it.

In a little while, under the high clump of wild hemp that lined the edge of the jungle, he found, first, the Colonel's horse. Its belly had been slit open and its throat had been cut. A dozen yards away he found the Colonel, half-concealed by some overhanging creeper that seemed to be feeding on his body. It was torn and bleeding, as though he had fought for a long time before they had killed him, and he wondered what freakish trick of the wind had kept the sound of the shooting from them. Colonel Ericsson's revolver and his boots and his belt had been carried away. And so had his head.

He called the others over, and they stood looking down in silence at the testimony of their enemy's savagery, and then they all looked at Pattman and waited for him to give them their orders.

The Major slipped into command with practiced agility. He placed the men carefully, taking advantage of every boulder, every tree stump, every crack in the ground that could be an obstacle, just as they had taught him in the old days at the Point; but he knew that the others had no confidence in his abilities.

The silence was all around them as he went to the edge of the canyon and peered down into its depths, knowing that there was a way down there and up the other side if only they could find it—or if only they dare try to make it. He knew that there was nothing left for him to do but stand and wait for the Moros to attack, knowing that the attack would come and that nothing could save them but the chance of a passing patrol. He could feel the antagonism of the others, not willful, but caused solely by their resentment that Colonel Jed Ericsson, the best soldier in the Islands, was dead and had left a lesser man to command them; the burden was hard on his shoulders.

*What does it matter*, he thought bitterly. *Tonight, we shall be dead, every man jack of us.*

He took Sullivan aside, pulling him by the arm into the shadow of the bushes. He said shortly, "You know these people better than I do, Sullivan. You think they're waiting for nightfall?"

Sullivan said slowly, "You never can tell, Major. If they think we can do them much damage in daylight, they'll wait for the dark. But they must know that a patrol could pass by here. Although they'll have scouts on the other side of the canyon looking for any signs of a relief party. I don't think they'll wait."

"They *are* waiting, Sullivan."

"Doesn't mean a thing. They could be waiting for reinforcements. The party that killed the Colonel may not be strong enough to attack our rifles. Or maybe they're waiting for their leader."

"Their leader?"

Sullivan shrugged. "Could be anybody. Malavisan, Jokiri, Hiyang—there are a dozen petty chiefs in these parts. I don't think it matters much."

"No?"

"Let's face it, Major. We don't have a chance. Does it matter who cuts us down?"

Pattman said stubbornly, "You could easily be wrong. There's some—some reason they're holding back for. If there's just a few of them."

"You were going to say some comfort, weren't you?"

"I was going to say some hope. But how can I be sure?"

There was bitterness lining the furrows that ran down his pale cheeks. He said again, "How can I be sure? I'm an administrative officer, not a campaign man."

Sullivan sensed that he was asking for help. He said gently, "Well, maybe there's still hope. They'll be expecting us back at Alfonso. They've probably sent out a search party already."

"Last pig hunt, we didn't get back till long after dark."

Sullivan had to admit it. "Well, that's true enough. So long as we can hold out for the night . . ."

"Wouldn't it be better to—to move on down the side of the canyon? Looks like there's a way down there."

"No. Worst thing we could do. String us out in a line and we're as good as dead. Keep the horses saddled and free to move about fast—we may have a chance. Besides, we'd never manage the litter down to the bottom."

Pattman said wryly, "You realize I'm picking your brains? Not really the proper way for a senior officer to behave."

"We'll need all the brains we can muster to get out of this, Major. If we can hold them off until they start worrying about us in the Fort . . ."

"And not a sound of them. Anywhere. It's hard to realize that they're really out there, skulking in the shadows. Watching us. Listening to us. Waiting."

"The Colonel's body. There's all the proof you need."

"Yes. I know." Pattman said suddenly, "Can we depend on Withers in a fight?"

Surprised, Sullivan looked across at the journalist. He was sitting on a stump, nervously fingering a lance that someone had given him. He said, "All he can hope to do with a lance is hold someone at arm's length for a few moments. But he'll certainly do what he can to save his own life."

"I'm not so sure. He looks to me like the kind that throws up his arms and shuts his eyes. Hoping."

"Maybe."

"Did you know he was mixed up in that business in Manila? What was his name—Rice?"

It was one of the minor Army triumphs. Rice, a journalist, had been accused of maliciously publishing false charges against the Army Administration. The Senate, conciliatory as always towards the gentlemen of the press, had caused Adjutant-General Corbin to demand an exhaustive inquiry from General MacArthur, who had been Military Governor for less than a year. MacArthur's reply had been firm to the point of arrogance, and Rice had been summarily deported; and Corbin's office had promptly dropped the matter.

"No, I didn't know that," Sullivan said. "All I know is that these journalists are a goddam nuisance."

"When they sent Rice back to San Francisco, Withers left Manila in a hurry and came down here."

"So?"

"Well—it proves he's got no guts."

"We'll soon find that out."

"Tonight, you think?"

"Don't try and force me to guess, Major. I could be very wrong."

"Sorry."

"Shall we get any warning?"

"Maybe. They'll start screaming first, and then they'll charge. A barong in one hand and a kris in the other. Some of them may have rifles, but I doubt it. If they had, they'd have used them already to pick us off one by one from under cover."

"From what I've heard, they'd rather fight with knives."

"That's the theory. They claim there's no pleasure in killing a man unless you can feel it personally. It's my guess that they're holding back until we're worked up enough with fear to give them a better battle. They know that a frightened man makes the best soldier."

Pattman was surprised. He said, raising his eyebrows, "Well, that's a strange philosophy. Tell the truth, I didn't think they knew the meaning of fear."

"They'd rather think of it as desperation. The terrible limit of resolve."

The Major, frowning, turned away. He said irritably, staring into the forest, "I wish they'd come out of there. We're sitting ducks and

[ 34 ]

there's nothing we can do about it. Nothing at all. Just sit. And wait. We're letting them pick the battleground, and it's not good."

"You're not contemplating sending one of us for help?"

The Major nodded morosely towards the shadows where the Colonel lay.

"That was a mistake in the first place."

"He was thinking of the Brigadier."

"Yes. I know that. But if he were still alive, maybe he'd know what to do now."

"We're doing the only possible thing, Major. Waiting. When they attack, we'll try and beat them off."

"If only we could guess how many of them."

Sullivan said slowly, "There may be a couple of hundred of them, or more. Who knows? Our only chance will be on the horses. If we hold our mobility as long as we can. Dismounted, we'll hold them off only as long as we don't have to reload, but on horseback . . ."

"None of us is Cavalry, Captain."

"But all of us can ride. They'll unhorse us pretty quickly if we stand still, but moving fast among them—a horse's hoofs are a pretty deadly weapon. If we use our lances . . ."

"Seven men, five horses."

"I know."

"That means Withers."

"I'm afraid so. But there's no alternative."

"Even so, how long can we last out?"

"Ever hear of the Battle of Otumba, Major?"

"No, I can't say I have. I'm not much of a student of military history. An administrative officer . . ."

Sullivan laid his rifle down, propping it carefully within instant reach against a broken stump. He fingered the long Bombay lance, feeling the edge of the blade with satisfaction. He said slowly, "They made these things to stick pigs with. I wonder if it ever occurred to them how like a pike it is."

"A pike?"

"Cortés. Hernando Cortés of Mexico. At the Battle of Otumba he fought two hundred thousand Aztecs with a force of less than two hundred Spaniards and two thousand Indians. What's more to the point, he killed twenty thousand of them; with swords and lances. Odds of a thousand to one, can you believe that?"

"Cortés had artillery."

"Not then, he didn't. It was four hours of hand-to-hand fighting. I grant you, the outcome was—well, a bit fortuitous, to say the least. But he kept his horses moving and rode up and down the flanks of the Aztecs, cutting them to pieces and moving too fast to be stopped. And he used swords and pikes to do it."

Pattman looked around the confines of the clearing. He said doubtfully, "There's not much room to maneuver."

"I know. Point is, if we keep moving, we should be able to hold on long enough. It's the best we can do under the circumstances."

"And you want to use lances instead of rifles?"

"We have three rifles, three revolvers, and a shotgun. How long do you think our ammunition will hold out? At close quarters?"

"Well . . ."

"Of course, we'll use our firearms too. But at the end—at the end, our lances will be the best weapons."

"What *will* be the end, Sullivan?"

He thought about it for a moment. At last, he said wearily, "Numbers. It all depends on how many of them . . . They must know that if we don't get back to Fort Alfonso in a reasonable time, a patrol will come looking for us. So, they must reason that if they don't act soon, we can become bait in a trap that will close on them. It's also probable that they've got scouts out on the other side of the river, watching for a relief party, and the moment a company leaves the barracks and heads this way, they'll move in on us. To get the bait before the trap can be sprung. They're not fools, these people. And they've all had enough experience fighting the Spanish and the Dyaks, the Dutch and the Portuguese before them, to know a great deal about guerrilla warfare."

Pattman raised his hands hopelessly.

"And there's no way for—for the bait to fight its way out of the trap."

Shrugging, Sullivan indicated the canyon that lay to the south of them.

"All right, so there's a path of sorts down there. There's a ford across the stream and there's a track up the other side. We'd be in single file, leading the horses—carrying a stretcher. What chance would we have there?"

"I suppose you're right."

"The decision's yours, Major. If we stay and wait for them, at least we'll have a chance. Not much, but—well, it's your decision."

"I don't like the idea of fighting on horseback."

Indecision. He knew that the Major had still not made up his mind. He made no attempt now to keep the scorn from his voice. He said, "Don't worry, Major. They'll unhorse you before you have time to feel too unhappy about it."

He was conscious again of the enmity between them. Conscious too that now, of all times, they should be sticking tight together. Trying to make amends, he said, "They'll go for the horses' hocks with their knives. That's when you'll need your lance. Strike down hard, as if it was a pig. They'll twist and turn under your hoofs like a good boar, and your problem will be to kill before the tusk strikes home."

"But there'll be more of them."

"Once your horse is down, find someone else in the same predicament and cover his back. Back to back."

The Major said, "It's nearly six. They're waiting for sundown."

"Maybe. I shouldn't count on it."

"I could do with some food. I wonder what happened to the bearers."

"They're Filipinos, remember. Their loyalty to us is dependent on two dollars and seventy cents a month."

Pattman smiled crookedly. "Plus clothing allowance."

"Still not enough to keep them on our side in case of emergency. One glimpse of a Moro, and they head for the hills. Can't say that I blame them. We've been telling them long enough that we're here to protect them. Just as the Spaniards did."

Pattman said sharply, "That sounds like treason, Captain. The Army's doing a fine job over here."

"The Army's getting itself killed off over here. We're through fighting the Spanish, so now we're fighting the Moros. And the

Dyaks. And the Bisayans. Only people we're protecting—we're protecting ourselves. We could do that just as well back home."

Staring at him wide-eyed, Pattman said, "I'm surprised to hear you talking like that. You, of all people."

Sullivan said tightly, feeling the bitterness of it, "I don't want to protect them. I want to fight, and that's not the same thing, is it? The Army's job is to fight, and that's all of its job. They're trying to turn us into diplomats. With celluloid collars. There's a cable on my desk at the Fortress at this very moment, from Washington, telling me we're not treating the natives gently enough. There's also a cable telling Washington about that business in Mulada; three officers and forty men murdered—out of a command strength of three officers and seventy-two men. So they expect us to put on celluloid collars and become diplomats. I tell you, Major, the Army's job here is to fight, to pacify. We're not protecting anyone except ourselves."

The sun was low in the west, touching the mountains with brilliant gold which faded away into blues and somber purple where the lower slopes had taken on a cloak of shadows. The air was suddenly cold and moist.

Somewhere close at hand a bullfrog started croaking, and the two men exchanged glances. Then a thousand other tiny, ugly throats took up the sound and the forest was filled with the reboant cacophony till it seemed to tremble with the intense vibration of it. Then, just as suddenly as it had started, it stopped again and all was silent once more.

Pattman walked off to look over the battleground for the third or fourth time. The canyon was a narrow slit that opened up in the hard earth to their south. He wondered if it could be used as a flank support, and then realized that as long as there was any path up the steep incline at all, the Moros would use it. To the north, the east, and the west, the forest was somber, dense, and silent. A bright-colored bird had been perched high on a branch that stuck out from an apitong tree like a twisted, broken finger, but now, even the bird had gone. The trees were tall and heavy with green and yellow foliage.

The clearing was not more than seventy yards across at its widest point, and the Major wondered, with anxiety, how the horses could maneuver there, with perhaps half a hundred Moros milling about under their feet with sharp knives and heavy barongs. Half a hundred? More than three hundred of them had attacked one of the new stone forts near Maymbung, less than ten miles from here. On the other hand, a group of only six "friendly" Moros, last week, had approached a working party of engineers along the beach and killed every man jack of them. Twenty American boys, decapitated. Three more of the troopers had been carried off, as prisoners, and he shuddered when he thought about what had happened to them. Six "friendly" Moros, apparently unarmed, begging for food or cigarettes or clothing. Sullivan was right, these were not people to protect. They were people to pacify.

The sky was losing its brightness, and he knew that they would not have much longer to wait. He said a few words to Baroni, and Stiles, and Wentworth, and then went and squatted on the ground close to the stretcher where the Brigadier lay. There was no sound or sight of breath, now, in the puffy, flabby body, and he wondered if he were dead. He touched his hand gently to the bloody white pad that the Colonel had strapped across the huge stomach; it was soaking wet, and he wondered if a man could lose so much blood and still live. When he placed his hand over the plump breast, he could feel the faintest heartbeat.

He went over to the horses and checked their girth-bands, nodded curtly to Withers as he walked past him, then stood on the edge of the canyon and waited.

The first warning, as Sullivan had said it would be, was a shrill scream.

It came from the forest immediately to their north, a long, high-pitched cry like the squeal of a wounded hog. Even before the answering call came from the canyon itself, Pattman was on his horse, shouting to the others. His voice was calmer than he would have thought possible.

"Horses! Get to your horses!"

Sullivan came running in and seemed to step into the saddle, his long legs swinging over with hardly a break in his pace. His lance was upright in its boot, the long steel blade high in the air. *"Let them see the sun on your blades," Cortés had said.* His Springfield was held in one hand, and the reins were twisted around his wrists. His was the first shot that was fired.

Baroni was next up, colliding as he mounted, with Stiles. The two Lieutenants exchanged quick looks in which—they were both very young—there was neither fear nor excitement, but only a fierceness which sprang, though in itself it was identical in the two men, from two vastly different forces. In Stiles, it was the outcome of his military training, a molding of his thoughts and his actions into the one finished product—a fighting weapon that could think clearly and act bravely, with no other thought except the contest itself and the defeat of the enemy. In Baroni, the emotions were quite differently rooted. He was slim, good-looking, courteous, and carried himself with a deportment that belied his humble origins. He had been close to Father Lupari, the Missionary in Maymbung. To Baroni, the Moros were the men who had captured the good Father Lupari, castrated him, and scornfully set him loose again. They were savages to be destroyed because they were not Christians, and as he flung himself astride his horse, there was no fear in him at all.

Wentworth was in the act of removing a small pebble from his boot when the call came, and he pulled at the straps angrily, knowing in a moment of panic that he could not fight a battle with only one boot on. As he stamped his foot in firmly and grabbed at his pistol, he saw that a Moro, the first one into the clearing, was heading straight for him, his small, dark, wiry body shiny with sweat. He wore a bright yellow turban, set well to the back of his head, with a red sleeveless jacket and long tight trousers held up by a purple cummerbund. The leather scabbard was at his side, but his barong was held high in the air, the sun catching the sides of the razor-sharp steel. Wentworth just had time to see with astonishment that Withers, far behind him, was unexpectedly charging forward with his lance held low, like a man about to vault over a high fence. It worried him, momentarily, that the lance was incorrectly held, and then the Moro was almost on top of him. He could see the violence and the venom that were bursting out of the fanatical brown eyes, shining now with hatred and determination. The bright blade fascinated him as it went up and out, and then he heard Sullivan's shot and saw the Moro's body leap into the air and double over as the heavy bullet smacked into his shoulders. He had done nothing to save himself, and now Withers was there too, driving his lance into the dead face, pulling it out and driving it in again with an obscene fury.

The clearing was full of them now, thirty or forty of them, running with short, quick steps towards the group of milling horses. He was still staring, fascinated, at Withers, when Stiles came charging up with his jobbing spear raised high. It looked like a picture out of one of his childhood adventure books, and the world suddenly came to life again as the panic left him and desperation seized hold of him. He fired twice, rapidly, expertly, and the satisfaction gave him back his courage as he saw one man drop and another clutch at his knee. He ran to his horse and mounted quickly, and then he was in among them, using his horse's hoofs as a weapon, pulling his mount up on its hind legs. He fired again and again until his revolver was empty, and then thrust it back into its holster and seized his lance.

He saw Sullivan at the edge of the clearing, rearing his horse up and swinging it around, and suddenly he was aware that one of the Moros had risen from under his feet, screaming shrilly, and was waving a bloody object at arm's length; with a spasm of nausea he saw that it was the Brigadier's head. He thrust his lance down and forward, feeling the point enter the Moro's armpit, and losing his hold as his horse stumbled and fell. The ground came up and hit him. A thin, wiry hand yanked at his hair, and he fastened his teeth, like a savage, on the wrist that came at his throat, twisting himself round and hitting out blindly with his fists, wondering how he had dropped the lance that was his only hope of survival.

Then Sullivan came charging in, and he heard the crack of a horse's shoe against a fragile skull, and the grip round his neck was gone. He saw that Sullivan, high above him on his mount, was grinning down at him, and he had time to wonder if the grin was fever or frenzy or fear, and then again he saw the red blade of a barong high over his head, and he lurched sideways, pulling his spear as he moved and thrusting it without pause into a thin brown flank that was exposed close beside him. Wherever he looked, there was sweaty brown flesh, and he knew that now they were packed tight around him and that he would never escape alive. He heard Withers, running towards him, yell his name, and saw that the journalist was using his shotgun now.

"Wentworth!"

It was the last sound he heard. A sharp, fierce pain of incredible intensity struck across his back, and then he was lying down with the blue sky of the evening bright and clean above him and no feeling at all in any of his limbs. He knew that his back was broken and he tried to say something, to call a withdrawal from the battle because the contest was no longer equal and it was time for him to retire, but when he tried to say, quite calmly: "All right, let's stop now and take a rest," he found that he could not even hear the sound of his own voice. And when he saw the face of a Moro close to him, lifting his head up for the final decapitation, he could only wonder why they had not heard him, why they were still fighting when he had called a halt. He did not feel the slicing of the blade that chopped at his throat.

Withers stopped dead in his tracks to stare at the bloody act, and then dropped his empty gun, raised his spear, and plunged it deep into the back of the Moro who was bending over Wentworth's dead body. He drove it home inexpertly, getting it hopelessly stuck fast in the bony skeleton of the ribs, and as he tugged it free he felt another spurt of blood gushing down the side of his leg and wondered where it came from. He was on the ground, then, lying on his side, wondering how he got there and wondering also, with credulous incongruity, what was the name of the man he was struggling with; what was his tribe, and what were his habits; where he came from and why he was fighting. A paragraph from his last dispatch was uppermost in his mind: *They do not know what they fight for; they only know that we, like the Spaniards we defeated, are foreigners . . . that we have come here to govern them, and therefore we are to be killed. Your correspondent has seen them in action and can report that they fight with the blind, skilled hatred of fanatics . . .*

There was no life in the flesh he was struggling with, and he felt the absurd horror of fighting with a dead man. He pulled himself clear and found that his left leg was broken; he dragged himself up against the stump of a tree—how could he have moved so far from the center of the clearing?—and clawed his way half-upright, jabbing with his lance at a bright green turban that obscured his vision. He saw a rifle on the ground beside him and bent down to retrieve it, and then all the lights went out suddenly, in absolute accord with each other so that there was nothing left for him at all. He could not even know that three of them were fighting over his dead body, clawing at the broken limbs, slicing with fury at the suddenly senseless flesh.

Pattman and Stiles were still fighting, both on their feet and fighting back to back, lunging out with their lances, stabbing in short sharp motions, a dead horse close beside them. Stiles was clutching a hunting knife in his left hand, jabbing his spear with his right, finding comfort in Pattman's ferocity behind him. The clearing was crowded with the Moros now, more than a hundred of them, patches of scarlet and yellow and green and blue, moving with lithe speed, clambering over dead horses and their own dead. The floor of the forest was wet with blood.

Baroni, his left arm sliced off at the elbow, was forcing his way towards them, fighting like a maniac. There was a long gash down the front of his face, and as he reached them he stumbled and fell, and in a moment his body was covered with the sweating mass of their sleek and wiry bodies as they slashed at his flesh with their weapons. A strong brown hand clutched at the black, curly, youthful hair, lifting the body up; and then a lightning blow with a long sharp blade across the side of the neck tore off the head in one swift cut. The body dropped back to the ground and lay there in its own wasted blood.

Sullivan was moving in again, the only horseman now, charging with precision along the edge of the seething mass, using a saber. A saber? Whose? He wondered where it had come from. He heard Pattman yell, "To me, Sullivan, to me!"

Swinging his horse round savagely, he saw that Pattman was alone, his back to a tree, using his lance and a kris. He forced his horse towards him, slashing as he went, and waited till the Major had fought his way over to Stiles, then he spurred his horse at the Moros who were closing in on the pair of them, feeling them go down under the sheer weight of his charge. As he swung round again, he saw a tall Moro with a yellow sash at his waist, standing face to face with Pattman. As he watched, he saw the Moro raise his barong and bring it down with a speed that he could not follow. All he could see was that the long blade, cutting through Pattman's crown, had reached a point below the shoulder before its motion was arrested. He saw the Moro drop the weapon, and clutch with both hands at the kris which, dying, the Major had driven into his chest.

Stiles was still on his feet. He was fighting methodically, working his way to a tree to shelter his back, jabbing with the spear and swinging his rifle like a club. His face was drawn, but his movements were cool and careful. He saw the long red lance, the Bombay spear that Sullivan had been so proud of. It was broken in two and stood like an inverted V in the center of the bloody clearing. A Moro sidestepped the quick swing of the Springfield and closed with him, but he dropped the rifle and twisted the man's own kris towards him, driving it deep into his groin, and when the man fell he stooped to pick up his rifle again, wondering suddenly why the sky was so red above him and why the blood was flooding into his mouth. He found that he was lying on his back and that his hands were empty, and then he clutched automatically at the long dagger that had lodged in his gullet, plucking it out, not feeling the pain of it. And then he died.

Now Sullivan was alone. The saber he had grabbed was part of his arm, an extension of it. It was old and rusty, and the hilt was sadly bent. The Moro who had carried it lay dead, impaled with the broken lance. He raised it again and again, slashing with a fury that was exaggerated beyond all reasoning, and dimly, beyond the borders of his madness, he heard the shrill calls of the Moros as they raged about him.

He knew he was alone now, and when they fell back he spurred his horse into them and swung his saber with a savagery that was beyond comprehension, wondering why they fell back from him, wondering why they did not clamber, by sheer force of numbers, over his tired body. They broke before him as he charged into them, then formed into a solid mass behind him, and as he whirled and charged them again, again they made way for him. Then one man, a tall, skeleton-thin Moro, carrying a curved bolo with the bright red tuft of hair at its hilt that denoted senior rank, seemed to separate himself from the others and stand alone, holding a motionless pose of authority, his arms flung back, waiting for the charge. He wore tight-fitting yellow trousers striped with narrow blue, and a green shirt, collarless and open down to the waist, that had been heavily embroidered in scarlet, purple, blue, and gold silk. He wore a U.S. Army bandolier round his waist and his feet were bare. His bright green turban was smaller than was usual, and one end of it hung down over his left ear. He stood delicately poised on the balls of his bare feet, his arms spread wide, waiting.

It was a ritual and a challenge. On both sides of him, the Moros had fallen back. The clearing itself was heavily strewn with the bodies of the dead, and Sullivan stared at the bodies of his friends, all of them headless now. They were bloodless, empty, yellowing carcasses, and already the blue flies were at work on them, buzzing hungrily. The sight sickened him, and he took up the challenge.

He pulled tight on the reins, jerking his horse's head up, then dug his heels in hard. The pony reared up high, his hoofs flailing, then lunged forward. At the other side of the clearing, the tall Moro waited, motionless. Sullivan raised the saber. He held the reins taut, ready for an instant jink to the left or right, and as the distance rapidly shrank between him and his target, he felt the blood pounding in his head.

He was on him, then, in a final burst of fury. But the Moro had gone. Knowing what had happened, knowing that his enemy was under the hoofs like a tusker, working at his horse's feet, he swung the saber round quickly to use it like a spear. The horse screamed and fell, and as he slipped from the saddle he saw the Moro chief leap quickly to his feet, clutching a bloody dagger.

He swung the saber again, up and out in a huge circle, as wide as his long arms would permit. And then he went down as they surged forward onto him, and the sword was wrenched from his hand. He fought with his fists, then, striking out blindly, knowing that his target was dense and resilient and all around him. He lifted one of them to his feet and hurled him bodily over the heads of the others, and, wondering why they did not use their knives, he struck out and kicked and gouged and pummeled until, at last, he fell exhausted.

He lay back and closed his eyes, waiting for the touch of the knife at his throat, for the clutch of the hand that would jerk back his head to expose the vulnerable windpipe. He knew that he was petrified with fear, and he kept his eyes closed, feeling irrationally that they were waiting for him to open them before they made the wicked caress. He wondered if the ritual of decapitation would be reserved for the tall skinny chief who had slipped so dexterously under his horse to hamstring it.

It seemed an eternity before he dared to open his eyes again, and in the final moments before he did so he felt himself hoping, praying, that he would open them on a clearing devoid of movement, deserted by the enemy; that some miracle had happened that would permit his life to be spared. He dismissed the thought as cowardly, and then, knowing it was the fear inside him at work again, he knew that there had already been one miracle. The Brigadier, the Colonel, Pattman and Wentworth, Baroni and the tow-headed Stiles, even the uncouth little journalist Withers—all were dead. Worse, they lay there headless and cut into pieces, with the flies and the ants crawling over them. Only he was alive. It was at least the beginnings of a miracle.

He opened his eyes then, and closed them again as he saw that they were still there, milling about him, shouting and snarling to each other. He wondered why he had not heard their voices all the time and knew that, shamefully, he had fainted.

He felt them tie his wrists tightly together, and bind his ankles, and then he felt a sharp blow under his chin that jerked his head to one side, as they thrust a bamboo pole between his trussed limbs. He squirmed with the sudden, unexpected pain of it. Like a slaughtered pig, he was hoisted unceremoniously onto their shoulders, his body hanging limp, his head uncontrollably lolling back.

He had caused it to be done so often. The pig hunt was a weekly

[ 46 ]

affair, organized for the senior officers of the Fortress, and it was he, Sullivan, the expert, who had always made the arrangements. Truss him up, he had said, truss him up and sling him on a pole, we'll carry him back in style to the Garrison. It was he, Sullivan, who had seen to it that the raffia-cord about the hocks was tight and strong, and that the happy bearers could handle the load on their shoulders, and it was he, Sullivan, who led the procession back into the Fortress, with the horses trotting cheerfully, and the bearers with their load plodding patiently along behind, and the other officers of the Garrison waiting for them with ribald jests (except when it was the Brigadier; then they were more respectful), and the whole convoy would wheel into the grounds and watch the grinning cook sharpening up his butcher's knife.

And now it was he, Sullivan, who was trussed like a pig on a bamboo pole, and the Brigadier was dead and headless, and the butcher's knife was a barong that did not need further sharpening, and the grinning officers were a crowd of scowling Moros, and all was night and there was nothing left in the world any more.

He closed his eyes and let unconsciousness sweep over him.

# 3.

On the slope of the mountain overlooking the sea, a fisherman from the island of Palawan, who had been forced by the heavy currents to land on Sulu, was staring at a clump of bamboo, his long cutting-knife loosely held in his hand. He touched the shiny staves with the tips of his fingers, feeling for the dryness and the brittleness of them, and when he had selected the one he wanted, he sliced it off at the base and sat down to cut a notch in its side. His movements were slow and methodical, and from time to time he looked up at his wife who was cleaning a fish he had caught with his spear, and at the children who were running about collecting dry twigs for the fire.

When the notch was cut to his satisfaction, he stood up and unwound the rattan cord that was coiled around his upper arm, and then he placed his bamboo stave carefully on a small bundle of dry grass, slipped the cord through the notch on the underside, placed his splayed, prehensile foot on it, grasped the end of the rope, and quickly lugged it through the V-shaped cut. There was a smolder of smoke, and then, clucking his annoyance, he tried again.

On the third pull, the dry grass burst into flame, and he bent down quickly and blew on it, while one of his children brought a few small sticks and watched them catch fire, and when he looked up at his wife he saw that she had stopped her cleaning and was staring into the valley below where the edge of the marshes lay. Her hand was pressed to her cheek, and instinctively the children were running to her. He followed the direction of her gaze, standing still and silent, a frail old man with a hollow chest in which the cage of the ribs was shadowed against the gold of his wrinkled flesh.

He could see the moving column of Moros that was winding its way through the marsh, and he placed his broad foot squarely on the fire he had made, smothering it before the smoke and the smell of it should betray his presence. Then, moving slowly because he did not want his children to know of the terror that was in his heart, he gathered his family round him and slipped silently into the shadows of the forest.

He did not come out again until the Moros had passed by. Then, winding his firecord round his arm again, he ran quickly with his brood down to the binta he had left on the beach, pushed his family aboard, and paddled quickly out to sea.

There was not a tribe in the islands that was not frightened of the Moros.

When Sullivan recovered consciousness, he was deep in the marshy swamps that he knew must lie along the southernmost shores of the island. There was a fearsome pain in his head, and he was still being carried, trussed like a pig, and slung from a bamboo pole by the wrists and ankles.

All around him was slime, and the long black roots of the mangroves stuck out fantastically like the tangled tendons of a decaying animal in a terrifying nightmare. The dank water splashed at his face as he swung to and fro, upside down, and once he had to hold his breath while his face was dragged for an interminable length of time under liquid mud.

The only sound about him was the splashing of the thin legs of his captors through the water. Even the customary sounds of the forests had gone. In the other-world silence of the swamp there were neither birds nor animals.

The pain in his wrists was tearing into him, pulling the muscles

out of his arms, and the strain of holding his head up was insupera-
ble. He fainted again, and when he came to he studied the men
about him as best he could, trying to force his mind into activity,
trying to reverse the upside-down picture he had of them. Two men
carried the pole he was slung to, while a dozen others were march-
ing with them. They moved in silence, and their weapons were
sheathed. He looked for the man who, it had seemed, had chal-
lenged him to individual combat, the man who had hamstrung his
horse, but he could not find him there. He tried to learn their rank
by studying their weapons, but there was insufficient that he could
see. The Moro who supported the rear end of the bamboo shaft
carried a sundang, the general-purpose machete of the lower orders,
and a bolo with a brass hilt, both of them stuck into the gaudy sash
round his waist. Beside him, a much younger man, with a Chinese
cast to his face, carried one of the fearsome talibongs, the four-foot-
long sword that was used for the ceremonial decapitating on the
battlefield. Its steel blade was curved, like a kris, and its handle
was of redwood inlaid with circles of ivory.

He swung his head round and found his personal enemy striding
along on his flank. He studied him carefully now, a tall, thin man
much older than he had first thought when he had spurred his horse
towards him and seen him slip expertly under its flying hoofs. His
face was thin and aquiline, and cruelly set. His pantaloons, soiled
with mud, were tight under the knee and billowy at the hips, and
his sash was made of striped gold silk. He wore an embroidered
shirt and a dark green jacket that was streaked with blood, and into
his sash an ornate barong was thrust in its leather scabbard. The
long straight steel of the blade broadened out near the hilt, and
the elaborate handle was huge, heavy, and finely wrought. It was
made of horn, and studded with bright stones that looked like
rubies, curved round in the form of an "S." On the other side of
his waist he carried a short curved sword of the kind called a campilan, with a red tuft of hair at the hilt. Sullivan knew that the tuft
denoted his rank, a senior officer. He twisted his head around to
get a better look at the man, wondering if this were their chief.
And then someone shouted something, there was a brief pause in

the forward motion, and a soldier stepped over to him and struck him lightly between the eyes with the handle of his bolo.

The world went black again.

He had no way of knowing how long he had been unconscious or how far they had carried him. It seemed but a moment ago that he was dragging his face through the mud of the swamp, closing his eyes tightly and trying to keep the filth out of his mouth and nose. Now, he was lying on hard earth, and it was dark all around him.

He found that his arms and legs were free, and he staggered to his feet, stumbling to a wall of bamboo stakes. He rubbed his hands over his eyes, trying to massage the daylight back into them, and then it became clearer a little and he saw that he was in a sort of shack, a hut made of light poles covered over with thatch. There was an open doorway, and when he went to it he saw that he was in a native village, a small one, no more than twenty or thirty huts. Their walls were made of matting, and their roofs were covered with palm leaves, but he saw that the whole village had been surrounded by a fortification built of earth piled high against a row of logs and reinforced with rolled-up matting and slabs of mahogany wood.

Within the compound, a group of Moro women and a few children were squatting on the earth preparing some rice. The smaller children were quite naked, and the older ones, like their mothers, wore only the universal jabul, a loop of bright cloth twisted casually around the waist. The breasts of the younger women were bare, but the older ones wore a sort of Mother Hubbard that fell loosely to their feet. To his surprise, no one paid him any attention at all.

He walked over to the breast-high palisade, feeling unsteady on his feet, and leaned against it, watching. A Moro soldier, dressed in a kind of uniform made up of a blue American Army shirt and native trousers, with a bandolier round his waist and a rifle, also American, slung across his back, passed him by without so much as a glance. He examined the territory carefully, trying to decide where he was.

Ahead of him was a tall mountain, volcanic, which he had not seen before, or at least could not immediately recognize. It was late evening, and it seemed to him that the sky behind the volcano was lighter than elsewhere. He felt at the mud on his trousers; the heavy drill cloth was damp, but not wet, and when he rubbed at the caked mud around his boots it flaked off and left damp patches underneath. An hour, then, since he had left the swamps? Two, or three, or four? Certainly not more.

He stared at the volcano again, sure now that it must be Mount Tukay, ten miles or so southwest of Jolo and close to the marshy swamps that lay to the west of Maymbung on the southern coast of the island. That meant they had carried him along the river course of the Tubig Palag to the mangrove swamp at the coast, and then turned west to the drier slopes of the impenetrable Mabingkang forests.

A movement high above his head caught his eye and he looked up and saw a brightly-clad Moro squatting high in the fronds of a palm tree. He saw that several other palms close by had twin ropes tied round their trunks, looped into two steps, one for the right knee and one for the left foot, and he judged that these were the lookout posts.

A Moro warrior, stripped to his waist, came out of one of the huts and took a bowl of food from the women close by, then went back again. He was astonished that no one seemed to mind where he went or what he did. He walked along the southern border of the palisade, leaning against it from time to time until his strength returned, looking out into the dense thicket and feeling sure that once he was out there he could run and they would never catch him.

Never catch him? The Moros could move through the jungle with the speed and silence of snakes. He climbed up onto the palisade and looked down. The outer edge was thickly lined with soldiers, squatting on the hard earth, their weapons laid across their laps. One of them looked up and gestured at him, and wearily he clambered back again. He continued his walk along the perimeter and came to a barricade that served as a gate. It was guarded by three warriors, thickset Monteses from the mountains, dressed in skirts made of beaten banana fronds. They stared at him curiously as he walked by them, but did not move from their positions. He found a group of Papuans, slim black men dressed in loincloths and copper anklets, their frizzy hair covered with ornamental headdresses and their faces brightly painted. One of them wore a ceremonial mask, and one of them wore a necklace of boar tusks. They carried long spears and ornately carved wooden bludgeons, and he wondered who could have brought Papuans, Monteses, and Moros together in apparent amity.

He reached another gate, and here a group of Moros, heavily armed, turned him back with a sign. One of them drew his kris and waved it, and the others laughed at the gesture.

He turned and went back the way he had come.

It was getting darker now, and some of the stars were coming out. He made a quick check and saw that he had been right in his first surmise of his whereabouts. At least, the mountain lay to the west of him, and he was quite sure that it must be Tukay. His limbs were stiff and his back was sore, and he was both hungry and thirsty.

The group of Moro women was still there, and he went up to them and lifted his hand to his mouth in the universal sign language. One of the women, a girl of perhaps twenty or so, stood up and handed him a gourd, indicating the earthenware pot that stood by the entrance to the hut. He took it from her and filled it. When he drank, he found that the water was brackish, tasting strongly of salt. He grimaced, and the girl laughed, then took the gourd from him and ran with it to another pot, filling it again and handing it to him with a giggle. It was fresh water, and he knew then that the other vessel contained a mixture of spring and sea water that the islanders to the far south always used when they came north, because the water on their own islands was heavily spiked with gypsum and they could not acquire the taste for clean water. He tucked the information at the back of his orderly, military mind, wondering how many different tribes and clans and sects were gathered together here, and why.

One of the older women, poking at the fire with a stick, said something in Moro-Samal and the young girl turned and scooped some rice into a bowl and handed it to him. He took it from her gratefully, and began eating it with his fingers, as they were eating, feeling the rich heat of it in his mouth, savouring the meaty juices in which it had been cooked.

The girl stood and looked at him, and then her dark bright eyes glanced up over his shoulder, and for no apparent reason there was a moment of sudden panic in him which he could not account for. He only knew that suddenly he was perplexed and frightened. He swung round on his heels and stared.

A man was close behind him, a white man. He was middle-aged, heavy-set with a brown, deeply lined face, queerly twisted in a sort of grimace that might have been meant for a smile. He was dressed in filthy khaki trousers and a bush jacket, belted at the waist, and he wore a slouch hat of gray felt that was obviously not American; it carried a band of buffalo-skin and a brass badge at the side. He walked with a limp so pronounced that his walk was almost a hobble, as though there were no power at all in the right leg, and he carried a short stave of ebony.

The moment of surprise passed quickly. Sullivan said, puzzled, "Well, how do you do?"

He knew that the fear was still inside him, and still he could not account for it. The cripple had hobbled to a halt. He fumbled in his pocket and took out a battered cigarette case. Holding it out, he said, "The cigarettes are your own. My name's Dawson."

Taking a cigarette, Sullivan felt that his hand was shaking. Dawson struck a lighter wheel with the heel of his hand, blew on the tow wick until it glowed brightly, then held it out. He was watching Sullivan carefully. He said, "And your name is Shay Sullivan. Captain, United States, Twenty-third Infantry. We know all about you, and you know nothing about us."

The fear flared into life. "We? Us?"

Dawson's twisted smile became more twisted. He said affably, "Why don't we sit down and have a chat?"

"I thought for a moment you were also a prisoner here."

Eyebrows raised: "But I am, my dear fellow. A prisoner, the same as you are."

"The same?"

"Well, not quite the same perhaps. I'm not a soldier. I have certain privileges. But a prisoner none the less."

"You're English, aren't you?"

Dawson sighed. "Still shows? After all these years? I haven't seen England since . . . hell, I don't remember when was the last time. Malay, Burma, Australia, Borneo, Papua—now the Philippines."

"Go on."

"Eat your food. I'm afraid it's not very good for an American taste—they've been spoiling you over at the barracks. There's supposed to be some buffalo steak mixed in with it somewhere, but you've got the women's portion so it's mostly rice."

Sullivan said sourly, "Well, at least they're short of food."

Dawson laughed shortly. His face creased into narrow, leathery rivulets.

"Short of food? Don't you believe it. But the men have been out fighting, and the women have been having an easy time of it. Things will change when they get back."

"Oh? When will that be?"

"Tonight, tomorrow, next week. Who knows? Come to that, who cares?"

"Would you mind telling me where we are?"

"I thought you knew. I saw you carefully calculating the direction of the sea and the volcano."

"Tukay?"

"Glad to see you got it right. We need a good mind in this little outfit."

Sullivan felt that his mouth was open. He said sharply, "Would you mind saying that again?"

"The old man feels that you might be useful to us."

*The "us" again.* Sullivan said irritably, "Suppose you tell me just who you are and what the hell you're doing here?"

"Why don't we sit down and make ourselves comfortable?"

Dawson went over to the fire and shooed the women away, and they cleared a place for them on the fiber mats, staring into the flames and keeping silent. Dawson said at last, "It's pretty simple, really. I've been here a long time now, more than two years. I suppose you'd call me a sort of—well, a sort of comic opera grand vizier. I advise the old man. I act as interpreter."

"The old man?"

Dawson went on, speaking slowly and carefully, "I ought to tell you, I suppose, that I'm not on your side."

Sullivan felt the muscles at the side of his mouth tighten. He said angrily, "A white man? And you're not on our side? You mean you're fighting with the Filipinos against us?"

"Get your facts right," Dawson said. "I'm not fighting. I'm just an adviser."

"Same thing."

"Not exactly. The Filipinos are fighting for independence. As far as I'm concerned, that's just a word, and nothing more." He added sarcastically, "In that respect, at least, I agree with your own government. Doesn't mean a damn thing. The Moros are fighting for— hell, they're fighting because they've never done anything else. They're pirates, bandits, robbers. Call them what you like. They fought the Spanish and the Filipinos, they're fighting the Americans and the Filipinos, and they're fighting the Dyaks and the Americans. All very simple. In other words, they're fighting anyone who doesn't belong to their own tight little organization. And occasionally, they fight among themselves." Mocking, he added, "Just like the civilized Western world."

"All right, I know my history. Now, what are you doing here?"

"Ah, it's a long story. Wish I had some liquor to offer you. Can't drink it here, you know, too many Moslems about, they don't like it. I have a bottle stashed away in the forest, but I have to be a bit careful."

Dawson stood up and hobbled over to the water-vessel. Gulping noisily out of the gourd, he turned and went on: "I told you, I'm a prisoner. I came here two years ago, looking for pearls."

"Pearls?"

"Oh yes, the Moros are great pearl pirates. They raid the Company beds, and they steal the pearls, and they sell them to the Chinese traders in exchange for anything they can lay their hands on. Cloth, pig iron, tools. I tied up with a fellow named Sulubu, from Borneo. Had a good plan. We'd offer modern weapons to the Moros in exchange for their pearls."

He broke off and came back to the fire. The flames lit up the twisted side of his face. He went on: "I was a good soldier then."

Tapping the side of his leg, he said, "This came later. In those days, I could handle a gun or a sword with the best of them. British Army, you know. We came across from Borneo in a binta, eight of us in a damn canoe that was big enough to hold maybe two. Never been so scared in my life. We traded around for a while, got a lot of pearls together."

"In exchange for arms?"

Dawson grinned. "Now don't start lecturing me on the morals of war. Where was I?"

"You were selling arms to the natives."

"Of course, we had to steal the guns in the first place. Started off up in Manila where the supply was the biggest, but it got too organized up there, so we came down south. We managed all right for a while, and then poor old Sulubu got killed. We had a run-in with a prahu-load of Moros and they slashed him to pieces. He's lying at the bottom of Tu'tu Bay somewhere, with a hundred thousand dollars' worth of pearls in his pocket. Quite a find for someone, what? So I made a deal with one of the Moros we'd captured. My Borneo boys wanted to eat him, but I said no. I said I wanted to do a deal with his boss, and he guided me in here. It was a good idea, because the old man is one day going to be the Sultan of all the Moros, and I shall be a man of considerable importance."

He sat down again heavily, slipping slowly down the side of his staff and tucking his feet under him with an awkward movement. He said again, "I'd give my soul for a drink."

The crickets in the forest had started their piercing shrieks, and somewhere a parrot squawked in the bushes. The fires were lighting the compound, now, and more men were coming in. There was a lot of commotion over by the main gate. Dawson paid no attention to it. He said sadly, "I could have been a big man. But greed—greed for wealth—my own fault, of course. The old man had gathered together a mess of pearls as big as . . . there was one single pearl there that would have set me up for life. But we were short of rifles. Your fellows were getting careful. I was supposed to go into Jolo and take a dozen Papuans on a raid. Can you imagine that? A white man leading a bunch of savages against an American fortress? So, of course, I said hell no. We had words. That night, I tried to get into the hut where the pearls were kept. They caught me. Thought I'd make a break for it and . . . Hell, in those days I could move through the jungle faster than they could, and I knew my own Borneo boys would stick with me. But they caught me."

There was an infinite pain in his face. Sullivan sat silent and watched him.

"They caught me, and I couldn't bluff my way out of it. I said to the old man, 'Don't try any funny stuff with me, you need me.' It was the truth, and he knew it. I'd been a staff officer, and I was worth my weight in gold to them. It was I who'd pointed out the advisability of bringing the different tribes and clans together. Not many, just a few Macabebes, a few Papuans, a few Monteses. Like this, when we have to go up into the hill country we take a couple of Macabebes along with us and we know we're safe. The local warriors leave us alone, because they won't fight their own people. When we go to Mindanao, we take along a few Visayans, and then we can concentrate our forces on the people we're after without worrying about attacks from the local natives. It's a higher principle of piracy. The old man knew that he needed me. So . . ."

He tapped his leg again, grimacing.

"They held me down on my belly in the mud, and one of the datos drew his ceremonial sword across the back of my knee. Just deep enough to slice a tendon in two. Now, I can walk, I can even run. But I can't get very far or move very fast. They wanted to make sure I wouldn't leave them. Clever, what?"

Sullivan said nothing. He could sense Dawson's deep suffering, the suffering of a broken, useless man.

"They used a thing called a pira. It's a sword the priests use. Sort of long-handled scimitar that's quite useless in fighting—the handle gets in the way. Relic of the old days, I suppose, when they had ceremonial sacrifices."

"And these are the people you joined. Your people."

Dawson shrugged. "So? Time heals everything except a sliced tendon. The old man's not a bad sort. And where can I go? I'm a deserter from my own Army. I lit out five years ago, in Malaya, when I saw a chance to get rich in a hurry. Now look at me."

He grimaced and indicated his filthy clothes.

"No. My only hope is that one day—well, it's possible. I'm still needed here. One day they'll forget what I tried to do. One day they'll see how important I can be to them, and by that time— who knows?"

"By that time the Islands will have been pacified and you'll be court-martialed anyhow."

Dawson laughed again, a short sharp bark that came from deep in his throat. "Pacified? You're mad. You'll never pacify the Moros."

"Sooner or later they'll see the advantage of the democracy we're trying to teach them."

It sounded smug, and he felt uncomfortable about it. Dawson took issue with him at once.

"You really believe that? The Spanish said: 'Do as we tell you or you'll be garroted.' The Americans went one better. They said: 'Love each other or we'll string you up on our beautiful new gallows.' You really believe that an intelligent savage will pay any attention to either of you?"

Sullivan said stiffly, "The British Colonial record—"

"Oh, balls! I'm arguing morality, not politics. And don't try to hit me there, it doesn't hurt in the least. My allegiance now is to myself and to no one else. No one."

He sounded cross, but Sullivan could hear the tone of loneliness under the petulancy. He said slowly, "They killed all the men in the party I was with. Every one of them. Why didn't they kill me? Why did they bring me here?"

For a long time, Dawson was silent. Then he said, sadly, "I suppose that's an important question. You're lucky. At least, you're lucky inasmuch as a man is lucky who has a chance to survive. Ever notice how we hang on to life at the end? We're all going to die bravely until the very last minute, and then there's nothing we wouldn't do for a few more ignoble moments. For the privilege of living a little longer, no matter how, we'll crawl for it."

"Some of us will."

Dawson said irritably, "Don't be so bloody pompous. We all will. You'll find that out in the course of time, if you live long enough."

"All right, why have they brought me here?"

"They think you can teach them how to fight." He said with a twisted smile, "You've been marked for promotion, Sullivan. The old man's had his eye on you for a long time. Remember that affair at Pitugu?"

The memory flooded back to him. It had been a long time ago, more than three months. A stupid, tragic affair.

They had gone to Pitugu, seventeen of them, two officers and fifteen men, to look for a rebel dato who was hiding in the little fishing village and to bring him back to Jolo for swift American trial. The dato had fled Pitugu the night before, and the Moros of the village appeared friendly and cooperative. The soldiers had stood around the beach chatting with the fishermen, exchanging cigarettes for fish, making themselves understood by signs, while the officers had stood a little apart, Sullivan and a young Lieutenant named Gillmore. Suddenly, at a prearranged signal, the peaceful fishermen had drawn their jungle knives and sprung upon the unsuspecting soldiers. One had been struck across the back of the neck and killed instantly. One trooper suffered a slash across the top of the skull from which his brains oozed out. Another dropped with a hatchet buried deep in his shoulder. The others, forewarned, had seized their rifles and started firing, and Gillmore and Sullivan had dropped to the ground and started a methodical attack with their pistols until their ammunition had run out. Three of the Moros had come running up the sand towards them, leaping in short, side-stepping jumps and waving their long knives. Gillmore had gone down at once, badly wounded in the arm, his hand hanging by a shred of flesh, and Sullivan had seized a Moro by the throat and thrown him bodily against the man behind him, then snatched the bush knife which had fallen from his grasp. He had lain about him like a madman, swinging it with a fury he had not known was in him. He knew only that his violence came from terror. Gillmore had staggered to his feet, had picked up a knife, and was fighting beside him, gasping and bleeding, and when he fell there was only one Moro left alive, a short, wiry man who moved on his feet like a ballet dancer, carrying two knives, one in each hand. As he moved away from Sullivan, pulling back and watching for the opportunity to charge, Sullivan had hurled his unaccustomed weapon deep into the man's throat. He had dragged the still-living Gillmore down to the water's edge, pulled him aboard a binta, and paddled with the others along the coast to Maymbung, where he collapsed from exhaustion and loss of blood.

He said now, remembering the horror of it, "Pitugu? Sure I remember."

"One of these fishermen was a pretty senior officer, the best man with a bolo. If he'd had a proper weapon, instead of the fisherman's jungle knife, you'd never have survived. But as it was, the old man was so impressed with your ability as a soldier he's been after you ever since. Three or four times, on your weekly pig hunts—you're lucky he didn't get you before this."

"And now? What am I supposed to do now?"

"You're supposed to teach them something about fighting in the American fashion. The old man's ambitious. He wants to use all the advice he can get."

Sullivan said tartly, "In the U.S. Army, we call that aid and comfort to the enemy."

"Yes. Yes, I know. Well, we'll see."

"You must be out of your mind if you think I'll agree to teach a lot of damned savages the arts of warfare."

Dawson was grinning at him in the firelight, the deep lines of his face shadowed against the gold reflection of the flames. He said cheerfully, "Let's be more specific. There's not much you, or any other damn Yankee, can teach them about that."

Sullivan said stiffly, "I come from Virginia."

"From Virginia?" Dawson stared at him blankly, then said carefully, "Oh, I see. I beg your pardon. As I was saying, there's not a great deal you can teach them, on general principles. But the old man is modest enough to know that he too has a lot to learn; most particularly, about American arms. We're getting quite a lot of them now, and while we know all about Springfields and Colts, some of the heavier guns need a little understanding. What's more, some of your Generals—Funston, Lawton, Kobbe—some of them have been achieving quite a degree of success in the kind of warfare the Moros themselves specialize in; guerrilla warfare. We'd like to know what kind of tactics you're using. What your overall strategy is."

"And you seriously expect me to teach them that? You're out of your mind."

"So you said. Yes, I expect you to do just that. The old man will gather a few of his chiefs together, and you'll talk to them about the way your General Staff is planning the suppression of the guerrillas, and I'll translate for you, and everybody will be happy. And when we get a busted Gatling gun in here you'll tell us what we need to repair it, and you'll help us with the repair. And then, you'll teach them how to use it. It's as simple as that."

"And if I don't?"

There was no menace in Dawson's voice. It was as if he were trying hard to avoid a threat. He said gently, frowning, "You will, my dear fellow, one way or the other. If you try and fight it—well, I don't know what they'll do. I suppose they'd just kill you. But a little mature reflection will make the point obvious. If you ever want to get out of here, as you presumably do, you'll have to go along with them, even if it's only a token acceptance."

Sullivan said thinly, "Are you trying to bribe me with offers to escape? Wouldn't you say that's a bit transparent?"

"No. Not really. But the old man's got ambitions. He's brought the warring tribes together and he wants to become the number one Moro. He probably will."

"And who, for God's sake, is the old man?"

Dawson said, smiling, "His name is Jokiri. He's a pirate, a robber, a soldier. And a man of considerable menace."

# 4.

Throughout the length and breadth of the islands, the whole country was in revolt against the bewildered Americans, who could not understand why the natives should not grasp the benefits of American sovereignty with eager hands. They had come to free the Filipinos from the yoke of Spain, and now the Filipinos themselves were turning against them in the name of Independence.

The strength of the occupying Army, under the battering of the guerrillas, had grown from eleven thousand to more than seventy thousand men. In the northern and central areas, progress towards pacification was slow but it was also apparent. In the south, however, the Army was fighting, not against a scattering of heterogeneous tribes held loosely together only by the dubious bond of nationalism, but against a far stronger enemy—a tightly-knit clan, three hundred thousand strong, whose only heritage was the practice of terror, and whose only trades were piracy and murder.

Even the excitable Spanish had displayed a wise caution in trying to deal with the Moros. Their policy had been the uneasy one: *Leave them alone.* They had paid the Moro Sultan two hundred dollars a month and naively hoped that he would somehow contrive to keep his unruly people in order, or if not, that they could

[ 63 ]

claim the Sultan as their ally and, equally hopelessly, try to discourage the more furious raids on their blockhouses.

Under the terms of the Treaty of Paris, the Americans took over this sick headache, and increased the Moro Sultan's stipend to two hundred and fifty dollars in gold. The datos, the Moro chiefs who owed a token allegiance to their Sultan, took care to insure that their loyalty should remain no more than nominal. They paid their taxes infrequently, and then only in accordance with what they thought His Highness deserved. They regarded him as an undersized, plump little man whose occasional affectation for European clothes could only mean that he had lost whatever Mussulman prerogatives he once held. His mild request that they leave the Americans alone as much as possible was a challenge to their manhood and an insult to their dignity. He made no efforts to control them, and the slaughter continued.

Out of the swamps and the hidden islands came the lesser chiefs. They gathered their murderous bands together, and they built fortified camps in the forests, throwing up earthen palisades heavily reinforced with thick slabs of mahogany and padded mats of coconut fiber. They sharpened their weapons daily, and the trade in the hand-beaten bolo was brisk. The blacksmiths squatted over their charcoal fires and their anvils, hammering out kris and talibong, bolo and capilan, quinbasi and the fearful barong. The handmade blades were finer than the famous Japanese steel, and they honed them to an astonishing degree of razor sharpness, testing them with the dreadful nonchalance of habit on the bodies of their captives.

A Moro's prime duty was killing. The Spanish, who, to tell the truth, had never bothered them much, were out of the way, and the newcomers from the other side of the world were trying to take over the Islands which they had always regarded as their own.

The time was ripe for slaughter.

Onto this bloody stage stepped Jokiri.

He was a name, at first, no more than a cipher who kept appearing in the reports that went to Manila, and then, later, in the reports that went from Manila to Washington.

At first it was *a minor chief named Jokiri*; then it became *Jokiri the Moro pirate*, and finally simply *Jokiri*, when his name and all that it stood for was known by every American in the Islands.

The soldiers would be ambushed, and as they lay in the grass and fired into the shadows of the bamboo thickets, they would mutter among themselves: "You think it's Jokiri?" And if someone shook his head and said: "No—Jokiri's over on Siasi," it was as though the skirmish were already over and won.

But they never *knew* where he was. Once, a fisherwoman came screaming into the market place of Jolo, waving her hands and shrieking that Jokiri's men were killing her family on the palm-bordered main road that led from the city, within sight of Asturias Fort and blockhouse Number Two. Within minutes, two Companies of the Twenty-third U.S. Infantry under Colonel James S. Pettit were running through the tall grasses of the hacienda which bordered the road, closing in and carrying their rifles with bayonets fixed. But Jokiri had gone, and the only evidence of his presence lay in the dried mud at the side of the road—four headless bodies, their limbs sliced off and lying scattered obscenely nearby.

The offense? They had been too friendly with the American troops.

The next day, Jokiri, with eighty-two men in a prahu and four bamboo rafts, had sailed up the Tubig Palag, slipping past the fortress at Maymbung in the darkness, and had attacked a work-party of Filipinos who, under the protection of a Company from the Fourteenth Infantry and two officers of the Battalion of Engineers, were constructing a blockhouse commanding the approaches to the delta. Eight Americans had been killed and eleven wounded. The Filipino laborers had made a desperate bid to escape into the bush and had all been hacked to pieces. The Moros had lost twenty-seven men to the steady fire of the Infantry, and four rifles, with nearly three thousand rounds of ammunition, as well as a number of barongs and bolos, had been captured from them. The rafts and prahu had been abandoned on the river. Jokiri had escaped into the impenetrable forests that lay at the foot of Mount Talipaw.

But before the troops could return to Jolo, Jokiri had struck again, within half a mile of the walled city itself, bursting into blockhouse Number One, murdering four Infantrymen and stealing seven rifles. He had also taken a Gatling gun, but had been forced to abandon it when the heavy wheels had sunk deeply into the rice paddies he had crossed on his escape back to the mountains.

The order had gone out to get him at all costs, and Colonel Williston had taken four batteries of the Sixth U.S. Artillery with elements of the Fourth and the Twentieth Infantry to sweep the western portion of the Mabingkang range where Jokiri was known to be hiding. Eight of his band had been captured, and among the thirty-four dead Williston had seen a Negrito, a Mangyan from Mindoro, four Papuans, two Monteses, and a Dyak.

Frowning, he had said to his Sergeant-Major, "I don't like it. This fellow's trying to bring the tribes together."

A mixed bag was unusual enough to worry him considerably. The Moros were fine fighters in their own rights, but their weakness had always lain in their chauvinism. Now, here was a band that included among its ranks many of the Moros' traditional enemies. It could only mean one thing—Jokiri had aspirations beyond the limited ambitions of a purely endemic pirate.

Sullivan had led two sorties against him, and once his men had been ambushed at sea by a roving party of Jokiri's men under his chief lieutenant Pangiran. The trap had been cleverly sprung after Sullivan and his troopers, in boats, had stopped to gather information from a group of fishermen who were stringing their nets in great wide cadences from the bamboo houses of their water-village. Jokiri, the fishermen had said, was on the other side of the mainland, but Pangiran and six of his Moros were hiding in one of the houses on the sea side of the tiny group of shacks that were perched on stilts over the faintly lapping surface of the water. Sullivan, cautiously, had sent his second canoe round on the eastern flank, while he himself had taken the west. They had paddled carefully forward, their rifles ready, a wary eye on their Filipino paddlers whom they knew they could never trust completely. There were eight troopers in each canoe.

Suddenly, Sullivan's frail craft had been seized from under water, the bamboo bottom had been sliced wide open, and as the binta sank quickly in the shallow water, half a hundred Moros had surfaced, their short stabbing krises in their mouths and their naked bodies dark and wet with the black mud in which they had lain concealed. Standing in wet slime to his waist, Sullivan had slashed out with his saber, calling to his men to clamber onto the platform of the nearest house. He had suffered a cut across the lower arm, and he had heard the swish of a barong over his head as he had run his opponent through. And then he had pulled himself up onto a flimsy board platform, and back to back with one of his troopers, had staved off further assaults until, by the grace of God, an unexpected burst of gunfire had come from the shore where a patrol which had lost its way had found itself on the beach, witnessing the battle in the shallow water a hundred yards offshore. The Moros, suddenly outnumbered and caught in a cross fire, had disappeared as unexpectedly as they had come. Sullivan had rallied his men and searched for their canoes; he had found none.

He had gone through the flimsy houses and found no trace of a living soul save the three trembling fishermen who had been left there to mislead him. He had burned the shacks to the water and had waited for the hidden pirates to flee the flames. But at the end of a four-hour wait he had been forced to concede the obvious—the Moros had gone.

Now, when Dawson said carefully, "A man of considerable menace," Sullivan had felt a tremor of excitement run through him.

Keeping his voice carefully scornful, hiding the fear that welled up inside him, he said, "And when do I get to see this savage master of yours?"

Dawson smiled patiently. He said, "I understand your feelings, of course. A white man . . . You'd naturally expect—well, some sort of help from me. But I ought to tell you, my dear fellow, I'm the only possible chance you have of ever getting out of this place. Common sense should dictate a common courtesy, even if you don't feel inclined to it. Don't you think so?"

Sullivan said again, stubbornly, "When do I meet this savage?"

"Pretty soon. He has great plans for you."

"Oh?"

"He's an ambitious man. He wants to modernize his Army. He feels that with a little training from an experienced and highly competent American officer, he could take on all comers and lick the lot of them."

Sullivan said, derisively, "And you really think he expects me to train his men? To fight against my own regiment? He must be an idiot."

"Well, maybe not." Dawson scratched at the lice which were crawling along the inside of his filthy jacket. He said, "The choice is not entirely up to you, either. He wants to find out if you're as good as you're supposed to be, first. If you are, then he'll offer you the job."

"And if I'm not?"

"Then you won't have to worry. Your head will be with the rest of them. With all your friends'. The Brigadier's, the Colonel's— What was that little civilian doing with you?"

"He was a journalist, fellow called—" He broke off suddenly, staring. He said tightly, "Am I to understand you were there? At the canyon?"

"No. But I got the news. I don't go out on their fights any more. My leg. What was his name?"

"Withers."

"Uh-huh. A lot of them are almost on our side, even if they don't really know it."

"You mean those misleading reports they send in?"

Dawson threw back his head and laughed. "Precisely. It's the prerogative of the press in the time of war to beat hell out of the Army with their bloody little pencils. You must admit you've had your fair share of it."

"Yes. I know. I suppose they have a job to do."

"I suppose so."

"Well, you can tell your boss I'm not interested in his proposition. I'm a soldier of the Twenty-third U.S. Infantry." His voice trailed off into a lame diminuendo, and he waited for Dawson to say something. It was easy enough to be heroic, talking like this across a small campfire with the crickets shrieking and all the harsh noises of the night forest coming to them from the blackness outside the circle of red-yellow light. He said sullenly, "I'm an officer in the Army of the United States. That should be enough of an answer."

"Yes, it should, shouldn't it?" Dawson's voice was mocking. He said affably, "But then, I grew tired of the Army. I wanted to live my own life. And when the time comes I prophesy that you'll want to live yours. You'll find that out. Tomorrow morning."

The fear was creeping up on him again. He said coldly, "And what happens tomorrow morning?"

Dawson had stopped scratching and was removing a ragged leather boot. Shaking the sand out of it, showing the filthy rag that was wrapped round his foot in lieu of a sock, he said casually, "They've got a public exhibition for you to participate in. The old man thinks that if you're as handy with a saber as they say you are, then you must be a pretty good man all round. It's the only thing they understand, you know. The use of a sharp blade. You could be the American Army's worst officer, but if you can fence well . . . How are you with a sword, truly?"

Sullivan said stiffly, "Adequate."

"Don't be a stuffed shirt. Tomorrow, you'll be fighting for your life with a barong. Individual combat. There's a fellow named Pangiran here, one of the old man's chief lieutenants. You ran into him once, in a village called Boyang, remember?"

Sullivan said steadily, "I remember. They tried to ambush us. Hid under the water."

"That's the one," Dawson said delightedly. "This fellow Pangiran—you stuck your sword into him and made him very angry, because no one's done that to him for a long, long time. He's got a bit of a reputation. Best man in the camp with a barong. I once saw him slice a captured Dyak down the middle from crown to crotch, one blow. He was just showing off, of course, proving a point, but I never saw anything like it. Fantastic."

Wrapping the rag carefully round his foot again, pushing his toe hard into the boot, he said, "You don't happen to have a spare pair of boots, do you? No? Where was I? Oh yes. How do you feel about fighting with a barong? Ever used one?"

"No," Sullivan said. "And I don't intend to start now."

"You will," Dawson said gently. "Believe me, you will. They'll hand you a barong, and Pangiran will make a quick slice at your neck. Believe me, you'll start fighting. Only problem is, will you be

[ 69 ]

able to win? Personally, I doubt it very much. In individual combat, it's always the toughest who wins, and Pangiran, my soft American friend, is tough."

Sullivan felt it was time to set the record straight. He said coldly, "I have no intention of reducing myself to the level of the Moros. I intend to get out of here and rejoin my unit at the first possible opportunity. And if they kill me in the attempt . . ."

There was a long pause. A woman came over and tossed a log of eucalyptus wood on the fire. Dawson took off his trousers and started rubbing sand into the seams to kill the lice. He looked up at last and said, "Yes? You were saying?"

When Sullivan did not answer, Dawson stopped work on the lice and twisted his face around, away from the brightness of the flames. Peering at him, he said slowly, his voice very quiet, "I'm probably a little bitter. Maybe we can do a deal together. Maybe we could help each other escape. Neither of us could do it alone, but maybe later on, when they relax their guard over you."

Sullivan said curiously, "And you've never tried to get away? Not since . . . ?"

"No. I wouldn't last for five minutes in the forest. All I can do is hobble. You saw."

"Yes. I'm sorry. But now they trust you? They leave you alone?"

"Sort of. Some of them do, some don't." He said with a twisted smile, "The old man knows I put too high a price on my life. It makes him despise me, but I have my uses. And perhaps, later on, you may be the answer."

"Then let's get out of here. Tonight."

"We wouldn't get past the palisade. It's manned, shoulder to shoulder. And at night they move like cats, and they can see like owls. We wouldn't have a chance. And it's impossible to cross the swamp. They have a way through, but we'd never find it, not without a guide."

"So? We stay here and rot?"

"We stay here and *wait*."

He was aware of a tremor in Dawson's voice. Dawson said with sudden nervousness, "And for Christ's sake don't talk about it unless I say it's all right. A surprising number of them speak a little English."

Sullivan was staring, flabbergasted.

"English? I don't believe it."

Dawson's wry humor returned. He said cheerfully, "I taught some of them myself. Not much. A few words."

"And—and Jokiri?"

"No, he doesn't." Dawson was studying his face intently. "But his daughter does."

Sullivan said nothing. He knew that Dawson was trying to tell him more, trying to ease some of the pain out in talk, trying to find comfort and protection—against what?

Beyond the darkness, on the other side of the houses, the commotion at the gate had died down. The compound was quiet now, with only an occasional group of warriors passing them, scarcely looking at them as they sat there in the firelight. Watching them, Sullivan thought: *These are the men I was fighting a few hours ago, the men I've been hunting like animals, the savages who murdered my troops.*

They carried their weapons carelessly, clutching them lightly or leaving them loosely tucked into the sashes at their waists. Some of the blades were without scabbards and shone menacingly in the yellow flames. One warrior was holding a loose tuft of grass, and was slicing it neatly as he walked by, testing the edge of his kris.

The mosquitoes were whining round Sullivan's ears, stinging the back of his neck, and he brushed impatiently at a soft, fleshy insect that was crawling towards the dried blood of a flesh wound in his arm; he winced as he felt the squelch of it. He said, "This—this thing tomorrow. It's all arranged?"

"Yep. Jokiri's given the order. Pangiran has shaved his eyebrows."

Sullivan shuddered.

"Juramentado?"

"I'm afraid so. He's shaved his eyebrows and bathed his body, and he's taken the oath before the priest."

Sullivan said somberly, "Doesn't that mean he knows he'll be killed?"

"That's the theory. If he kills you, he'll be taken into Jolo under

[ 71 ]

a pile of fodder that's being delivered for the garrison horses. He'll finish there the work his oath imposes on him."

"From what I know about it," Sullivan said, "a juramentado doesn't stop killing until he's dead. It seems to me he might try and take you along too. Doesn't that worry you? Another white man, another Christian?"

Dawson said quickly, "I'm a Mohammedan. I changed my faith a couple of years back."

"That was very thoughtful."

"Planning, dear boy. Looking to the future. I learned enough to convince their priests that I'm a true subject of Allah. You'd be surprised what a help it is."

"I can imagine."

"So I've nothing to fear from Pangiran, or any of the others. A lot of them take the oath, once in a while, you know. Makes me glad I'm not a Christian any more."

"And if I kill him?"

"Glad to see you're coming round to the idea. If you kill him, your troubles are practically over. It will convince the old man of your astonishing prowess and you'll have a brilliant career ahead of you. Military adviser to the next Sultan of the Moros. But you realize it won't be easy to kill him—a juramentado. They seem to go on fighting long after they're dead. Like a chicken with its head chopped off. Only this chicken carries a very nasty weapon."

"Barong, you said?"

"Yep. It's a lot heavier than your saber. And a great deal sharper. Hell, you've seen what a barong can do."

"And I'm not coming round to the idea."

"You can hardly refuse, can you? What are you going to do, stand there and let him slice you in pieces?"

"No. I suppose not." He said disgustedly, "A Roman spectacle."

"Sort of."

"Anyway, what makes him think I can teach them anything? There's nothing wrong with the fighting abilities of a Moro. They must know that."

"They can't understand why the fat and flabby Americans stand up so well under their attacks. They know it's not merely a question of your superior numbers, or your artillery. They know it's not physical strength, or stamina, because you don't have either, not by their standards. They think it's some sort of—well, if they knew the word I suppose they'd call it discipline. So, tomorrow you'll have a chance to show them what it is. They'll make an attentive audience."

"And if I can—I'm supposed to murder this man in cold blood? Is that it?"

"Believe me, old boy, your blood won't be cold after the first couple of minutes. If you're still alive."

He could feel the cold night breeze on the back of his neck, and he felt himself shiver. He said shortly, "Right now I could do with some sleep."

The weariness and the stiffness was coming over him. He went with Dawson into the hut he had left, and lay down on the rush mat on the earthen floor. He wondered if his life was as cheap a thing as he'd been trying to pretend. He knew that he hadn't convinced Dawson. And he knew he had not convinced himself, either.

He was asleep before Dawson, scratching at his armpit again, had left the hut and gone out into the smoke-scented darkness of the compound. He awoke once, a little later, in the terror of a nightmare, and turned over to his stomach and forced the awareness of his condition far to the back of his mind.

Tomorrow he would worry about it. For the present, only sleep. Tomorrow . . . tomorrow . . . The night was dark, and still, and silent. Even the night birds had ceased their squawking, as though they too sensed the tension that hung over the camp; as though they too were pondering the problems that the morning would bring, and, like him, were shivering at the thought of the peril and the shame of it.

The wood-smoke hung in the air over the fortified village, lingering on the dampness that came up from the putrefaction of the swamp. His own courage was the softly thinning smoke, and his fear was the putrefaction.

Fitfully, at last, he slept.

[ 73 ]

# 5.

THE FIRST THING THAT SULLIVAN SAW WHEN HE WOKE UP WAS A barong.

He had slept, uneasily, on a bamboo mat spread out on the mud floor of the hut, and he woke with a start to find that daylight was already streaming in through the doorless opening, breaking in a bright beam across his face. He opened his eyes quickly, wide awake at once with military instinct, reaching out for his rifle or his saber which, he was sure, were in their accustomed place close by his cot. He fumbled in a moment of panic before he remembered that he was a captive, and that the Moro standing beside him had not come to kill him. He struggled to his feet and wiped the night-coma from the corners of his eyes, rubbing a hand across his face, feeling the stubble of his beard.

The Moro was silent beside him; he held out the barong for Sullivan to take, and then went out, without a word, moving softly on bare feet, his body sleek and shining as he went through the doorway into the bright outside.

Sullivan felt the weight of the barong, moving his arm up and down, twisting his wrist, getting the feel of it, touching the edge of the blade and marveling, against his will, at the incredible sharpness of it. He drew it gently across the back of his arm and watched the dark hairs that gathered in a shaved clump of blackness, and when he looked up again Dawson was there. The Englishman was leaning heavily on his stick, and he had a black cheroot sticking out of the corner of his twisted mouth. He said, grinning, "Well? How did you sleep? Not as comfortable as the barracks, is it?"

Sullivan stretched the vestiges of sleep out of his cramped limbs. Holding out the barong, he said, "This what I'm supposed to fight with?"

"Uh-huh."

"And there's no alternative?"

"Sure there is. Tell 'em you won't fight. See what happens."

He was still grinning, but there was an undertone of fear in his voice. He said flippantly, hiding his worry, "They'd simply use you to test their blades on. If you fight, at least there's a chance."

"A chance for you, you mean."

"That's right. For both of us. Sure, I've got a stake in it too. First of all, Pangiran's a bit of a bastard, you know, gives me a bad time, and if you cut his bloody head off it might give the rest of them cause to respect us—to respect a white man a little more, don't you think?"

"And with me dead you'll never get out of here."

"That's true. But for Christ's sake keep your voice down."

The flippancy had gone now. Looking nervously at the entrance behind him Dawson said, "They're all out there, waiting. Gathering together from all over the damn place." His good humor returning as quickly as it had gone, he went on: "One service you're performing for your fellow soldiers, even if they don't know it, is that every Moro for twenty miles around will be here today, so they'll rest more peaceful in the Garrison. That's something, isn't it? You want to clean up a bit? Freshen up?"

"When is this—this Roman spectacle scheduled?"

Dawson shrugged. "Oh, some time this morning. Any time. Your guess is as good as mine—you think these people carry watches? Come on, I'll take you down to the stream."

"Oh? I'm allowed out of the camp?"

"Don't worry, they'll be watching us. Both of us. Are you hungry?"

"No. Not particularly."

"There's some meat if you'd feel like some. Buffalo. Not bad."

They went out together and crossed the compound to the small gate at the palisade. A Papuan warrior, dressed in a loincloth and carrying a long spear, was squatting on the ground, his feet spread out under his thin buttocks. He rose on a word from Dawson and pulled back the timbers that constituted the crude gate. A moment later they were in the forest. Dawson said, "Looks easy to make a break, doesn't it? But they're all around us, ten or fifteen of them. We wouldn't get more than a hundred yards. And even if we could give them the slip, there's that bloody swamp to cross."

"There must be a way across it. There's no deep water."

"No, but have you ever seen wet quicksand at work? You go down in the mud till it sucks at you, pulls you down—I've seen it. Nearly got caught myself once. I was out foraging with some of the boys, following in their footsteps, so to speak, and I lost my footing. They watched me go down, laughing at me, all of them. When it was up to my neck, one of them threw me a length of vine and hauled me out. Can you imagine that, they laughed. Wanted me to understand that without them I couldn't get a couple of hundred yards away. Well, now I know. We don't try and cross that swamp till we can get a guide."

Sullivan said thoughtfully, "Tell me about this man—what's his name? Pangiran?"

"Pangiran. He's a dato, a minor chief. He usually fights with a barong and a kris, one in each hand, and he's ambidextrous, so watch out."

"Two weapons?"

"No. This time, just a barong. The old man's a stickler for protocol. He thinks you'd be at a disadvantage with a kris. You must admit it's pretty fair-minded of him."

Sullivan said carefully, "And I imagine Pangiran is a rival for Jokiri's crown. Is that it?"

Dawson threw back his head and laughed.

"Exactly. Glad to see you're catching on. Sooner or later, someone would have killed Pangiran, so don't feel too bad about it. Another thing—you know about the talibong?"

Sullivan said briefly, "I know."

It was a long, curved, single-edged sword that every fifth warrior in the Moro army carried, and was used for decapitating the enemy wounded. They had told him about it at the base. There were earnest students of enemy tactics who sat on teakwood armchairs in the hot Headquarters building and lectured the officers on the methods and the weapons against which they would be fighting; and there were fervent journalists who, eyes gleaming, drew pencil sketches of the Moros' fearful tools to excite an expectant audience back home.

Dawson said, "Don't let it put you off, but there'll be a soldier standing by, dancing around the edge of the fight, waiting for one of you to fall. He'll be quite harmless, but—well, he'll get carried away, and if he thinks you can't get up he's the head-cutter. A ritual."

"And Pangiran?"

Dawson shrugged.

"To a talibong soldier it doesn't matter a damn whose head he gets. The lower ratings. Same as in any other army. All he has to do is make sure that his own particular job is done properly. And his particular job is to slice off a head with one blow. Yours or Pangiran's, why should he worry whose it is?"

They had reached the edge of the stream and Dawson had stripped off his jacket. His flesh was taut and firm, and there were two scars running across his left shoulder. He knelt down on the rocks and threw the water up into his face in native fashion. Watching him, Sullivan felt a shudder of revulsion as he took off his dark blue shirt and his pale blue trousers and stepped in his underpants into the cold, fast-moving rivulet. He felt the black mud give under his feet and staggered to the rocks close by Dawson where the water was cleaner, then sank down till he felt the cold freshness of it round his chest. He rubbed at the dried blood on his arms, trying to massage the stiffness away from them.

The forest was darkly alive with sound. There were birds squawking angrily at them in the trees, and once a small monkey hissed at them and scurried up the trunk of a palm. The liana vines hung down thick and heavy, and there was a bright purple cluster of flowers that he knew were poisonous. In the mud on the other side he could see the tracks of a small buffalo that had come down in the night to drink.

He stopped his washing when he heard the rustle in the bushes, and looked back over his shoulder. A group of women came down to the edge of the water and stood for a moment looking at him. They carried earthenware pots on their heads, and they were dressed in jabuls which they wore tightly tucked round their waists; their breasts were bare. And then he stared in astonishment.

One of them, a tall, slim woman of twenty or so, was lighter in color than the rest, and her features, though heavy, were Eurasian rather than Mongoloid. Her nose was straight, with no trace of the thick nostrils of the other women, nor was she as dumpy as they. She carried herself without the bowlegged waddling of the others, and her black hair hung down her bare back instead of frizzling bulkily on the top of her head. As she saw Sullivan looking at her, she stopped and made a subconscious gesture with her hand; she made as if to cover her breasts. And then, she lowered her hand and her eyes and walked steadily with the others to the water's edge. He watched her, wondering, as she stooped and filled her vessel, lifting it easily onto her head again and moving back in the direction she had come from. She paused, then, waiting for the other women, looking back at them. Sullivan watched her, waiting for a sign from her that she had noticed him, but she turned as the other women came up and in a moment she was gone. He stole a quick glance at Dawson. Brushing the water off his chest with the flat of his hand, Dawson said casually, "The old man's daughter. Let him see you looking at her like that and you'll be in trouble."

"But—but she's *white*, for God's sake!"

"White? That's all a point of view. Are Dagos white? I suppose they are. She's Spanish."

"Spanish?"

"An adopted daughter. The Dyaks captured her when she was a child. She was only six or seven, too young for a concubine, so they took her to a sort of slave market in Borneo, together with a lot of handsome young Spanish soldiers they'd caught at the same time. The old man's people happened to run across them, and you know the Moros when they see a Dyak. They carved hell out of the Dyaks and rescued the girl. Don't ask me why. She was still in shock, but the old man says she just clung to him. I suppose he took a fancy to her, thought she might be worth something when she got a bit of a figure on her. Anyway, he took her on his prahu, and in the course of time he adopted her. Again, don't ask me why. He's not a very strict Moslem, and in any case he could easily have divorced one of his wives to make room for her. But—well, I don't know. Now she's his daughter, and that's all there is to it."

"But a Spanish woman—here!"

"She's not Spanish any more, she's just another Moro. Better looking, perhaps, but . . . Tell the truth, I rather fancy her myself, but I fancy my skin more. Lay a hand on her, and I tell you, friend, life just won't be worth living any more. Take my word for it. And we'd better get back. You ready?"

Saying nothing, Sullivan climbed out onto the rocks and slipped into his clothes. He could not get the memory of the girl out of his mind.

The duel began in the early afternoon. He was resting in his hut, listening to the excited sounds that filled the compound, dreading the event but knowing there was no way to escape it, when Dawson came in.

The Englishman sat down on the earth beside him, squatting like a native, and said, "You've got a few minutes before they're ready."

He fumbled in his pocket and pulled out a small bundle of leaves that looked like a twist of tobacco. His voice low, he said urgently, "Eat this. Chew it well, hold it in your mouth as long as you can, then swallow it."

Frowning, struggling to his feet, Sullivan said, "You might at least tell me what it is."

"It's a narcotic."

"Are you mad?"

"Don't be a fool," Dawson said angrily, "Pangiran is a juramentado. He's taken the oath. You know what that means. He'll fight long after the breath's gone out of him. You know how these fellows are. You'll need every bit of help you can get."

"But a drug isn't going to help me."

"It will." Dawson shoved it into his hand. "Take it. Take my word for it. It's like—it's like hashish, like marijuana, it speeds up your reactions. All right, it'll give you Dutch courage too, but chew it. If you won't take it for your own sake, take it for mine. As I told you, I've got a stake in this too. Go on, take it."

Hesitantly, reluctantly, wondering first if he were doing the right thing and then thinking wearily, *Well, what does it matter anyway,* he took the bundle of leaves from Dawson's grubby hand and tentatively tasted it. It was sour, bitter, pungent. "Go on, eat it," Dawson said again, and he wondered if he was being deliberately poisoned. Then he knew that Dawson was right. He, too, had a stake in the outcome of the battle. He stuffed the wad into his mouth and began chewing. His saliva dried up and the tears came into his eyes, and as he chewed he felt the harshness of the liquid burning his throat. Dawson slapped him on the back and said cheerfully, "That's the spirit. You know what? I think you've got a pretty good chance. Remember, ignore the talibong man. Keep your eyes on Pangiran. Go first for the arm he's not using so that he can't switch hands and confuse you. Go for his neck. Go for his guts. Hit him anywhere you can, but hit him. One good slice is all you really need."

Sullivan picked up the barong and tried the balance again, as if it were a borrowed saber. The fear was growing to a climax now, and he could feel the heavy beat of his own heart. Dawson said, "Two other things. The old man's here, watching. And that stuff you're chewing—Medina gave it to me for you."

"Medina?"

"The old man's daughter. The girl you had your eye on. Don't ask me why. And keep quiet about it, too. I suppose I ought to say good luck."

Dawson held out his hand, and when Sullivan took it he was surprised at the strength in the grip. The Englishman held on to it and said slowly, "You'll have to fight hard, Sullivan. There's no other way. Think of it as a saber. I don't have to tell you how important it is."

He dropped his hand and turned his back. Sullivan swallowed the sickly wad in his mouth and strode out after him. His head was swimming and he felt a little drunk. He said to himself, *Well, what the hell, we only live once.*

There were two or three hundred of them there in the sun that struck down to the center of the compound, squatting round in a circle and waiting.

To one side there were thirty or forty Papuans, their slim bodies doubled up, crouched close to the earth. They wore loincloths and held their spears upright between their thighs, and some of them wore brightly painted masks; others had pins of ivory through their noses and wore brightly beaded amulets. Their shields were leaning against the grass walls of the huts behind them. A group of grass-skirted Monteses, heavy, thickset, stolid, sat together where a baobab tree cast its great shadow across the earth. Beside them there were a dozen Mangyans, wearing striped cloth kilts and head-dresses of parrot feathers. There were Negritos, and Visayans, and Tagalogs, and Malays, and even a scattering of Samals. He wondered about the ambitious man who could bring the warring tribes together like this, wondering what cause they could have in common. They were all armed to the teeth.

At one side, close by the best hut in the compound, a shelter of palm fronds had been mounted on tall bamboo poles, and under it sat a chief. He wondered if this were Jokiri, and he heard himself ask Dawson in an astonishingly loud voice: "Is that the old man over there?"

He shook his head to drive away the dizziness, wondering what had prompted him to speak, feeling that he was drunk, and frightened because of it. He saw Dawson look back at him in surprise, and then turn and continue on his way.

They were ceremonially dressed, the Moros, in their best clothes; tight bright pantaloons and decorated jackets, with colored turbans and embroidered shirts. Even some of the women, who stood close under the shadows of the huts, wore bodices of gaudy cloth, as though this were a festive occasion that demanded their best array. He thought he had never seen so many colors gathered together in one place, and then Dawson turned and sat down on the mat next to the chief.

[ 81 ]

He walked towards the center of the clearing, his barong gripped tightly in his hand, and he knew that a new, unexpected determination had come to him. He was walking straight towards the proud, silently evil chief and he was going to hack at his head with the unaccustomed weapon and the devil with it. Let them cut him to pieces afterwards if they cared. It was his duty as a soldier to kill his enemy, and he knew that his true enemy was not Pangiran but Jokiri. His head was swimming, and he heard Dawson yell, his voice coming from a long way off, *"Behind you, Sullivan!"*

He was not conscious of the volition, but his knees bent quickly as he slipped to a crouching position, slewing his body round instinctively and holding his weapon high over his head. He was scarcely conscious of the charge as Pangiran came at him, moving, it seemed, incredibly slowly; he knew that the narcotic had speeded his own reactions to the point of fantasy.

He remembered Pangiran now, remembered him standing tall and straight in the shallow water that time at Boyang, standing silent and expectant as the narrow canoe came at him. He remembered lunging forward with his saber and feeling it bite deeply into the flesh at the side of the shoulder. He remembered his fierce elation as the undulation of Pangiran's dropped kris had caught the sun when it hit the water. Now, the same Moro was coming at him again, the blade of his barong held horizontal to the ground and a little to one side. Sullivan sprang to his left and heard the blade whistle past him.

He stood still, then, waiting for the second pass, watching Pangiran's sudden turn like the jink of a pig-pony, and for a moment the two men stood facing each other. The Moro leaped to the side, and danced back again, moving like a dancer in short, graceful leaps, waving his blade in the sunlight, seeking to distract his adversary with a display of gymnastics. Sullivan waited. He was calm now, quite calm, forcing himself to think of his weapon as a saber, holding it out in the on guard position, not taking his eyes from the Moro's face. He saw that his eyebrows had been shaved clean, and there were traces of white powder on his cheeks; his clothes were all white. He waited for the prancing to stop, knowing that he could move fast when the time came, and then the barong whistled past his face again and he knew that he had ducked clear from a blow that would have taken his head off. He swung his arm up and out then, throwing his weight into the blow, and he felt a surge of excitement as he saw the scarlet flow of blood that gushed out of the Moro's side, seeping into the white cloth of his shirt, and spreading down the side of his tight trousers.

He ran in fast for the follow-up, counting his steps and measuring the distance, and Pangiran slipped under his arm and slashed at him as he twisted his body away from the blow, feeling the hot searing of it across his chest. He was moving fast now, faster than he had ever moved in his life, and there was an elation in him that he could not understand. They stood facing each other again, and he saw that the Moro's face was expressionless, dead, dulled, and lifeless; but the razor-edge of the barong was weaving slowly from side to side, and learning his lesson he waited for the charge. When it came, he stepped to one side and slashed with cold precision, bringing his arm high in the air and savagely down again, swinging his blade like a woodchopper. He felt it slice deep into flesh, felt it twisting against bone, and as he tried to drag it free, tugging it viciously out, he felt an unbearable pain in his side and he screamed out his agony.

They were both on the ground now, slashing at each other without conscious decision, fighting blindly like animals, and for a moment the only sound was the parry of steel against steel. Sullivan felt the blood sticking to his hand between the flesh and the smooth rosewood of the handle, felt that he was using his shoulder to swing the weapon, felt that his movements were slowing down. He rolled over to his side and struggled to his feet, clutching at a bloody jacket with his left hand and swinging his barong up in a cruel arc aimed at the Moro's stomach.

There was no reason to his fighting now. He felt that the life was gone out of him, and he knew that his adversary was losing blood fast, more blood than a man could lose and still live. He pushed himself clear and brushed the sweat from his eyes, squinting in the sunlight, drunkenly swaying, resisting the impulse to charge in for the kill, and when the Moro came at him again, swaying from side to side, he stood his ground and lunged forward, getting in too close for the slash that came at him, getting close in under it, feeling the dull pain in his back where the brass haft of his enemy's weapon caught him across the kidneys, feeling the hot edge of it as it was pulled back. He knew that he had run the man through, and he tugged the blade free and moved back. He was appalled by the spectacle that confronted him.

Pangiran was still on his feet. His left arm had been sliced completely off at the elbow. The gray mass of his intestines were hanging down the front of his belly and his face was covered with blood so that only the gleam of the eyes seemed to penetrate the ghastly, crimson flood that was his head. The right arm, that still held the barong, was slashed and useless, but he stood swaying on his feet and preparing for another charge.

Shaking with fear and horror and disgust, Sullivan stood swaying, watching, waiting, feeling the earth reeling around him, seeing the faces of the crowd in a blur of hatred, not hearing their voices except in sporadic bursts of sound. He watched the Moro stagger towards him, watched the barong come up again and swing out and up, and then he saw him fall to the ground and lie there, breathing, bleeding, splayed out like a crucified, bloody animal. In a daze, he saw one of the soldiers move forward into the circle, moving slowly, almost casually. He saw the skinny hand grasp the Moro by the hair and lift up the head, and as he closed his eyes he heard the sickening sound as the talibong cut through the vertebrae at the neck, and he fell to his knees and was sick. He felt the dull blow as the ground swung round and hit him, and then it was dark and peaceful and quiet. The only sensation he had was of wetness, and he knew that he was slipping and twisting himself in pain in the morass of his own blood.

He came to his senses much later. It was dark, and at first he wondered if he were blind. Sound swayed into the orbit of his hearing and then swayed back again into silence. He opened his eyes painfully and all he could see was a light, like the flame of a candle, close to his face, and out of the depths of his coma he heard Dawson's voice, trembling and hesitant. "Coming to, old boy? Coming to?"

He closed his eyes, and when he opened them again he saw that Dawson was leaning over him, grinning, holding a spluttering wick sunk in a lump of tallow. Its light was yellow and smoky, and the smell of it sickened him. He tried to move, but he could not, and the ground under his back was hard and painful. He heard soft mutterings and knew that Dawson was not alone, but the effort to revive himself was too much for him and he let himself slide back into unconsciousness. The pain in his body was unbearable, and he knew that he could only fight it by willing himself back into insensibility.

He opened his eyes again and saw that it was daylight, wondering how the night had passed so quickly, wondering how he had survived it at all. He twisted his shoulders round and saw that his limbs were heavily padded with cloth; he was bandaged like a mummy. He heard himself groan, and then Dawson was standing over him again, looking down on him and scratching at his head.

Dawson said, "Well, I'd never have believed it."

Sullivan looked up at him and tried to speak. He was seized with a fit of coughing, the pain shooting through him savagely. Dawson crouched down quickly and said, stupidly, "Don't do that, old man. Don't die on us now."

The coughing went away and there was only pain left. He said weakly, "What happened to Pangiran?"

"They cut his head off. Don't you remember? That was some fight. I was really proud of you."

He felt the ground swaying around him, and he heard Dawson's urgent voice: "Some more water—quickly."

There was a wet pad on his head and he could feel the water trickling into his eyes. He heard Dawson say, "That's better. That's the idea."

He opened his eyes again, and it was the girl who was bending over him. Her hair was falling over onto the ground close to his face, and he could detect an oily perfume in it. He tried to smile at her. She was wearing a bodice, now, like the upper-class Moro women from the towns, but her shoulders were bare and he saw that her skin was smooth and clear. The touch of her hands on his head was soft and gentle. He felt the tears coming into his eyes, and he was ashamed of them. He lay still and thought about the barracks and the men and the horses in the stables—anything to take his mind off the agony of his position. He heard Dawson say cheerfully, "You'll be all right. Just a question of time, now."

Then the blackness came over him again, and he slept. And when he awoke once more, the sun had gone to the other side of the hut and was casting eerie shadows under the overhang of the rush roof. The pain in his limbs had given way to an intolerable stiffness, but he could move them now, a little. He saw that the padding on them was a crude form of bandaging, and when he pressed at it gently he felt a dry, crackling substance underneath like the leaves of a cigar. Both arms and both legs were heavily covered with the brown cloth, and there was another bandage across his chest from stomach to shoulder. He tried rolling over on his side, and he nearly fainted from the pain in his kidneys, and at last he called out weakly, "Dawson? Dawson? Are you there?"

A shadow fell across the doorway and he saw one of the Moros standing there, looking at him dispassionately. He said, "Dawson—get Dawson." The Moro turned and left, and a moment later the chief himself was there. Sullivan stared at him, half in fright and half in fascination.

There was no doubt in his mind that it was Jokiri. He was taller than average, nearly as tall as Sullivan himself, and the muscles across his bare chest rippled like those of an animal running in the sunlight. He wore tight Moro pantaloons of red and gold striped silk with a green sash at his waist. He had no shirt, but wore an open, sleeveless jacket of blue cloth richly embroidered in silver cord. He wore no turban. In the strap round his waist he carried, on the right, a kris with a blade that was both fluted and perforated and was decorated on its ivory handle with pigeon-blood rubies and discs of mother-of-pearl; on the left was the long terciada, the heavy ceremonial sword which denoted his senior rank. Both of these weapons were fitted at the hasp with two long steel studs between which the user could catch the blade of his opponent's sword and snap it in two like a twig.

Sullivan stared at him, and then said hesitantly, "Jokiri?"

It was hard not to regard him as just another Moro. He had to force himself to believe that this was the most feared dato of them all, a man of ruthless savagery whose slightest whim was law. He met Sullivan's eye without speaking, his face expressionless. It was the face of a brutal maniac. His eyes, Mongolian in slant, were close together, his mouth was small and thin-lipped, his nose was aquiline and pointed, and the yellow cheeks were hollow like those of a man long sick with tuberculosis. His ears were small and sharply pointed, like the pictures he had seen as a child of the gnome who lived at the bottom of the garden. But there was nothing gnomelike about his expression; it was an expression of proud impatience, mixed with a kind of latent virulence that seemed ready to burst out in an explosion of temper. He looked Sullivan straight in the face, unspeaking, for a long time, then turned and spoke to someone behind him.

It was the girl, Medina, who came forward, and behind her Sullivan could see the faces of two Papuans who, he found out later, were her bodyguards. She came close to where he was lying and looked at him without expression, and said, haltingly, in English, "This is my father. His name is Jokiri. He is the chief, and one day he will be Sultan. He will tell you that when you will be better you will work for him."

Feeling at a disadvantage, he said slowly, "Does your father speak English?"

"He speaks only Moro-Joloano and Moro-Samal, and a little bit Spanish."

"I have to thank you for helping me."

He was remembering her hand on his forehead. She said quickly, quite calmly, "It is better if nobody knows that I gave it to you."

"I wasn't thinking of that. Where is Dawson?"

Jokiri turned and spoke to her, and there was a long conversation between them. Then she said, "My father will tell you that I will help Dawson to take care of you. When you will want something, there will be someone here who you will send for me."

"Will you tell me your name?"

"It is Medina. Before, I was Spanish, a long time ago. Now, I am Moro like my father Jokiri."

"Yes, I know. I was told."

[ 87 ]

He was trying to establish a bond of secrecy between them. She said again, "I will help you to be better. Then you will help my father Jokiri."

The chief turned abruptly and went out, and in a moment his daughter followed him. Sullivan was left alone. He turned heavily over onto his stomach, burying his face in the straw-stuffed cushion under his head. He thought of the green fields of his parents' farm, and the copse that stood on the top of the hill beyond the gentle river that wandered quietly, peacefully through the valley; of the white fence that contained the restless energy of the young horses, and the big roan that stood more than seventeen hands high and could jump like a kangaroo . . . of the red-roofed barn that had just been painted before he left, and of the ancient walleyed dog that was chained in the yard at the back of the house. He thought of his mother, and of his sister, and he wondered if he would ever see them again.

# 6.

THE RAIDS INCREASED.

The war against the Filipinos, which was the occupying Army's *raison d'etre,* had settled into a process of attrition, during which the temper of the fighting was hotter in the States than it was in the Islands. The cynics were already beginning to call it the Hearst War; inflammatory press reports arrived from the professionally excited journalists who had flocked there once it was seen that the war was not really too dangerous, and back home the fever of Imperialism swept the country. Letters from soldiers in the field were published in a thousand home-town papers, and sharp editorials were written by men who had never been beyond the confines of their own home towns. When the news was scanty or dull, it could always be colored by the "eye-witness" format, and books on the new possessions appeared like flies in summer.

It was nearly a week before Sullivan was able to move about with any degree of ease. The wounds healed slowly, but they healed well. Each day Medina came to him with lubigon leaves soaked in water, which she pressed against the deep slashes and bound into place with torn rags; and when the poultices dried out, she replaced them. His arms, his legs, his chest, were deeply stained with the dark purple of the juice, but the wounds did not turn septic, and in the course of a few days the gashes began to close up and the process of healing set in.

He was well fed, on fish and buffalo meat and rice, with sometimes a ration of yams or sweet potatoes. He came to know the life of the village and to accept it, and the villagers came to accept him.

It was not much of a village. Unlike most of the Moro compounds, it was on dry land, above the level of the mangrove swamps, and it was well fortified against attack. He spent his first pedestrian morning examining the structure of the palisade that ran round all sides of the compound, wondering how it would stand up under artillery fire, and deciding that a few well-placed shells would blow it to pieces. Dawson came hobbling up to him and stood watching him for a while. He said, "Yes, I know. Artillery would make a hell of a mess of it. That what you were thinking?"

Sullivan nodded.

"And yet they seem to be contemplating a stand here. I thought the Moros believed in the theories of fluidity."

"You can't store heavy guns on prahus. This place is going to be an arms depot. And it's not fortified against the Americans. It's meant to hold off the Dyaks, that's all."

"Oh? And what's supposed to happen when the Infantry comes this way?"

Dawson grinned.

"They won't. We're well hidden here, and there's only one way into the village. Across the swamp. The Dyaks know we're here, but the Americans don't. Whenever an American patrol gets near the marshland, they're attacked by a Moro patrol which then retreats and entices your fellows up onto the mountains where the battle is gently disengaged. It's getting to be a habit. And no patrol could ever come across the swamp."

"They will, one day."

"Then they'd never get back to bring up the artillery. Not one of them. When are you going to be ready to start work?"

"I have no intention of starting work."

Dawson said slowly, "Unless they begin to have some sort of

confidence in you, you'll never get out of here. You know that?"

"I'll get out. Sooner or later."

Dawson changed the subject. He said, "How's it going with Medina?"

Sullivan turned away and sat down under the shade of the palisade. He sat on the ground with his legs stiffly crossed under him, like a Moro, and changed his position when he saw Dawson's twisted smile. He said slowly, "I don't understand. After all, she's a Moslem, now, and yet . . ."

"Yet she associates freely with you?"

"I must say it surprises me."

He was beginning to feel troubled every time she came to him.

"She has ambitions, dear boy."

Sullivan said sharply, "What's that meant to suggest?"

"She's after you. There's enough Spaniard left in her to make her want a white husband."

"But—but her father . . ."

"If her father knew just exactly how free and easy she is, then maybe things would be a little tougher for you. They keep a fairly strict eye on her, but after all, she's the daughter of the old man. There's nobody much who's going to interfere with her when he's out of the camp. To tell the truth, Jokiri rather encourages it, when he's here. He thinks that some sort of association with the better elements of the occupying Army will add considerably to her culture. He makes me give her English lessons. But just in case you should get any ideas—he takes it for granted that you know what would happen to you if you should lay a hand on her. He's quite sure your friendship will remain platonic. If you don't believe me, take her to bed one day and see what happens next."

Sullivan said stiffly, "I wish you wouldn't talk like that."

Dawson's attitude was offensive to him. Grinning, he said, "Come off it, my sexless American friend. I've seen you peeking down her bodice. Don't tell me you wouldn't like to get on top of her. Only thing is, make sure no one's looking."

Grinning obscenely, he gestured at his crotch.

"They'd take these off for you in a matter of seconds. Then where would you be?"

The Englishman did not really trouble him very much; it was more that he was troubled with himself. His position, for an officer of the Twenty-third U.S. Infantry, was quite intolerable. He was a prisoner, but a favored one. He didn't like it. There were other American prisoners with the Moros. He had taken pursuit columns out after them, frequently, and when he caught up with them he had always been appalled at the sickening condition his men were in; they were half-starved, barefoot, exhausted, and bloody. Their wounds were generally unattended, not because the enemy took a particular pleasure in letting them bleed to death, but because they were contemptuous of physical injury. It was one of the major differences between the savages and . . . *Are we coming down to their level?* he asked himself.

It was a hypothetical question that had long worried him. *We are fighting to impose upon these savages*, he said to himself, *the advantages of American democracy, and they are fighting an invader in order to preserve their way of life. We treat our prisoners with good will while we prattle of amnesties. We shudder when we see them slice off a man's head with a talibong. But do they recoil when they see us open up a man's stomach with a mortar shell? Is there a degree of the responsibility for slaughter?*

He said to Dawson, somberly, "Tell me something. The Moro dies without any trace of fear. Except when we hang him. Why?"

Dawson rubbed his hand over a stubbly chin. The saliva was trickling out of one side of his mouth. He said, "They've been killing each other off for a thousand years. In battle. They've got used to being decapitated. Even the Spanish garrote—the Spaniards were here long enough, and used it often enough, to make them get used to that too. Then the Americans came and set up their gallows all over. It makes them wonder about you because it's new. And they don't like anything new." He said sourly, "If you're here long enough, they'll get used to that as well. But meanwhile, allow them the privilege of not liking your civilizing influences too much."

"You don't like us, Dawson, do you? The Americans?"

"No offense, dear boy. I just don't like anyone who interferes with the accumulation of my personal wealth. If you'd only leave the Moros alone, I'd soon be grand vizier to the new Sultan."

"And meanwhile—a British Army Officer, gone native, fighting with a savage band of pirates and cutthroats. You must feel a great pride in your Regiment."

Dawson came over to him, and for a moment he thought that he would strike him across the face with his staff. He waited for the blow, but it did not come. Instead, Dawson said gently, "I have only to raise my voice, you know. They'll cut you to pieces."

"I know."

He could not feel hatred. He felt only contempt, and even this gave him cause for sympathy. He wondered what he would do in a like position, and said abruptly, "I'm in the same boat myself. I should have killed Jokiri when I had a chance. If you had not shouted, I'd have gone for him instead of Pangiran."

"And died bravely for your country?"

"Let's drop it, shall we?"

Dawson said pompously, "There comes a time for all of us when circumstances preclude our behaving as we have always been taught to behave. Then you can either fight it or go along with it, whichever you like. I chose to go along with it. I don't regret it. Not really."

He wondered if Dawson were trying to delude him or himself. He said nothing.

The bandages came off his arms a week later. It was Medina who removed them.

She came to his hut, unexpectedly, in the early evening. He saw that her Papuan bodyguard was standing respectfully at a distance under the bamboo, waiting for her to come out or to call them. She squatted on her heels beside him and gave him a cigarette. He knew, every time American supplies came into the camp, that there had been another raid somewhere—that his men were being killed—that sudden screams were filling the night while he lay here in a thatched hut with an earthen floor, drinking sour water out of a gourd and eating rice and fish with his fingers, washing his hands delicately before and after the meal, like a native. It was almost symbolic that now, so soon after his capture, he was accepting this life as easily as he accepted the cigarette from Medina's slim fingers, watching her steadily while she lighted it for him with a twig of burning wood from the fire outside in the compound.

She peeled off the dirty bandages, saying nothing, pulling away the pads of lubigon and washing away the purple dye with cold sea water. The scars were long and deep. One of them ran from the shoulder clear down to the waist, an angry, indented weal that he knew would be there for life. Another gash across the left wrist had incapacitated two fingers of his hand. A slash across his chest had left a gouge that had scored the bones of his ribs. Looking at them he said, "I'm lucky to be alive. You've done a good job."

She looked at him for a while without speaking. Then, "Tell me about your home."

Dawson had told him what to expect and what to do. As she worked on his bandages, he told her about the green hills and the cool forests and the yellow, waving fields. He spoke to her of the city and the neat frame houses and the green lawns. She listened intently, and he knew that a picture was returning to her, and that this was what she wanted, what Jokiri wanted, to bring back to her the semblance of—what could he call it? Of civilization? He said bitterly, "Our people were fighting each other too. There was a long war . . ."

Talking to her, sitting there in the grubby hut with a pile of dirty bandages on the floor beside them, he wondered if she were moving closer to his life, or if he were moving closer to hers. He said abruptly, "Do you want to stay here all your life, Medina?"

There was a sudden panic in her eyes. She said quickly, "This is my home. Jokiri is my father."

"You're Spanish, not Moro."

"I am a Moro."

"Each day, less and less."

She was wearing a long voluminous garment round her waist, divided like a pair of baggy trousers, and a skin-tight bodice that flared out over her hips, with a long plaid called a patadiong over her shoulders. Her clothes were clean, bright green and scarlet. He said,

"Look at yourself. You dress like a Moro. But like a Moro who wants to be a Spaniard."

She flushed deeply, and when he saw her again, later in the evening, she was wearing only the jabul round her waist, leaving her breasts exposed. She stood for a while in the door of his hut, looking at him, wanting him to notice her and to see that she was, in spite of all he had said, a true Moro. He was puzzled and disturbed, and he knew that the disturbance was not only in his mind; it was in his loins as well. He said angrily, "You wanted to see me?"

She came forward then, holding out a long curved sword, a campilan, with an ornamental wood handle heavily inlaid with silver. There was a tuft of red hair attached to the haft, which meant, he knew, that it was to be carried by an officer of senior rank. The leather scabbard was inlaid with ivory. She said, "My father will want you to carry this with you, always."

He stared at her in surprise. She said slowly, "It means that you are one of us."

Bitterly: "A Moro. Like Dawson."

"You must not feel unhappy because of it. My people are good people."

"I'd rather be among my own. And I suspect that you would too."

"You must not talk like that."

He could not keep his eyes off her. She stood slim and straight and—*poised* was the word that came to his mind. Her long black hair, unkempt but shining with coconut oil, hung down over one shoulder; her skin was smooth, olive-colored, and unmarked with the tiny pockmarks the other women had; her breasts were splendidly formed, set high and wide and full; her waist was as narrow as a boy's, and where the jabul clung tightly against her leg he could see that her thighs were long and smooth. He felt himself shivering with the desire for her, and when he took the campilan from her he laid a hand on her upper arm, knowing that he did so to find out if she would draw away from him. She did not. Her eyes were solemn and steady and she did not move. Still touching her arm, he said slowly, "I do not believe that you want to stay here all your life."

She said nothing. He knew that he was trembling. Then she

turned and went out of the hut. He followed her to the entrance, and stood watching her as she moved across the compound to her own house. He watched the two Papuan warriors, their spears held high and their painted shields slung across their backs, move after her and take up their habitual position on each side of the entrance.

He was suddenly aware that Dawson, standing over by the fire and a little way beyond its light, was watching him. He turned and went back into the hut, and as he lowered himself gently onto the mat, Dawson came into the doorway, grinning at him unpleasantly. Sullivan said wearily, "They've given me a sword. What's that supposed to mean?"

"It means you're a man of importance. They'll put you to work pretty soon. It also means they trust you."

"That makes me a traitor."

Dawson shrugged.

"If you want to assuage your ego—trust or not, you couldn't have escaped. Your conscience can be clear on that point, at least."

"What's that supposed to mean?"

Dawson threw away his stub of dead cheroot and came quickly into the hut. Squatting down, peering up into Sullivan's eyes, he said quietly, "What about Medina? You know she's after you?"

"Nonsense."

"Take my word for it, old boy. Point is, are you prepared to make use of that knowledge?"

"Go on."

Dawson edged closer to him. He said, "Look. We could both get away from here if we knew just where Jokiri is. He's out of the compound almost all the time, but if he's close enough to get back here quickly—you see what I mean? We'd never get far enough away to give us any chance at all of getting to Jolo. But if we were sure that he was—well, more than a couple of days' forced march away from the camp, we might make it. And the only way we can get that priceless piece of information is from Medina. She'll know where he is. Nobody else will. And she might show you a way across the swamp. In exchange for what she wants."

"You make me sick, Dawson."

"Oh don't be such a bloody prude. She's been making sheep's

eyes at you ever since you got here. You're tall and handsome and virile—everything a young maid wants. All right then, put her on her back and make her happy. She'll do anything you ask her."

Sullivan said furiously, "A week or two ago you were telling me not to lay a hand on her."

"That was before I realized how she felt about you."

"And you expect me to—to betray her like that? For your personal gain?" He knew that he was being pompous again, and he knew that he was sick to death of Dawson's acute perception of his thinking. He said, "Forget it, Dawson. I'll get out of here when the time comes. I don't need your help. Or hers."

Dawson was interminably scratching at his lice. He said eagerly, "It's the only way, I tell you, the only way we'll ever get out of here. Look—for all we know, the place might be practically unguarded now, at this very minute. There are less than twenty warriors in camp, but—where are the rest of them? Across the other side of the island? A hundred miles away on Mindanao? Bottled up in a canyon trying to fight their way out of an American trap? Or just a mile or two away in the mangrove swamp? Which is it, Sullivan? Tell me where they all are and I'll tell you what your chances are of getting out of here."

"I don't disagree with your arguments. I just don't like your methods."

"Hell, you'd be doing the girl a favor. She's aching for it."

"You make me sick."

"So you said. But take my advice, old boy. That girl is your passport back to Jolo, and mine too. Put her on her back, play with her for a while. You'll see how she responds." His eyes gleaming, he said, "Then all you've got to do is tell her. Tell her you want to cross the swamp. Ask her how far away the old man is. I tell you, she's aching for you. I know her, and I'm telling you the truth."

He knew that Dawson was right. The revulsion in him was turning to anger. He said shortly, "First of all, her relationship with me is—is merely friendly. Secondly, I have no intention of making love to a woman for my own personal gain. And thirdly, shut up."

Dawson said disgustedly, "Of all the bloody Yanks they had to pick you."

[ 97 ]

He went out and left him there, disturbed, angry, and frustrated.

A moment later he was back again. Standing in the doorway he said, "Almost forgot to tell you. The old man's due back in a day or two. He'll expect you to stage a nice course of lectures to his senior officers."

"Lectures!"

"Somebody will translate what you say. Me, probably."

"But—but what the devil can I tell them?"

Dawson shrugged. "What do I care? Tell them about Ulysses Grant and the battle of Shiloh. Draw a few maps in the sand—you know the sort of things. Nothing they like more than arguments about tactics. I take it you've read your military history?"

Sullivan said stiffly, "My people served with Jeb Stuart."

"Then tell them about Bull Run. They'll love it."

Sullivan bit his lip and said nothing.

When darkness came and the moon rose up in brightness over the tops of the trees, he went over to the palisade and leaned against it, wondering if they were watching him, staring out into the black and eerie silence of the forest and thinking.

He had a friend in the Garrison, a young Lieutenant of the Scouts named Desting, a man who could move through the brush like an animal. He was one of the old school of scouts who quickly adopted the ways of the natives and could outsmart them at their own game. Desting had told him one day, sitting on a high bluff overlooking the sea, "You can always get away once you know where you are. Keep moving north or east or west, in a straight line, over everything. Sooner or later you'll find a place you can recognize."

Now, he looked up at the stars, trying to work out the direction of Jolo; but the stars were pale beside the bright moon. He wondered about the swamp, asking himself if it could truly be impassable.

There was a rustle in the bushes outside the palisade, and as he waited and watched, he heard Medina coming up behind him. Turning, surprised, he said quietly, "Isn't it late for you to be wandering around by yourself?"

He could not see the two Papuan guards, but he knew that they would be within sound of her voice. She said slowly, "I saw you look to the forest. I think perhaps . . . Do you wish to go back to your own people, is that it?"

He hesitated, then, "Of course."

"My father will not allow. He has told the warriors, you may move in the village where you wish, but you must not go outside. If the warriors see you outside, they will kill you."

Staring at her somberly, he said, "In the forest, they would not find me."

"They will find you. In every tree, there is a warrior. Always."

He looked up into the foliage of the thorn-tree that stood close to the palisade; he could see nothing. Pointing to the clump of greenery at the top, she said, "There—two men. Also in the baobab tree. And at each corner of the village. I do not wish them to kill you."

"Is that why you came out here? Were you watching me?"

"Yes, I was watching you."

He wondered how long she had been standing there in the silence, before she had approached him. It disturbed him not to know why she had been watching, and it disturbed him to know that she was interested enough to observe him, unseen, as he moved around the compound. The firelight was reflected in the smooth skin of her body. She still wore only her skirt, though the night was cool. Remembering what Dawson had said, he spoke to her very quietly. "Why do you watch me? Why are you afraid for me?"

She said, hesitantly, looking for the right words, "Because here, in the camp, the young men—there is no one. Only, when I see you, my heart—it beats faster. There is a feeling inside me . . . here . . ."

"It is a long time since you spoke with—since you saw someone of your own kind."

"My own kind are Moros. But here, inside me . . . if you touch me, you will feel my heartbeat."

He did not move. She took his hand gently and laid it on her breast, pressing it close to her. He could feel the nipple hardening under his touch and he knew that he was trembling. He said hoarsely, "Someone—someone will see us."

When he tried to pull his hand away she held it there firmly, caressing herself with it, forcing him to feel the firmness of her, waiting for him to draw her into the shadows of the trees. She said, speaking very quietly, "Why are you afraid? There is nothing to fear."

"If we should be seen . . ."

"I am the daughter of the chief."

"Then you should know it would be dangerous."

"It is not dangerous."

Her eyes were puzzled. She could not understand why he did not take her, there and then, in the deep grass among the bushes. He said awkwardly, "It is not—it is not the time."

"They say that in your camp in Jolo, the servants bring you women at night."

"Sometimes. It's not the same thing."

"Why is it not the same thing? Do you not think I am beautiful? Is it that?"

"No—no, it's not that at all. Only . . ."

"Is my skin too dark? It is not darker than the other Moro women."

"No, but—you're not one of them . . ."

He flung up his hands helplessly, pressing his fingers into his eyes, shaking his head. "I do not know. Perhaps—perhaps if I were not a prisoner here . . . I do not know."

She pulled his hands from his face, pulling them behind her back and holding them there, drawing herself close to him. She said slowly, "If you wish that I speak to my father . . ."

He did not know if it were meant as a threat. In a sudden panic, he said again, "Medina . . . someone will see us."

The strong scent of her hair was thick in his nostrils. He clutched her to him for a moment, holding her tight, and then broke away sharply and turned and left her standing there, looking after him in puzzlement.

When he went back to his hut, he threw himself on the hard floor, wishing that she would come to him, and yet fearing this too. Once, he stood up and went to the doorway and stood looking out into the night, darker now that the moon had set, watching the pinpoints of the dying embers across the compound, feeling the misery and the oppression and the loneliness.

He knew that escape was of paramount importance; but he could not forget the vision of her, standing there in the half-darkness, waiting for him to love her, offering herself to him, standing with her long slim back close to where the grasses were a cushion behind her for them to lie on, knowing that a step into the shadows was all that had been required of him. He lay on his stomach and thought about her, worrying. It occurred to him that Dawson had probably been watching them from the dark doorway of his hut, watching and grinning and hoping, feeling a vicarious excitement as he watched.

He got up and lit one of the cigarettes that Dawson had given him, pulling on it nervously in the silence, waiting and wondering in the lonely darkness, and when the morning came he went down to the river, to the rocky pool where the stream was fast-running and clear, and stepped out of his clothes and into the cold fresh water.

He soaked his shirt and started trying to get the grime out of it, and then some of the women came down to do their washing. One of them, a girl he had seen with Medina that first time, came over and took it from him without a word, and he watched her while she beat at it with a rock, pounding the soil out of it. In a little while Medina came down too, stepping into the pool and throwing the water over her body. She looked at him, unsmiling, saying nothing, and then she went over to the young girl and took the shirt from her.

It was a gesture, and as she wrung the water from it and shook it out, she looked over to him and smiled secretly, as though by her action she had established her claim to him. One of the women said something to her in Moro-Samal, and they all laughed, and suddenly he felt ashamed of his behavior the night before. She was soaking the blue shirt in the water again, pounding it on the smooth boulders, the water gleaming on her body, and she looked up at him and laughed, showing the bright flash of her smile. The long black hair fell over her shoulder and onto her breast, and she tossed it back with an eternally feminine movement, touching her hand to her forehead so that the drops of water ran down her forearm.

He lay back in the pool and let the water run swiftly over his chest, and in a little while the women finished their washing and, gathering up their soggy bundles, went back to the village. Medina waited to lay his shirt out on the warm grass, and stood for a moment watching him. Her wet skirt was clinging closely to her thighs.

He said nothing, lying back and watching her. Then she slipped out of her jabul, letting it slip down to the ground at her feet and stepping out of it, and for a moment she stood there quite naked, the water glistening on the long slim flank of her. In accordance with Moslem custom, the hair on her body had been removed, and the shock of it stung him with a little spasm of—was it revulsion? Because her body was so—so white?

Then she tied a fresh skirt around her waist, turned, and went back the way she had come. She paused once at the edge of the forest to turn and smile at him; and then she was gone.

# 7.

THAT NIGHT, THE DYAKS ATTACKED THE VILLAGE.

It began when one of the Montese headhunters who was standing guard at the small gate suddenly clutched at his stomach and fell without a sound. For a moment, no one seemed to notice it, and then another man fell silently, and then a third. A Papuan warrior yelled and threw his spear, and in a moment the camp was in an uproar. The men came tumbling out of their huts, wielding their barongs and running for the palisade.

Sullivan leaped to his feet and ran outside, and then Dawson threw himself out of nowhere and pushed him to one side; he heard the sharp hiss as a dart from a blowgun sank itself into the thatch behind him. He jumped up again, ran back into the hut and picked up his campilan, and when he came out again he went quickly with Dawson, fast as the Englishman could hobble, over to the borders of the barricade. A small, wiry man with light brown skin and long black hair, his nostrils dilated, leaped onto the palisade and drew back his bow, then fell, as the shaft left the string, with a thrown kris buried deep in his groin. A group of Papuan warriors were stabbing furiously down into the thick mass of small bodies that were clambering up onto the timbers, and in a moment the compound was full of them.

They ran lightly, the Dyaks, and quickly, armed with bows and spears and knives, and the Moros fought against them with a savagery he had never before witnessed. Dawson was standing with his back to a tree, using a barong and a pistol, and he wondered at the marvelous agility of the man in spite of his leg. He saw an orderly body of Papuans run to Medina's hut and station themselves around it, their spears poised ready, their painted wooden shields held firmly in front of them to form a protective cover. Someone stabbed at him with a spear and he sidestepped and slashed out with his campilan, cutting the weapon-hand off at the wrist. He heard Dawson yell, "Look out! Blowgun!" and again he heard the sound of the dart.

He ran along the palisade, to where a dozen small men were seething forward, and he slashed into them, towering above them and wielding his blade like a seasoned expert. He fought against the stiffness that was still in his arms, cutting and ripping, hacking and slashing, hewing and chopping like a madman. He was conscious of a fierce heat behind him, and he fled from the flames of a burning house that collapsed about him in a shower of sparks. Soon, the whole compound was in flames, and in the red heat and glare a hundred men, indistinguishable save by their weapons, were shrieking and milling about, slashing at each other with a frightening ferocity.

He found himself alone, and saw that Medina's hut was burning. The Papuans who surrounded it were gone, some of them dead on the bloodstained earth around it. He ran towards the flames, bursting through them, feeling the searing heat of them, and saw her clutching a spear, bending down to grasp the kris of a dead Moro who lay at her feet. He threw himself at her and sent her sprawling to the floor, then dragged her forcibly away through the flames. She fought him until he shouted, "This way—under the palisade!" and then she let him pull her, dropping her weapons and running with him. He had lost his campilan, and he looked round for something to take its place. A Dyak came screaming at him, brandishing a spear, and he sidestepped and used his fist, grimacing with the pain as he hit the small hard head, then pulled Medina to the ground under the protective covering of the fallen palisade timbers. He lay tight beside her, pressing her to the ground, and the battle went on all around them.

It was growing weaker now, and the smell of blood was heavy in the air. Through a rift in the timbers, he could see that the chief's house had collapsed and was burning steadily; it was the only house in the compound that was built on a stone foundation. He watched it for a moment, knowing that underneath its base there was room for the storage of weapons, room to find shelter too.

He watched for the opportunity, and then grabbed Medina by the arm and yanked her vigorously across the compound again, throwing her bodily under the house and slithering in beside her. He forced her deep into the darkest corner, pulling a smoking timber that burned his hand, thrusting it into position to hide her, quickly piling up loose rocks to make an adequate shelter. She held him then, putting her arms tight around his neck and not letting him go, and he said urgently, "I must go—I must fight."

She clutched at him fiercely and said, "No! Please—stay with me."

He lay close beside her, hearing the screams and the yells and the fierce sound of the flames. The heat was almost intolerable. He said, "All right. I'll stay—if the Dyaks . . ."

He broke off, not knowing how to say it. She was trembling with fear, clutching him tightly round the neck. He could feel the smoothness of her flesh against his bare arm. She said, "They will go soon. They will not wait for Jokiri to come back."

"Jokiri?"

"He is close by. A runner will tell him news of the attack. They will know this, and they will go soon, before he can return."

"Better lie still. Keep quiet. We're safe in here."

The wooden planks over his head, a few inches above him, were smoldering. He moved over a little, but moved back when he felt a gentle drip on his neck and knew that it was blood. He whispered, "It's getting quieter."

"They are going away."

"Maybe. Maybe they've won."

"No. I do not think so."

He whispered, "Does this happen often?"

"Many times. They make an attack, and then they go. It is quickly over."

"Are you frightened?"

"No. I am not frightened. Not now."

She was pressing her body against him. He moved his hand up to her breast and pressed it gently, feeling the warmth of her. Her hips stirred and pressed themselves against his, forcing her loins tight against him. Clumsily, trembling, he fumbled at the knot of her jabul, tearing his hand on the silver brooch that fastened it in place, and when he had removed it he rolled over on top of her and transmuted all the heat and the ferocity and the fear and the passion that was around him into a personal thing that was now only between him and her. The tension burst inside him in a fierce ecstatic spasm, and all around him was nothing but silence and a terrible stillness.

He was gasping for breath when he lay back. She put a hand on the blood that was flowing down his arm, and then touched her own body with it, on the breast, leaving a red smear that he covered with his hand. They lay back together and waited, listening to the silence, hearing now the murmur of voices in the distance, hearing too the groans of the wounded and the butcher sounds of the talibongs that told him the Moros had defeated their enemy and were systematically and dispassionately beheading the Dyak wounded. He shuddered his revulsion, then struggled to his knees and looked at her. He did not know what to say.

He heard Dawson's voice in the distance, calling, "Sullivan? Sullivan?" His voice was weak with pain. He crawled outside, then, and saw the Englishman sitting propped up against a tree, his legs stuck out incongruously in front of him. He was stabbing himself in the arm with the point of a kris, grimacing in agony. Sullivan clambered quickly to his feet and ran over to him. He said gruffly, "Here, give me that."

"Dart from a blowgun," Dawson said, whimpering. "It's heavily poisoned, got to get it out . . ."

Sullivan gripped his arm tight above the wound and levered the steel dart out. It was tipped with yellow feathers. He made a deep incision across the wound and squeezed the flesh around it to force the poisoned blood out. He fished in his pockets for a cigarette, and put one between Dawson's lips. He said, "Will they be back, the Dyaks?"

"No. I doubt it. This happens all the time." His voice was heavy with pain. "Sea-Dyaks. They bring a prahu-load over, land in the night, make a hit and run attack, and by morning they're on the high seas. Jesus . . . I wish I had a drink."

"Do they have an antidote for this stuff? The poison?"

Dawson nodded. "Just make sure it bleeds—there's a poultice they make. We lost a lot of men."

Looking around the compound: "So did they."

"They must have known that Jokiri was away. He's probably off on the other side of the island."

"No. He's close by."

Dawson looked at him sharply, squinting into his face. He said nothing. They went over to the palisade to get away from the heat of the burning buildings, and in a little while Medina came over with a group of women, looked at Dawson's arm, and then went away and came back with a bundle of leaves, which she gave Dawson to chew, standing there solemnly and waiting while he ground it to a pulp with his teeth. He spat it out into his hand and gave it to her, and she placed the pad carefully over the wound and bound it into place with a piece of red cloth. Then she turned and went back to her house; it was a heap of smoldering ashes now, and she looked down at the bodies of the Papuans, and then went off into the darkness.

He did not see her again for the rest of the night.

Two days later they were sitting together by the water where he had first seen her. Medina was silent. Her legs were drawn up under her and she leaned back on one arm so that he could see and admire the splendid curve of her breast. She had given up wearing her bodice, now, and he sensed that it was because she knew the pleasure he found in looking at her, in touching her, in letting his hand move slowly over the soft, taut skin. He knew that it was strange to her that anyone should find pleasure in the contemplation of a woman's breast, that she thought only the hidden parts could rouse him. He wanted to tell her that it was something to do with the color of her skin, but he could not find the words.

Jokiri was away from the camp. And as always, during his absences, there was a lessening of the tension in the village. A warparty had just come in with a load of medical supplies; when he asked her about it, she turned away from him and said nothing, and he sensed that she was feeling a sense of guilt as he watched the Army bandages and surgical instruments being carefully sorted out by the women. One of them had sniffed cautiously at a bottle that he knew contained iodine, and then had taken a tentative sip of it, spitting it out in disgust and throwing the bottle away into the forest. He wondered how many of his men had died trying to carry those supplies to one of the outlying stations. When he insisted, she said somberly, "We have learned to need these things too."

When he did not answer her, she changed the subject abruptly. She said, "Where did you learn how to fight like that—with a barong?"

"That? Oh—it's very much like a saber. Only heavier."

"You fight like a Moro."

He knew that she meant it for a compliment. He said bitterly, "The only thing I'm good for."

"You must not be angry about this. It is good to fight well."

"Yes. I know."

He lay back on the grass and listened to the gentle sound of the water.

"The only thing is—with me, it's—it's instinctive. When I fight, I lose control. Completely. Once a fight starts, and I get in it, it's all out of my hands. I've no more restraint than an animal. It disgusts me and it sickens me. And I'm frightened of it."

She was silent, watching him, feeling his loneliness with him. He rolled over and put his hand on her hip.

"Don't you understand, Medina? For a man like me, the Army's the only possible life. My family—we've been soldiers, always, so it comes naturally to me, and yet . . . I'm not so sure that the good Lord didn't have something else in mind when he made man. We're supposed to be a civilized people, and when we come face to face with these primitive savages we see just how civilized we are. Looks to me like there's nothing much to choose between us."

"But you love your Army, do you not? A good soldier . . ."

"Sure I love it," he said passionately. "It's all the life I've ever known. And I know what it's doing to me. It's sucking the life out of me. I know that and I want to escape from it, but how can I? You can't break away from your whole life like that."

"I did."

He stopped short, looking at her. Her eyes were clear and calm. She was telling him that a new way of life had been forced upon her and that she was happy because she had accepted it without question. He said slowly, "I can't believe that you've really accepted all this."

"I have accepted it. Jokiri is my father now, and these are my people. It is a good life. You would like it too."

He drew away from her slightly, wondering if she noticed the gesture. He said quickly, "And your real parents? Your father and mother?"

"They are dead."

"Killed by what you now call your own people. The people you say are yours."

"No! They were Dyaks!"

"The same thing."

She looked at him in surprise. "The same thing? I do not understand you."

He sighed and waited a little while before he answered her. Then he said, smiling so that it would not hurt, "To you, all white men are the same now, aren't they? The Americans, the Spanish, Dawson . . ."

"Yes. Yes, of course."

"Well, to me—Moros, Monteses, Negritos, Dyaks. They're all the same too."

"Natives."

"If you want to call them that."

"Is this why . . . why you do not like to love me?"

He rolled closer to her, feeling the need for her, putting his arms tight around her. He said urgently, "You know I like to love you —but not here."

"At night, only?"

"When it's dark."

"Why must you hide this? It is good to love in the sunlight too. Better, even."

"Don't you understand? If someone found out . . ."

"My father is the chief. I will do what I want to do."

"Yes—yes, I know that."

He was worrying about it, feeling the distaste of his own caution. He said heavily, "We can't—we can't bring it out into the open like that. It presupposes too many things, Medina."

At the back of his mind he was aware of their two opposing desires; of his own, which was for immediate and temporary gratification, and of hers, which was for a permanent relationship. He feared discovery, and he knew that she courted it.

Now, he saw that she was hurt, and guessed that she knew his reasoning. Smiling, he said quickly, "Is there sunlight under the bushes?"

She threw back her head and laughed, then, and she got quickly to her feet and ran, and he ran after her, and in a little while he caught up with her and threw her to the ground, rolling over and over in the wet grass with her and laughing like a schoolboy.

Then he looked up and saw that the long black roots of the mangrove trees were splaying their tenuous tentacles out close by, and he knew that they had run to the edge of the swamp. He was suddenly aware that she was not laughing any more, and looking at her quickly he saw that there was an unaccustomed hardness in her eyes. She said tightly, "There is no way across the swamp, Shay."

The lust had gone out of him. She jumped up suddenly and ran back to the village. He watched her go, and then got to his feet and stood leaning against the black trunk of a giant tree that was wet with green and yellow moss. When he walked a few paces further on he saw that the black, slimy water was spread out in front of him as far as he could see, dark and bleak and filthy. A snake moved in a tree close by, and somewhere in the distance he heard the startled cry of a bird that echoed in the uncanny silence.

A crocodile was asleep on the bank, its huge mouth wide open and a bird pecking at the rotted food around the filthy yellow teeth. The vines were twisting themselves like living things around the searching roots that struggled out of the feculent mud, and everywhere there was the odor of putrefaction. He thought that he had never before seen a place so terrifyingly rotten, where even the air was laden with the smell of death.

He turned and walked slowly back to the palisade.

The camp was rebuilt within a week. Day and night they had worked, sinking heavy poles of ironwood into the ground and tying long slats of woven coconut-fronds to the horizontal thorn-twigs with short lengths of raffia and wet palm-fiber that tightened, when dry, into a stiff cord as strong as steel.

Jokiri had returned from his raids, and had listened impassively to the recounting of the battle and to the telling of the dead, sitting on an upturned wooden box in front of his house, his evil eyes unblinking as they showed him the Dyak heads they had taken. Watching, Sullivan had heard someone speak his name, and the chief had looked across at him and then at his daughter, and had nodded in silent appreciation. Dawson, then, squatting in his accustomed place at the chief's feet, had looked at him and grinned, and he knew that his stock was rising among the Moros; he could find no comfort in it. A saranda, a teller of tales, had come forward and chanted his own version of the battle, waving his sword and throwing his arms about in fine mimicry of the fighting. A huge meal of fish, and chicken, and frogs, and rice, and eggs that had been scrambled in rancid coconut oil had been served, in small silver dishes on immense brass trays, and then a group of Moros brought out their gongs and the long kulingtangan and beat them through the night until the first red streaks of the dawn were appearing in the sky.

Jokiri had gone on his way again, and only fifty warriors had been left in the compound. A Gatling gun had been manhandled in, its breech cracked open and its wheels splintered. A load of ammunition had arrived on a buffalo-cart, and Sullivan knew that there had been another raid on one of the blockhouses.

The brief quarrel with Medina had been forgotten. He stood that night at the door of his hut, waiting for her, and when she came in the darkness he clutched her tight to him and whispered, "You know that I can't live without you."

She came to him every night after that, and their love-making was silent and animal and disturbing. There would be a rustle at the thatch wall of his new shack, and a moment later she would slide in beside him, touching her finger to his lips. She would chew on a piece of betel nut while her fingers explored his body, and then, before they made love, she would kneel down briefly and put the half-chewed wad and a germ of wheat in a small gourd that she brought with her, touching the floor close by it with her forehead and then calmly lying down and waiting for him to take her. Her love-making then was urgent and unbelievably fierce, but he always had the feeling that she was insisting on a Moro ritual, and a fertility ritual at that, because she wanted him to know that in spirit she was a true Moro and that he must take her as such; it was a defiance of all that he was trying to teach her, of his efforts to draw her away from her primitive custom. It angered him to know that in spite of it all, the warmth of her body was the only thing that mattered to him in these heated moments; and when she had left him, even immediately after the act when he was resting, exhausted by her violent demands, he knew that soon he would need her again and that she was fast becoming the most important thing in his life.

Jokiri came back and went again. The village had grown once more as though it had never been destroyed. Only the chief's house, which was built of mahogany planks hand-split from the solid red trunks, remained to be completed. The dead had long been buried. The bodies had been sprinkled with salt and camphor, and a kris had been tied to each dead wrist; the gongs had been sounded, and the carcasses had been covered with earth; the site of each grave had been marked with a sliver of bamboo and a coconut-shell full of water.

And within another ten days, the village had returned to normal. Time passed; and only they stood still.

Dawson said to him one night, squatting on the ground beside him and shoveling some rice into his mouth, "You'd better be careful, friend. I saw you and Medina yesterday."

Sullivan looked up in alarm, wondering how much he knew, then turned away. Dawson wiped the back of his hand across his mouth and said, "If I see you, some of the others might. Just thought you ought to know. You needn't worry about the women, they're all up to the same tricks, but the men . . . especially the Papuans. Well, maybe they won't talk, but if Jokiri finds out . . . Needn't tell you what they'll do to you."

Sullivan said nothing. Dawson gulped down the remains of his meal and began to wash out the gourd with sand. He said nervously, "I saw you getting mighty friendly with her. It's none of my business on the face of it, but if you're screwing her I think you ought to tell me. For your sake as well as mine."

"I wish you wouldn't talk like that."

"Don't worry. I'm not an officer and a gentleman any more."

"Still no need to talk like that about her."

Dawson was watching him carefully, probing his mind. He said, "You really ought to tell me, you know. It could be the easiest way out of here."

"When we first met, you went to some trouble to tell me that you were on their side. Not on mine."

"I know. But when there's a chance to get away like this—it's too good to turn down. There comes a time . . ."

"Well, there's nothing to tell anyway."

"Nothing?"

"You heard me."

"I see. Well, I wish you'd make up your mind to forget your stuffy American inhibitions. It could make things a lot easier for all of us." He paused, squinting at Sullivan as he dusted the sand out of his bowl. "You're telling me the truth, friend?"

"Not that it's any business of yours. But it's the truth."

He wondered how he could lie so easily.

Dawson stood up abruptly. He said, "I'm supposed to take you to the old man's house. He wants to talk to you."

There was a moment of panic again. He said slowly, "So that's why you wanted to know about—about Medina and me?"

Dawson grinned at him quickly.

"If the old man has any suspicions, then I want to be forewarned. He wants you to talk with his daughter, help her along on what he fondly thinks is the road to culture. But that doesn't include getting between her legs. And if you've been doing that, my friend, then I want to know about it in advance."

Sullivan, sick of him, said, "Let's go. What does he want me for?"

"You're going to give his senior chiefs a lecture."

Sullivan swung around on him. Dawson said, shrugging, "Well, you knew you'd have to. I told you, a long time ago."

"But—but it's impossible."

Smoothly, Dawson took his arm and led him towards the chief's house. He said gently, "I told them you would like to talk about the great war in your own country. I said you'd tell them all about Gettysburg. Surprisingly, they've heard of it. I said you'd draw them some lovely maps in the sand. There's a dozen of them up there waiting to hear you speak, and you'd better not disappoint them. In case you don't know it, someone told the old man that you fought well against the Dyaks, as well as a Moro . . ."

*There it was again . . .*

". . . and they're really proud of you. This can help us both a lot. In a few weeks you've got closer to the old man's heart than I have in two years. Makes you think, doesn't it?"

Heavily, Sullivan went with him up to the long-house.

Jokiri was sitting in regal splendor, dressed in silk and silver, on an upturned box that had once held cans of tomatoes. His personal bodyguard was standing behind him, their campilans drawn, the firelight glinting on the blades and on their smooth, oiled bodies. A dozen or more senior datos and warriors were sitting in a circle on the hard-packed earth in front of the long-house, and slaves were tending the fires that lit up the area, poking at them and stirring the flames into brightness. Dawson took his place at Jokiri's feet, and Sullivan was left standing there, awkwardly, his gaunt frame restless, not sure how to behave or what he was going to say. He was trying to convince himself that what he was about to do could cause no mischief—a friendly chat on a subject he was well versed in, a talk from one soldier to another. He forced the guilt of it to the back of his mind.

Jokiri made a long speech, and at last Dawson stood up and said, "In effect, old boy, His Highness welcomes you, and thanks you for your splendid efforts on his behalf against the pagan Dyaks who presumptuously took advantage of his absence to beat up the camp. He also understands that you were instrumental in saving the life of his beloved daughter Medina, which I must say is the first I've heard of it, and from now on, therefore, he regards you as his son, with all the privileges and responsibilities attendant thereto. He wishes me to say that they are beginning to understand why the Americans are meeting with such success against their warriors, now that he sees one representative of their forces more closely, at closer quarters. There was something about admiration for warriors which I didn't quite understand, but I don't suppose it matters. He has been told that you will speak to them about the great battles which took place in your own country, and news of which has reached even these tiny islands, and he will be happy to learn the reasons which caused the armies of the South to be defeated. I think that's about all he said, and now, old boy, you'd better bow deeply and look as though you mean it."

Hesitantly, Sullivan bowed. He was sick with hatred of himself, and of Dawson, and of the Moros.

Some of the men from his own Regiment had been sent to China to join the International Expedition that was trying to put down the Boxer Rebellion, and the kowtow to native chiefs was already becoming a scornful synonym for cowardice; but there was nothing else he could do.

His hatred increased when he saw that Dawson, squatting again at his master's feet, was slowly grinning at him. He knew the reason for the grin. Dawson was saying to himself, and it was clear on his face and in the gleam of his eyes, *That makes you a renegade, friend, like me. The difference between us is slowly being diminished. I told you it would be. I told you you'd do anything for a few more moments of inglorious life.*

He could think only of his mother's delicate, well-kept hands that dusted the saber which hung over the door and which the General had given to his father before he died. No one else was permitted to touch that saber, and his father would sometimes say, his tired voice filled with pride, "Jeb Stuart gave me that, with his own hands, just before they killed him. Makes a man mighty proud."

There were more speeches by the datos, and Dawson, full of good humor, told him that they were extolling his virtues as a warrior; beyond the perverted pride that was forced upon him by their eulogies he could feel the depth of his guilt. But when the time came, he took a stick and drew a line in the sand to represent the Gettysburg and Hanover Railway, and then began again the game that he had played so often in the Headquarters Building in Jolo, where there were salt shakers for infantry and wineglasses for cavalry. He began hesitantly, at first, and then, astonished by the intense interest of the datos, he warmed to his subject, scarcely conscious of the drone in the background that was Dawson interpreting for them as he went along. And after it was all over, and Jokiri had ceremoniously and gravely thanked him, he went back with Dawson to the new hut they had built for him, and they sat in the firelight at the entrance, smoking their cheroots and saying nothing.

He worried the thing over in his mind, and then, when Dawson took off his jacket again to examine the scar left by the blowgun dart, Sullivan said, "You're right, you know."

Dawson looked up in surprise.

"About Medina?"

"No. About—about the war, that sort of thing. I'm teaching savages the elementary principles of tactics. You said I'd resign myself to the idea."

"And have you?"

"No. Not really. All the same, once I got started . . . It was only later I realized the damage I could be doing."

"Don't let it worry you. We're all renegades at heart."

"What did you mean when you said 'about Medina'?"

"I'm still wondering if you were telling me the truth."

He knew that Dawson was watching him closely. He said as casually as he could, "Of course I was."

"A couple of weeks back you'd have been a good deal more pompous in your denials."

"I'm getting accustomed to your insinuations."

He was trembling. The need to keep his secret from Dawson was almost overpowering. He said, "About getting out of here. If and when the time comes—are you sure you want to come too?"

Dawson could not keep the excitement from his voice. "Of course. I told you. But we've got to know where Jokiri is. Unless he's more than a day's march away, we won't have a chance. And that means off the island. Almost anywhere on Jolo, he's within striking distance of us. They move fast, these people. It'll take us a day and a night to cross the swamp, and then another day at least to reach the road. Even there we won't be safe."

"Could you find your way through the marshes?"

Despondently: "No. It's full of quicksand. *They* know how to cross it, but I don't."

"If we keep going east?"

"In the swamp? You think there's a highway to safety?"

"Could we—could we bribe one of the men to lead us across?"

"The quickest way to certain destruction."

Dawson was squinting at him, waiting for him to say it. Knowing this, knowing that Dawson knew what was in his mind, he said defiantly, "If we took Medina with us? Would she be able to guide us? And willing?"

Dawson was delighted. Grinning, he said, "That's my boy! Just tell me when you're ready."

Turning away from his grinning, maniacal face, Sullivan said, "We'd need food. Or at least, water."

"Don't worry about that. I can always lay my hands on the rice we'd need. More important, we'd need guns. I can get those too. You wouldn't try to leave me behind, would you?"

"No."

"I believe you, Sullivan. You may be a morass of inhibitions, but I think you're honest."

Sullivan said sarcastically, "That means a lot to me."

"I'll bet. We'll need guns and barongs and food and water."

"Barongs? I never want to see one again."

"For cutting our way through."

"Oh."

"You're serious about this? You really mean to make a break for it? You'll ask Medina to help us?"

He would not answer the last question. Instead, he said, "I have always intended to make a break for it. There's something despicable about an officer going native."

Dawson said sadly, "You have a wonderful talent, Sullivan, for making me feel miserable at the wrong moment."

Sullivan smiled quickly. It was the first time he had felt well disposed towards Dawson. He said lightly, "I was thinking of myself. I suppose there's not much to choose between the two of us any more. Only thing is, I still think a lot of myself. You don't, do you?"

"Of you? Or of me?"

"Of yourself."

"Well, regrets never did anyone any good. I was a good officer once. If we ever get out of this I'll show you my medals. Now—well, look at me. If I had any regrets I'd have to kill myself. Since I don't want to do that, ergo, I don't think about it. It's a state of mind. One day I'll find what I'm looking for."

"And what's that?"

"Money," Dawson said promptly. "Pretty simple, eh? But I never in my life wanted anything you couldn't buy if you had the price. Just now I'd like to buy a bottle of Scotch."

"Do you realize that I've been here for nearly four weeks?"

"That long? I've been here for two years. Don't really know what I'd do in a civilized community."

"How long will it take you to get a couple of rifles when we need them?"

The excitement was stirring in him again, affecting Dawson by its contagion.

"A few minutes. I know exactly where to lay my hands on them. Those Monteses sleep like logs of wood. They've got plenty of rifles. Cut a couple of throats. A last friendly gesture."

"Is that necessary?"

"Squeamish?"

"I don't like unnecessary killing."

"You're in command."

"Yes. Let's establish that right now."

"Certainly, Captain."

Dawson put his jacket back on and stood up. He said cheerfully, "I'm quite happy to put my future in your hands. You're the kind of man who needs to feel he's in command. The military machine. Without that, my friend, you'd be a dead duck. Give my respects to your girl friend."

He went over to his own hut and left Sullivan staring at him.

When he got inside, Dawson carefully opened a hole in the thatch so that, unseen, he could keep an eye on the back of the house where Medina slept. He was chuckling to himself as he sat down to wait and to watch; he said to himself, enjoying the joke: *You can't do business with a righteous man. These bloody Americans . . .*

He lit a cheroot and waited.

The moon had set and the night was black when, straining his eyes and his ears, Dawson detected the briefest movement at the back of the little shack. He did not hesitate, sure of what the movement meant. He sprang to his feet and stood for a while in the cover of his doorway, looking across the clearing to where the two Papuan guards were crouched over their fire, turning a piece of buffalo meat on a stick over the red embers.

Silently, dragging his lame leg behind him, he slipped out and into the dark shadows of the giant bamboo that stood close by, pressing himself deep among its cold staves. He had stripped off his clothes except for his trousers, and his dark skin merged invisibly with the mottled darkness about him. He held his breath and listened, and then Medina appeared, standing motionless in the shadow under the eaves, looking carefully at the other huts and listening. She wore only a jabul, and in the darkness he could see the smooth line of her breast. Dawson, the excitement rising in him as he thought of her lying under Sullivan's loins, had never found her more desirable, and he felt that his mouth was dry; he licked at his lips nervously. He waited until she moved, and then slipped out from his cover and stood by the water barrels where, he knew, she would pass.

He knew where she was going and he knew that he had discovered all he needed to know. But he knew, also, that Sullivan would never demand from her the information they had to have; knew, at least, that his gentle susceptibilities might easily stand between them and their chance to escape. He knew that he would have to act himself, and act quickly now that the time was ripe. And above all, at the back of his mind was the gnawing fear that perhaps they would go away together and leave him there to face the violent anger of Jokiri.

He slipped among the bushes and waited for her, telling himself that this was blackmail and the easiest way to get what he wanted, wondering what else he could demand from her and wondering if he would have the nerve. When she moved again, he put out a silent hand and laid it on her shoulder.

He felt the sudden gasp of fright that rose in her as she swung round at him, and saw the fear go from her face almost at once. It hurt him, badly, to know that she was not afraid of him, and he gripped her by the shoulder and moved his head to one side, indicating the area under the apitong trees where, he knew, they could whisper together and be undisturbed. There was one thing only that he had to say, and he knew this was the moment to say it: *"If you want Sullivan alive, get him out!"*

It would be enough. He knew that an argument with her in the middle of the night, with sentries and patrols prowling around, would be fraught with the most terrible danger. But she was on her way to her lover; her resistance would melt in the heat that enveloped her.

All he had to say was: *"If you want Sullivan alive, get him out!"* The rest could follow later. Once she feared for Sullivan's life, the rest would be easy. But it had to be now, as she was going to him, as the passion was rising in her. If Sullivan would not press her for the help they needed . . . He tugged at her arm and felt her, in a moment of panic, resist him. Then, with an urgent gesture for silence, she went with him. The two of them moved like shadows, part of the forest, part of the darkness and the silence that were all around them.

Reaching the darkness under the trees, he cupped his hand at her ear and breathed the words he had rehearsed. He said, so softly that he himself could not hear the words, "*If you want Sullivan alive, get him out.*"

He dropped her arm then, and was about to turn away. The panic burst inside him as he saw her staring, in sudden alarm. He swung round in terror.

Two of the Papuans, their war masks on their faces, their weapons at the ready and their shields held forward, were standing close behind him. He heard the squeal of terror that came from his own throat, and then one of the warriors raised a war club and brought it down with a sickening sound on the top of his skull. He crumpled to the ground and lay silent.

# 8.

Bolo men and armed robbers from Tambang mountains attacked two Companies Fourteenth Infantry, Henderson commanding, at Suda, Tuesday morning; driven and pursued with loss to them of eighteen men. Casualties, killed three, wounded seven. Co-ordinated attack by second band on Armory Maymbung resulted in capture by robbers of eleven rifles, thirteen thousand rounds ammunition, one disabled Gatling gun. Co-ordination of two attacks and excellent tactics suggest new enemy leader better skilled than usual. Henderson busy pursuing robber bands Island of Sulu with good results . . .

Henderson came back from his drive three days later, and admitted that he had achieved absolutely nothing. He was buttonholed in the garden outside Fort Asturias by a thin, slow-speaking newspaperman who had just arrived to take over from the late Arthur Jensen Withers.

"Major Henderson?"

"Yes?"

"My name's Reed."

Henderson thought he looked like one. He said politely, "My pleasure, Mr. Reed."

[ 122 ]

Reed fingered his notebook slowly. He said, "Let's make a deal, Major. Some of our boys have been giving the Army a bad time. I know that, so you don't have to tell me, all right? And I don't like it any more than you do. All I want to report is the truth—without whitewash, without lampblack. So what do you say, you want to talk about these robbers?"

"If I will be accurately reported, Mr. Reed."

"You have my promise. I'll show you my dispatch, and you can cut out anything you don't like."

Henderson said suavely, "Couldn't that be construed as censorship? If I remember correctly, the Adjutant-General has been under fire from your people because the Army thought it should stop the more blatantly untrue reports from the field. The *Examiner* called that censorship."

"I'm on your side, Major. If you don't want to talk, I'll have to get what I want from the Moros in the town."

It was always a difficult problem. They had their duty, too, the journalists; it was to give the public what they wanted, to send in stories that would sell newspapers. They kept to the truth, where possible, and surely nobody could object to a little heightening of color, to a little dramatic touching up here and there? There were some of them, admittedly, who sat in Manila, in the comfortable hotels or Army messes, and dreamed up fantastic actions in the field, but these were in the minority. Most of them were hard-working, courageous writers who saw in the long protraction of the hostilities an opportunity to infuse their readers with the kind of fierce pride that had stood solidly behind the soldiers throughout the war. The official reports would sometimes have made pretty dull reading; the public wanted something more exciting, and the journalists were there to give it to them.

Henderson sighed.

"All right, come and have a drink."

They went over to the open-sided reed house that had been built at the shady end of the garden to serve as a Mess, and sat down on wooden easy chairs which the local natives had made for them. Henderson poured two glasses of whisky and said curtly, "All right, what do you want to know?"

Reed was flipping over the pages of his notebook. He asked, "How many men in your column, Major?"

"Companies I and K of the Twenty-third Infantry, two Batteries of the Sixth Artillery waiting for us at the end of the drive."

Reed said sharply, "The Twenty-third? I thought they were over on Iloilo?"

"They were. We're getting reinforcements. Not enough, but some."

"I see. And I'm surprised. I take it that's an indication you're stepping up your operations here? On Sulu?"

"Correct."

"Why, Major? At this stage of the war?"

"We've had our bellyful of the Moros. They're giving us a lot of trouble these days."

"And what did you achieve on this drive, Major? How many enemy casualties?"

"We killed about eighteen of them. We lost three men."

"And you captured . . . ?"

"None."

"I see. Any truth in the rumor that there were some Papuans fighting with the Moros?"

"Where did you hear that?"

"Is it true?"

Henderson nodded his head. "It's true. I'd like to know where you heard it."

Reed said primly, "We have sources of information which are sometimes better than those of the Army. In the market. Is it a fair deduction that they have a leader now who has a little more of the—the power of persuasion than heretofore? Wouldn't you say?"

"It doesn't prove a thing."

"But you admit you're up against a combined force for the first time?"

"Yes. I admit that."

"Any idea who the leader is?"

"No definite information."

"My sources say his name's Jokiri."

Henderson bit his lip.

"You seem to be well informed."

"There's no reason why I shouldn't be. It's my job. You think you'll catch him?"

"I do."

"Can I quote you?"

"I suppose so. We all like to think we're doing the best we can."

Reed finished his drink and got up. He said softly, "Like I said, I'll let you see the dispatch before it goes off. Anything you don't like . . ."

"Sure."

The Major read the report over that night. It was long and rambling, and told him a great deal about his own operation that he had not known. He realized that Reed had been talking to his Moro informants in the market and was getting both sides of the story. At the end of the dispatch there was a note about him personally:

Major Henderson, representative of the best of our boys over here, who is in command of the operation aimed at putting this pirate where he belongs, on the end of a piece of good Manila rope, told me that he is confident of catching the robber chief. I wouldn't be surprised if he does, too. This Moro leader Jokiri is no ordinary pirate but a man of intelligence and unbelievable ferocity who has succeeded in getting a formidable force under his brilliant command. But I prophesy he's met his match in Major Henderson . . .

Two nights later, a Moro laborer, bent double under a load of firewood for the barracks, deposited his barong with the sentry at the gate to the fortress, in accordance with regulations, and carried his load inside the compound. A moment later, he dropped his wood, drew a small kris, and plunged it into the sentry's neck. Before he died, the sentry just had time to see that the Moro's eyebrows were shaved, and with his dying breath he gasped out "Juramentado!" in the hope that someone would hear him. But the sound that came from his throat was nothing more than the hiss of escaping air. He pulled the trigger of his rifle and was dead before the shot left the barrel. The guard came tumbling out, dropping to their knees and firing carefully, and four of them were sure that their bullets had found their mark; but the juramentado ran on, burst into the officer's lines, and before one of the cooks sunk a cleaver into his skull, killed seven people—two Tagalog girls, a Negrito servant, three soldiers of the Provost Guard, and one officer.

The officer was Major Henderson.

Sullivan woke late that morning. He was accustomed to waking instantly when the six o'clock sun came through a gap in the trees and hit the side of his shack, but this morning he was late. There was a twisted knot of disquiet deep down inside him which he could not account for; he wondered if it were merely a touch of sadness because Medina had not come to him that night. He went across the compound and saw that there were more soldiers there than was usual; he wondered if Jokiri had come in during the night. At the gate, the Montese guards pulled open the barricade for him, as they did every morning, and he went down to the stream for his morning bath.

He stripped off his clothes and entered the morning-cold water, feeling the iciness of it against his limbs, splashing it into his face and over his chest, then drying himself on his blue shirt. When he came back into the compound he fancied that the Monteses were staring at him. He was sure that they were muttering among themselves. It disturbed him, like anything else that he did not fully understand. His heart beating hard, he went to the door of his hut and stared over to where the chief's house stood. The reed matting over the entrance was closed, which meant that Jokiri was there, and there was a group of Moro datos gathered around it. He looked over to Medina's hut. The Papuan guard had been increased to four men.

He knew now that something was terribly wrong. Forcing back the rising anxiety in him, he walked over to her house. The guards closed their ranks and one of them grunted and shook his head. He went away again, puzzled and frightened.

Dawson's house was on the other side of the compound, beyond the women's eating place, and he thought he would go over and see what Dawson could tell him about it all. As he crossed the clearing, he stopped short, frozen with sudden panic; there was an ear-splitting scream that came across the silence to him. It was like the sound of a boar that has felt the lance bite deep into his neck, and for a fraction of time he remembered the hog that had sliced its tusk into the Brigadier, the Brigadier whose head had been lopped off his almost dead body in the bloody clearing by the canyon. He turned and ran.

The terrible sound had come from the chief's house. Fully expecting the datos to stop him, he pulled up at the entrance, but they drew back for him, and when he hesitated one of them took him by the arm and guided him inside; it was a friendly gesture from one warrior to another. Trembling, he let himself be led in front of Jokiri.

The chief was sitting on his ceremonial stool of inlaid mahogany, his bodyguard standing taut and rigid behind with their barongs drawn, and the long staff of office, brightly tufted at the top, was held at the chief's back by a Dyak slave. It was darker inside the long building, and for a moment he could not clearly see what it was that lay on the floor in front of Jokiri.

Then the blood left his face and the saliva stuck in his throat as he saw what it was. It was Dawson. He was quite naked, and his flesh seemed to gleam in the half-light. His wrists were tied with fiber-rope to a bamboo pole above his head, and another pole at his feet secured his widespread ankles. Four Moros held the ends of the two poles to the ground, squatting astride them and bearing down with their wide brown feet. Dawson was struggling savagely, and there was blood at his wrists where the tight cord was cutting into them. He saw Sullivan and screamed out, "Sullivan . . . stop them . . . stop them! They're going to cut me!"

He stared at the Englishman in horror, his mouth trying to find words that would mean something. Dawson screamed again, his voice high-pitched with terror, "They're gelding me, Sullivan! They're going to geld me!"

A young warrior stepped forward, holding a terciada in his hand. It was an ornate, ceremonial sword—the most beautiful weapon he had ever seen. He threw himself forward wildly, and seized the warrior by the waist, and then some of the datos moved forward and dragged him back, hanging onto his arms as he struggled to free himself. He threw them to one side with fierce bursts of physical violence until Jokiri raised an impatient hand and one of the Papuans stepped forward to throw a rope of bejuco vine around his neck, tugging his head irresistibly back. He stopped his struggles as the rope bit deep into his throat, and then he saw for the first time that Medina was there too, standing by the curtain that divided the chief's sleeping-quarters from the rest of the house. She was staring at him and her eyes were wide with fright. There was a message in them, imploring him.

The warrior he had attacked moved forward again with his terciada. He bent down, crouching at Dawson's middle, and then drew the blade deftly, quite gently, three times in three short strokes across the crotch, then leaned forward and held out the testicles in his bloody hand for the chief to see.

Dawson was silent now, and for a moment Sullivan feared that he was dead. But when the warrior cut the plaited cords that bound his wrists and his legs, he rolled over, clutching at his mutilations, crouching for a moment on his elbows and knees. Sullivan too was free now, and saying nothing he went forward and gently helped the Englishman to his feet. The datos moved back for him as he helped him, sobbing, his tears making rivulets of clean flesh on his grubby face, out of the chief's house and across the compound to his own hut. The ceremony was over.

Sullivan went to the water barrel and brought him a drink, and then made a pad of wet wood-ash and bound it carefully over the wound, and sat beside him to wait. Dawson said nothing. He stared ahead of him and brushed at the wetness on his cheeks, and when Sullivan lit a cigarette and held it out for him he did not even take it. His face was pale and drawn, and his eyes were heavy with suffering. For a long time he sat there, his eyes vacant as though the life had gone from them. Sullivan tried to speak to him; he would say nothing.

At last, he went away, and he sat in his own hut, wondering what had happened and what was to happen in the future. No one came to him, and when it was time to eat he went out and took a bowl of fish and rice from a group of women, and carried it into Dawson's hut. Dawson was still sitting in the same position, still staring vacantly at the rush wall. He put the gourd down beside him, and said gently, "If there's anything I can do . . . anything I can say . . ."

Dawson did not answer. Sullivan waited a little while, and then he left. He took some food over to his own house, and ate it in silence.

He knew that the time had come for him to escape, that he could not wait any longer. He was trembling, and the sweat on his neck was wet and cold. And while he was turning over in his mind all the dangerous things he would have to do, he looked up and saw Dawson standing in the entrance, leaning heavily on his stick and looking at him. He got quickly to his feet and went to him. Dawson pushed him savagely aside and lowered himself painfully to the ground. Sullivan sat down opposite him, took out two cigarettes and lit them, handed one to Dawson, and waited.

Dawson said at last, "You'd think it would hurt, wouldn't you? It doesn't, really. I always used to wonder why the horses never whimpered when we did that to them. Now, I know. It doesn't hurt. Doesn't hurt at all."

Sullivan said nothing.

"You know, I ought to blame it on you. Tell the truth, I don't know why I don't kill you for what they did to me. Only one thing . . . we've got to get out of here. Should have done it a long time ago. Would have done, if you'd had the guts. Why didn't you tell me you'd taken her? Medina."

Sullivan could only stammer at him, "But . . . What do you mean by that?"

"I mean by that," Dawson said furiously, his voice a whisper, "I mean that you've been taking her to bed and doing nothing about it to get us out of here. I told you that's all you had to do."

"What's it to you, Dawson?"

"What's it to me?" The Englishman's voice was filled with hatred. "You saw what they did—you ask what's it to me? You really don't know? After what you saw them do to me?"

A new horror was creeping over him. He said quietly, "Go on, Dawson. You'd better tell me the rest of it. What happened?"

"I'll tell you all right," Dawson said, his voice uncontrollable with pain and rage. "I tried to talk to Medina last night—in the darkness when everybody in the camp is supposed to be sleeping. They caught me. They must have examined her—one of the priests, most likely—and found out that she's not the bloody virgin she's supposed to be. They're Moslems, Sullivan, don't you realize that? It's important to them. And they thought it was me." He said savagely, "I told you, damn your eyes, I told you. I said I wanted to know if you were screwing her, and you had to lie to me about it. We could all have been out of here, all of us, and now—now look at me." The tears were coming fast from his eyes, unheeded. He said, whimpering, "A eunuch, Sullivan, a man like me—for the rest of my life. You know what that means to a man? Can you understand what that means to a man like me?"

There was a long pause. Sullivan said at last, "Why—why should they be so *sure* that it was you? They know that Medina and I spend a lot of time together."

"Yes, you bloody idiot, in the daytime. But let them find you holding hands with her after dark and see what happens. To the Moros, the time for fornication is after dark. There's no privacy in their houses, they all sleep together, the whole family. So when they want a bang, they have to wait till after dark when the children can't watch. And the unmarried ones, they sneak out into the forest at night, can't you understand that? As far as they're concerned, any young girl's maidenhood is safe in the daylight. Around the camp, anyway." He said bitterly, "Why do I have to spell it out for you? If you used your brain as well as you use your balls we'd have been out of here by now."

"I still don't know why they'd assume it was you."

Dawson threw away the end of his cigarette and said sullenly, "Give me another cigarette."

As he lit it, he said slowly, "Well, that was my fault, I suppose. I told you, I tried to talk with her last night. If I'd waited till morning . . . I was pretty sure you were playing around with her, more than you'd let on. You don't lie very well, you know. And I was pretty sure that your fancy inhibitions wouldn't let you make use of her, so I thought I'd better have a talk with her myself. I should have waited till morning, but I thought . . . Hell, I thought that if I caught her while she was hot with the need for you, she'd see my point of view just that much quicker. And while I was talking to her, one of the Papuans hit me over the head with a bloody war club. During the night they sent for Jokiri, and the rest you know. If only you'd told me, for Christ's sake! They like to keep their girls *intacta*, except the whores, and once the priests found out . . . There's already a lot of bad blood between the old man and the priests; he hates their guts and they know it. So a thing like this . . ." He said obscenely, "As soon as they found out she'd lost it, they put two and two together and made six."

Sullivan sat silent for a moment. Dawson went on, "I could have told them it was you. Only thing is, to tell the truth, I didn't think they'd believe me. They'd caught the two of us whispering together in the moonlight. Must have been pretty obvious to them that it was me, once they found out."

"I'm sorry."

"Sorry! That's a bit of an understatement, isn't it? The whole idea was you'd find out her father's movements, get her to help us. If you'd done that—if you'd been half a man—" He broke off, then said bitterly, "Half a man."

Sullivan said abruptly, "I'm not trying to clear myself, but—all right, I've made love to her. Every night for some time now. Only . . ."

"Only what, Sullivan?"

He bit his lip. "I shouldn't be talking like this, except that—well, under the circumstances . . ."

"For Christ's sake!"

"Well, I've been making love to her, but—she was not a virgin." Dawson was startled out of his anger. He stared at Sullivan.

"Are you sure?"

"I'm sure."

"You could easily be wrong, you know."

"I'm good and sure."

"I see. Like that."

They sat together for a while in silence. Sullivan said at last, awkwardly, "I mean no—no disrespect to her when I tell you this. I don't usually go around . . . Well, you know what I mean."

[ 131 ]

"A good thing you did tell me. It complicates matters very considerably."

"How's that?"

"It's no longer a matter of enticing her from her father. Now, it's from her lover."

"Jokiri? You must be out of your mind!"

"Who else?"

"But it couldn't be!"

"On the contrary, he's the only one it could be. Take my word for it. Any suspicion against some handsome young Moro—he'd slice his head off without giving it a second thought."

"That coarse old man . . ."

"He's less than forty years old. Each of his legal four wives is a woman of some political importance—the daughter of some tribal chief who Jokiri wants to keep in with. So, he captures a pretty young European girl from the Dyaks and wants to make her his wife. Normally, he'd simply divorce his oldest wife, in accordance with accepted custom, but how can he? He'd antagonize one of the tribal chiefs, and weaken the position he's so carefully built up. The answer's obvious—make her a concubine and keep it secret. That explains why he adopted her. I told you, the man's got brains. He thinks."

"It's horrifying."

Dawson said viciously, "It didn't seem to worry you when you thought it was some young Moro boy."

Sullivan looked at him sourly and said nothing. He knew that Dawson must be wrong. He said heavily, "We'll have to get out of here, soon. There's no doubt in my mind now. None at all."

Dawson said bitterly, "Well, that's a relief. Pity you couldn't have come round to my way of thinking a little earlier. First opportunity you get, find out where the old man is. He's going out this evening on a raid. With the grace of God it might be far enough away for us to get clear. Find out. Ask her. She'll tell you. But be careful. They'll be watching her like a hawk. First chance you get."

The chance came sooner than he expected. That evening, when he went down to wash at the stream, she came and joined him. Her Papuan bodyguard, four of them now, stood respectfully to one side as she crouched down and dipped a jabul in the water. He said quietly, "Can we talk?"

She did not look up.

"Yes. Of course."

"About Dawson. He told me he'd tried to talk to you last night. He told me why they—why they did that to him."

"I had to tell my father it was him."

He dropped the shirt he was washing and stared at her in astonishment.

"You had to tell him what?"

She said calmly, "I told my father that I was going into the hut to meet with Dawson. If I had told him it was you, he would have done this thing to you instead."

"But—but . . . Good God! You saw what they did to him! If you'd said nothing . . ."

"If I had said nothing, they would have learned that I was going to meet you."

"How could they?"

"Perhaps one of the women has seen us."

He turned to her slowly. "That puts me in a hell of a position. Another man punished for my—for what I have done."

"It is best like this."

It was the slow degradation of his quality. He had felt it first the first time he had sat on the ground with Dawson, his legs crossed under him like a Moro, like a native, knowing that the denial of his small white prerogatives was the first step on a long road that led to complete savagery. Now, he did not feel much more than a trembling of the conscience that, not too long ago, would have driven him to the edge of guilt's desperation. He said abruptly, "Now, they will be watching you very carefully."

"Yes. It is true."

"How can we be together, then?"

She said steadily, "Only if we go away from here."

"All of us? You and me and Dawson too?"

"If that is what you want."

"It's what I want."

"All of us then."

"Can you find a way across the swamp?"

"Yes."

"Are you ready to go soon? As soon as—as soon as the chief leaves the camp?"

"Yes. He will go tonight."

"Where to, Medina? How far will he go?"

"He will cross the water to Tapu."

"Tapu! That's fifty miles!" He said excitedly, "How long will he be gone?"

"Two days. Perhaps three."

"Then we go tonight, Medina. Are you sure this is what you want?"

"It is the only way you can love me."

He said uncomfortably, "There's only one thing, Medina. Are you sure you're ready to leave—to leave Jokiri?"

"I will leave him."

He wanted to ask her if the chief was her lover, but he did not have the courage. He said slowly, "No one must know about this. And—and can you leave your hut? Your bodyguard? The Papuans?"

"They will not know."

"All right. I will talk to Dawson. If we meet outside the compound . . . Can we do that?"

"Later, I will tell you where we can meet. I must find a way—I will tell you later. When we make food tonight."

"I'd better get back."

"And when we go, you will love me again?"

He said steadily, "I will love you, Medina. I think I will always love you."

He put a hand out towards her, and she said quickly, "Not now. Not here."

He saw that she was carefully getting on with her work as she talked, pounding her wadded jabul with a stone, beating the sodden mass of it on the rocks at the edge of the water. He knew that she was not as free as she had been before, and that the Papuans were there, watching her. He said, "When we go together, we will be together always."

Not looking at him: "I would like that, Shay. I want to be with you always."

"I'm asking you to marry me, Medina. To be my wife."

For a little while, she stopped working, and just knelt there, staring into the forest. Then she said, very low, "If this is what you want, Shay."

"You know I want it. And you?"

"You know also that this is what I want. To go back to—to my own people. But I am afraid."

"Afraid of what, Medina?"

"When we go to Jolo, when you see your own American people again, you will not want me any more."

She turned and looked at him steadily. He said urgently, "Medina. I love you. I want you. I want you to be my wife."

"Now, yes. At this minute, yes. But after . . ."

"Always."

Her eyes held his for a long time. He smiled suddenly and said, "This is a hell of a way to propose."

She did not answer his smile, and he knew that she still did not believe him. He said again, "I want you to be my wife, Medina. To be always together. Always."

Only then did she drop her eyes. She said softly, "All right. But now I must go. They are watching us."

"And tonight we go away, together."

"Yes. Tonight. I will talk to you again when we make food."

She turned and left him then, and as he wrung the water out from his shirt and shook it, standing up and brushing the soil off his trousers, he felt, for the first time in weeks, like a soldier again.

The bright lights of the fires were throwing their quivering shadows all around him when he went over to Dawson's house. He half expected to find that Dawson was dead, or had been taken again by the warriors. He could not believe that escape was so close at hand. But the Englishman was there, smoking a black cheroot and clutching a whisky bottle.

Indicating the bottle, he asked, "Where did you get that?"

Dawson grimaced at him, holding it out, offering it to him.

[ 135 ]

"Had it stashed away for a long time. This seems as good an occasion as any to open it up. The hell with them."

Sullivan took the bottle from him and drank, wiping his mouth with the back of his hand. He said carefully, "Are you feeling—do you feel all right?"

"As well as can be expected."

"Trying to get drunk?"

Scornfully, Dawson said, "On one bottle? It would take a dozen of them."

"You'd better be good and sober tonight."

Dawson, understanding at once, looked up at him sharply. He said softly, "I'll be good and sober. Tonight?"

Sullivan sat down close by him. Keeping his voice low, he said, "Jokiri's going over to Tapu."

"He's left the camp already, I saw them go. The rearguard follows him when the moon comes up. To Tapu? Are you sure?"

"Positive. He'll be gone for at least two days."

"That's my boy! In two days, we should be able to reach the road. How do we get across the swamp?"

"Medina will come with us."

"Excellent! I'll get guns."

"Two good rifles, as much ammunition as you can lay your hands on. What about a compass?"

"Might be difficult, but—well, we can manage without if we have to."

"Food?"

"I'll wrap up some rice and some meat. We won't need very much."

"Water?"

"I have a water skin somewhere. I can get another. We'll find plenty."

Tapping the cork firmly into his bottle of whisky, he said, "And we'll take this along too, might come in handy. The problem's going to be getting over the palisade. It's pretty well guarded."

"Medina will tell us later where we can meet."

"Jesus—after all this time. It'll be good to live like a European again. Where will I go, Sullivan?"

The excitement was gleaming in his eyes.

"I guess it won't be easy for you. Perhaps I can help in some way. With your knowledge of the Moros, maybe the Army can use you."

Dawson twisted uncomfortably.

"Would they have to know about—about me? A deserter has a pretty thin time."

"I don't see why I should mention it."

"You're a good fellow, Sullivan. Maybe I've never really . . . Tonight then?"

"Tonight."

Sullivan went back to his hut and examined the keen edge of his barong, and repaired the stripped sole of his boot by cutting small holes in the leather and threading it with tightly plaited raffia. When he went out and stood by the fire where the women were cooking the rice for the evening meal, Medina came over and sat with them, saying nothing.

A little later, there was a commotion when three or four Moros began dragging an ornamental brass cannon of local manufacture down the slope that led to the stream, and a dozen heavily armed Monteses followed them shortly after. He knew that the rearguard was moving out and that there were not more than twenty or thirty warriors left to guard the encampment. All day the Moros had been preparing for a new battle. Two of the Dyak slaves had been dragged, tightly bound, into the center of the compound and lashed to a tree, and some of the young Moros had tested the edges of their weapons on them, casually slicing across their flesh until all the blood had left their mangled bodies. It was their custom, but the sight of it had sickened him.

One of the women got up to find more wood for the fire, and Medina said softly, "When the house burns. Behind the big tree."

Not looking at her, he said quietly, "And you can find a way across the swamp?"

"Of course. There is a way."

"You're quite sure you want to do this, Medina? Quite sure?"

"Yes. This is what I want to do."

"And you've no regrets about leaving your—about leaving Jokiri?"

"It is time that I must leave him and return to my own people."

Trembling, he said, "And there is no one else—no one you will be sorry to leave behind? No one else?"

She looked across at him then, and then lowered her eyes, understanding what he was trying to say. She said stubbornly, "I have told you. I will come with you."

"Then we'll wait for you."

"Behind the big tree. My house will burn, and then you must go there."

He looked across at the big baobab that stood in the corner of the compound, and she nodded her head and smiled at him. He got up and went over to Dawson's hut.

Dawson hobbled up onto his feet quickly, his eyes aflame. He said eagerly, "Well, are we going?"

"Soon. She's going to fire one of the houses. We meet behind the baobab tree in the corner there."

A shadow of pain crossed Dawson's lined face. He said grimly, "We met there once before."

"This time, we'll be on the way out."

"Are you sure you can trust her? Medina?"

Sullivan said uncomfortably, "I think so. I—I made a sort of bargain with her."

"Oh?"

"I told her—I told her I'd marry her. I know that this is what she wants."

Dawson stared at him for a moment and then said cheerfully, "Well, that's a promise you obviously won't have to keep."

"It's what I want too," Sullivan said stiffly. "After all, she's not a Moro, she's a Spaniard. And I'm—I'm in love with her."

It was hard to talk about it. Dawson said, grinning, "Sure."

"I love her very much, Dawson."

"It's your business, dear boy," Dawson said affably. "After all, if she thinks you're going to make an honest woman of her, she'll do her best to get us to civilization. I should worry."

Sullivan turned on his heel and went back to his hut. He could never trust himself to argue with Dawson. And a little later there was a sudden shout outside, and when he ran out, clutching his barong in an agony of excitement, he saw that the shack on the other side of Medina's house was on fire, the flames bursting fiercely out of the dry thatch walls. The Papuan bodyguard had run from their place at her door and were quickly tearing down the hut that stood next to it to prevent the flames from spreading. He looked across and saw Dawson, his stave under his shoulder, hobble quickly across the compound, and then he ran to the rear of the big baobab and waited in the shadows. The warriors were running about the clearing, throwing water from the big earthenware pots onto the flames, tearing away the adjoining rush walls with their bare hands. He saw that the palisade behind the tree was unguarded. Dawson came hobbling over, two rifles tucked under his arm and a swaying bundle of bandoliers over his shoulder. He thrust a rifle into Sullivan's hand and said thickly, "This is it, old boy. Where is she?"

Sullivan looked all around him in desperation. Medina was nowhere in sight. He climbed quickly up onto the palisade, noting with satisfaction that there was no one guarding it, and when he leaped down on the other side, Medina came running to him out of the woods, holding out her arms and saying, "*Quickly—this way —this way.*"

He turned, then, and shouted to Dawson, and as the Englishman struggled up onto the barricade he moved to him and helped him over, taking the bandoliers from him, and then in a moment the sound and the heat of the fire were behind them; and a little while later it was no more than a red light that flickered far behind them as they ran together through the darkness of the forest. He called to Medina once, when she was far ahead of them, "Dawson . . . he can't run so fast." She slowed down and waited for them, her breast rising up and down with her heavy breathing, urging them on and saying, "Quickly . . . we must go far before they find that we are not there . . . quickly . . ."

The jungle closed in on them, and she began using her long bush-knife, the curved sundang, like an expert, hacking away at the heavy lianas and bejuco vines that obstructed their passage. Sullivan was close behind her, with Dawson leaning heavily on his shoulder, an arm around his neck, his gray features taut with pain and excitement. They did not stop until they had left the compound half a mile behind them, and then they sat down for a moment and listened. Faintly, they could still hear the shouts of the warriors in the village, and they knew from the sounds of their voices that they were still busy with the spreading fire. They could see the bright glow of it in the sky to the west of them, and Medina said calmly, "They will think that it is another attack by the Dyaks. They will not want to leave the village now."

Sullivan nodded. Assuming command now, he said brusquely, "Then let's be on our way."

There was an elation inside him. In a few weeks he had escaped from his savage captors, he had found a woman he could love, and he was on his way to rejoin his unit. The difficulties which he knew must lie ahead of him shrank to unimportance in the perspective of his triumph.

They climbed to their feet and moved off into the jungle. Its night sounds were a frightening symphony about them, and when, following Medina's footsteps carefully, they came to a bush-knifed path that led into the pestilent waters of the marshes, the dampness dripped off the trees and soaked their clothes. The wet mud closed about their feet; the thorns tore at them; and low-slung tentacles of vine and roots tripped them and flung them to the ground. Their clothes were ripped and their bodies were streaked with bloody scratches. The mosquitoes closed in on them in stinging clouds, and the small unnamed flying insects squelched under their slapping hands.

The stench of putrefaction was all about them, but they were free.

# 9.

THE YOUNG LIEUTENANT STRETCHED HIS LEGS AND STOOD IN THE
saddle, raising the binoculars to his pale-blue eyes; he was tired,
stiff, close to exhaustion. Close by, the horses wheeled in a tight
turn and waited, tossing their heads and champing at their bits.
Behind them, the white group of buildings that was Jolo seemed
to shimmer in the heat of the afternoon sun beyond the flat green
carpet of the haciendas.

The troopers of the Third U.S. Cavalry, who had but recently
arrived from Luzon on special assignment, wiped at their sleepless
faces, brushing the sweat off their foreheads. The Lieutenant put
his glasses back, swung his arm in a wide circle, and shouted an
order. Wearily, the troopers moved into place behind him. On the
brow of the hill immediately ahead of them, a detachment of men
from Company F, Signal Corps, was setting up its helios and
stringing telegraph wires out; and to the far south, Batteries H and
L of the Third Artillery were wheeling their heavy guns into position, manhandling them up the slopes of the hill that overlooked
the wide sweep of the sea beyond Mabingkang. Further to the
west, three companies of Infantry were entrenched in a strong position with the cliff on their left flank and the river on their right.

[ 141 ]

Two Macabebe Scouts, for whom the blue-eyed Lieutenant was searching, came in from the hill on his right, riding their small ponies hard, reining in wildly close beside him. They spoke together in low tones for a moment, and then the Lieutenant called for his runner and sent a message to the H.Q. position which had been established in a small valley on the other side of the river. It read, simply, explicitly, and sadly:

The Scouts have returned. They have found no indications that Jokiri is within the circle we have drawn. All information suggests that he escaped during the night and has gone to the island of Tapu. Shall I withdraw?

He ordered the troops to dismount, they sat up their portable kitchen, and they cooked their breakfast. It was the first good meal they had eaten in three days. They had bacon, and bread, and fried pancakes made with corn, and coffee.

When Sullivan, Dawson, and Medina reached the swamp, it was already daylight. Sure now that their escape must have been discovered, and that runners would be slipping through the forest to look for their tracks and to cut them off, they had pushed on at a merciless pace, forcing their way through the thickly tangled bushes, bursting through the thorns, hacking sometimes at the turbulent vines that seemed to reach out for them and fasten themselves around their bodies. When they sliced at them with their knives, great skeins of them fell heavily from the treetops and lay in festoons around their feet.

Their clothes were already in shreds. The bejuco vines, in their natural state, were long tough cords as thick as a man's finger, pliable and enormously strong. The vine was of uniform length from root to tip, and at its end there was a wide spray of leaves among which were hidden huge bundles of recurved thorns that seemed to seek out their clothing and fasten themselves in it. It made a vicious weapon in the jungle's struggles against the encroachment of man.

They sank down onto the wet moss of a small clearing in the marsh and rested. Dawson's face was pale and drawn, and it was clear that the forced march of the night had been too much for him; but when he looked across at the others he grinned and jerked his head derisively back at the camp they had left. Sullivan was panting with the exertion, but it was good to feel a rifle in his hands again. He carried the barong, too, using it as a machete in his fight against the jungle.

Only Medina seemed unmoved by the effort they had made. Her bare feet were cut and bleeding; there were thorn-slashes down the sleek sides of her body; her bodice was little more than a ripped rag and her bare flesh showed through the rents in her jabul. She had wound a wide sash round her waist, and now she took from this a bundle of food and opened it out, spreading it wide on the grass and offering it to them. It was cooked rice into which fish had been pounded and heavily spiced with pepper and cumin. They ate in silence, and drank from the water skin into which Dawson had poured a little of the whisky, then lay flat on their backs to let the strength seep back into their limbs.

She said, at last, somberly, "We must go on. If we do not cross the swamp soon . . ."

Sullivan asked her, "How long will it take us to cross?"

"Until tonight. There are many crocodiles."

"I know. We have rifles."

"Yes," Dawson said. "The best way to tell them exactly where we are. Now our trail isn't as clear as all that."

Sullivan said sharply, "You expect to fight crocodiles with barongs?"

"We may have to. Start firing off our rifles, they'll be all around us in two minutes."

"We'll see," Sullivan said. He felt the need to assert his military authority. "The main thing is that we should get across the swamp as quickly as possible. Once we're over on the other side . . . Well, it shouldn't be hard to find the track that runs from Maymbung to Jolo. Let's move on, shall we?"

They clambered wearily to their feet, feeling the sleeplessness heavily in their bones, and went down the steep slope to where the roots of a huge mangrove lay spread out like the tentacles of a monstrous octopus, reaching with its hard black fingers deep into

[ 143 ]

the slime at the water's edge. The vines hung down in festoons from its branches, deep yellow and green and purple; the poisonous colors, he thought. Gingerly, he put one foot into the water. The mud squelched at him, oozing up and sucking him down. He held out his hand and Medina took it, then held her other hand out to Dawson. In a slow line, linked together, they began the treacherous crossing.

It was the only sound about them, the steady, sucking sound of the mud. There was an evil scent to it, the scent of decay and rot and filth. A bird swooped down and flitted across their path, and soon the monotonous humming of the insects started again. The frogs began their croaking, a monstrous cacophony that pressed down on them out of the lonely emptiness. Sullivan muttered, "I tried to bring a platoon over here once. We nearly lost all of them."

He was peering about him in the smelly morass. A crocodile was sunning himself on the bank to his left, and he pointed at it silently, then gripped Medina more firmly by the hand. His rifle was slung over his shoulder, and there were three full bandoliers around his waist; his barong was thrust through them, and the sun shone on the wet and shining hilt above the stained leather scabbard.

They reached a drier elevation where the wide buttressed roots of a gutta-percha tree spread out like the feet of some monstrous prehistoric bird, covered with moss and sprinkled with fallen apex leaves that had small silky hairs on the underside. A second tree had been felled close beside it, with the branches lopped off and circled with neat incisions where someone had been collecting the sap. He turned to Medina and raised his eyebrows, but she shook her head and smiled at him, meaning: *Not my people; we do not use these trees.* They sat down to rest for a moment on the broad roots, and he scraped a slug off his leg where a thorn had ripped a long tear in his trousers, feeling its teeth bite into him as he swept it away in disgust. There was bamboo growing nearby, and he went over and cut three staves, slicing their ends into sharp spears with his barong, and then they moved on again, walking into the sun, feeling the heat of it on their faces.

The water came up to their waists, now, and wading was more

[ 144 ]

difficult. They had to force their feet out of the mud that tried to suck them down, and he worried about the deeper patches where, he knew, a man could sink to a revolting death in a few seconds, but Medina seemed to know where the path was safe. From time to time she turned and said, "No . . . this way . . . through here," as though she had come this way many times before.

They found a small canoe, a binta, hidden under a canopy of cut foliage, and they stood by it for a while, looking around them for the owner, but not finding him. Medina said quietly, "One of the guards—he will be near here somewhere."

Sullivan whispered, "Shall we take it?"

She shook her head. "It is better not. It will not be easy to use, the way we must go."

He wondered if she was, even subconsciously, thinking of the Moro who had concealed it there, not wanting to leave him lost in the swamp. But soon they reached a broad patch of dry ground and he realized that it would have betrayed their passing had they been forced to abandon it there.

They cut back on their tracks, swinging away with the sun on their backs, and it was a long time before they came to the wet mud again and turned once more west. She stopped then, suddenly, her body poised lightly in midaction, her head thrown back, listening, and then she dragged them hastily under the cover of a clump of foliage. They sank down deep into the water, pulling the leaves about them tightly. His heart beating fast, his rifle held high, Sullivan waited.

He could hear nothing at first, and then there was the gentle lapping sound of paddles, and in a moment a long canoe swung into sight, with seven or eight Moros aboard. One of them was standing up, peering around into the darkness of the undergrowth, a blowgun held delicately in his hand. Sullivan held his breath. He watched a crocodile swimming lazily away from the canoe and knew that if it came too close, they would have to fight. The impulse to cough was almost irresistible, and when an insect settled on his neck and sank its tiny teeth into him, the urge to slap at it was almost overpowering.

The canoe moved away smoothly, with only the somnolent

sound of the paddles and the sporadic croaking of the frogs coming to them in the silence. They waited a long time, keeping quite still, till they were sure that it had gone; and then they moved quietly on until they reached dry land again and floundered like netted fish onto the leaf-covered earth. They lay there gasping for a while, feeling the strain in their muscles. Sullivan looked up at the sun, low on the horizon now. He said, his voice very low, "Another hour and it will be dark."

"We cannot move at night," Medina said. "We must find somewhere to sleep."

"And the others? The Moros?"

She said gravely, "At night, they will be looking for us. But I am afraid—I do not know the swamp as well as they know it. If we will be lost . . . Only when it is day we can move."

He said nothing. It was against all his military training to sit still while the enemy moved, but he knew that she was right. The knowledge that they were so dependent upon her irked him. Dawson said cheerfully, "Well, a night in the bush won't hurt us."

He had recovered his good spirits, though his eyes were wan and his face was pale and sickly. He seemed to have forgotten the tragic events of the previous day, but Sullivan knew that sooner or later the pain and the sorrow of it would catch up with him and leave him a broken, useless wreck. Again the necessity of holding his command came over him. He said carefully, "We'll stop on the next patch of dry ground. Cover ourselves with foliage, and keep still. It won't be easy, but if they're going to catch up with us, let's make sure at least that they don't find us."

He said to Medina, "You think they will have sent men from the camp to look for us? Before Jokiri returns?"

"Yes. They will send one man to tell my father. They will send perhaps ten or twenty men to find us, so that when Jokiri returns he will know where to go."

"Then we've only a small force to deal with for the moment. You realize—if they find us, we shall be killing your own people?"

She said steadily, "They are not my own people. I am Spanish."

He exchanged a silent glance with Dawson. He said slowly, "One of us must keep watch all night. Dawson and I will take turns."

[ 146 ]

"I can watch too. I am not tired."

"Good. The next good patch of land. There's not much daylight left to us."

They slipped into the water again, feeling the cold of it now, shuddering with the sickly smell of it, wading forward towards the light red patches that showed where the sun had gone down, and when they came to a huge mangrove tree that spread its roots for a hundred feet in all directions, he looked up at it and said, "Up here? A good place to wait out the night?"

They stood under it for a moment, shivering with the cold, staring white-faced at the height of its great branches. Dawson nodded. "No footprints to give the show away. Plenty of room up there."

Sullivan slung his rifle more closely about him and pulled himself up to the lower branches, then held out a hand for Medina. She climbed quickly and easily, and he braced himself in a fork of the trunk and tugged at the vine that Dawson was helplessly trying to clamber up. Soon, they were together high above the water, wedging themselves tightly in the tremendous broad spaces of the upper limbs, feeling the dry comfort of the hard bark under their hands.

He took off his wet shirt and handed it to Medina. She shook her head and wrapped her arms around her body.

"Go on, take it."

"I am not cold."

"You will be. Take it."

"I think I am more used to it."

"Take it. Please."

She hesitated, knowing that it was a matter of principle with him, then took it and put it over her shoulders. He reached across to her and wedged himself close in beside her, watching Dawson struggle into a kind of relative comfort just below them, leaning his head back and closing his eyes.

She said quietly, "Sleep for a little while. I will watch."

Sullivan shook his head. He said, smiling at her, "Sleep now. I'll wake you later on."

She nodded. He called down softly, "Dawson?"

"Uh-huh?"

"Get some sleep. I'll wake you first, you wake Medina."

"Sure."

"We must keep very quiet."

There was no answer. He knew that Dawson, exhausted, was already on the borders of unconsciousness. He put out an arm and let it fall round Medina's shoulder. The thick wool of his shirt was rough and soggy under his arm. She put her hand on his chest and her head on his shoulder, and she closed her eyes, saying no more but sleeping soon like an animal that falls into a coma whenever he is tired. He wished he could smoke a cigarette.

He had no knowledge of time. Once or twice his head drooped and he had to force himself awake. His arm under her was cramped and painful but he did not want to move it, and he passed the time by making himself ignore the insects that bit into him, drilling himself with a kind of masochistic pleasure into not moving, into keeping a stillness that was unnatural, making a game of it. The night birds were all round them, and he wondered what a spectacle they must present if those birds had the gift of thought. A twig broke off above his head and slithered down his bare chest, and he imagined for a horrified moment that it was a snake. He heard the quiet rustle in the leaves where an animal moved, a lemur, perhaps. Medina stirred and was suddenly awake, and she pressed herself closer to him so that he looked round in alarm to see what had awakened her; but she smiled at him in the meager light of the night sky and whispered, "Go to sleep. I will stay awake."

His voice no more than a murmur, he said, "Dawson . . ."

"Let him sleep. I am not tired any more."

"All right. Wake me soon."

He put his arm tighter round her, feeling the warmth and the softness of her, feeling the urge for her body again. He slipped his hand down inside her warm, damp bodice, feeling the roundness of her breast, and he slept.

When he awoke again, the rising sun was beginning to color the sky behind them. He shuddered with the icy cold and stretched his cramped limbs, then froze into immobility as Medina, wide awake and staring, laid a finger on his lips, then pointed into the dark shadows below them. He looked down quickly and saw that

Dawson, white-faced, was looking down and reaching cautiously for his rifle.

Far below, one of the Papuan soldiers from the camp was standing at the base of a narrow palm tree that leaned out over the water. He was cutting a vine with the blade of his spear and binding it into two tight circles. As Sullivan watched him, he looped one circle around his knee, and the other round his ankle, and then, easily and swiftly, he began to climb the trunk of the palm, sliding the vine-loops up with him as he went. When he reached the top, he pulled himself into the thick mass of the fronds and turned to look around him. He saw them at the precise moment that Dawson fired. His eyes went wide with surprise, and then the shot rang out and the bullet caught him squarely in the center of the throat and jerked his black-maned head back sharply. He made no sound, but toppled slowly backwards, his long black hands slipping with unconscious tenacity from the smooth bark of the tree, his body crashed against it, and he hung there, suspended upside down, his knee still hooked in the circle of liana-rope, and the blood, bright red against the black, trickling down over his face and into the huge mass of ivory-pinned black hair. The knife he was wearing at his inverted waist fell from his belt and splashed into the water below.

Sullivan said urgently, "It will take them some time to find where the shot came from. Come on."

They scrambled down from their perch, falling pell-mell into the shallow, black-mud swamp, grabbing their rifles and heading into the cover of the floating plants. They heard a shout far behind them as they pressed forward, and they reached dry land again and ran until the mud sucked at them once more and they sank deeper and deeper into the filthy water. Sullivan said, gasping, "You know where we are?"

Medina was moving ahead of them. She turned quickly.

"I know. We must go this way."

Dawson was struggling along in the rear, dragging his crippled leg in the mud, slithering to his knees and clambering painfully up again. They saw two Moros in a small binta far over on their right, and as they moved away the binta turned and came towards them, the two men shouting at them and one of them drawing his barong.

Sullivan turned round, steadied his rifle against the trunk of a tree, and fired carefully. The barong caught a flash of sun as it spun from his hand and the Moro fell backwards into the water. The canoe kept on its course, one man now moving his paddle and the frail craft slipping over the shallow water with incredible speed. It was quite close now, and Sullivan waited until it was almost on them, sighting his rifle. As it came to a sudden stop, he fired, a careful, precise, and point-blank shot that drilled a hole in the center of the Moro's forehead. He looked quickly at Medina and saw that her mouth was set in a tight line. Saying nothing, he pulled the canoe towards them and in a moment they were all in it and moving fast and erratically over the swamp to the clump of bamboo that meant another patch of dry land.

They stopped again from sheer exhaustion when the sun was high over their heads, sending up clouds of stinking steam from the water about them. The pain of moving was unbearable as they dragged themselves among the roots of a banyan tree and lay along the broad plateau of its bark. For a long time, none of them could talk, and the only thought that was in their minds was that they would never leave the stench and the filth behind them and reach dry land again. But a little later on they came to a broad flat stretch of forest where the sun had penetrated the trees and gently warmed the ground, and gratefully, they sank to their knees and fell once more on the friendly grass. They lay like crucified figures, their limbs stretched out to soak up the sun and dry the pain out of their bodies.

Dawson, his mouth drawn and his cheeks taut, was on the verge of collapse, and in a while Sullivan went over to him and stood looking down at him as he lay there, not moving. He said, "It's not easy, I know."

Dawson opened his eyes. Grimacing with pain, he said, "I'll get there. Don't worry about me."

"Man's capacity for pain . . ."

"And for survival."

"Yes, I suppose that's it. We'll soon be there. Tomorrow, the day after."

"I'm beginning to wonder if it's worth it. I was quite happy back there until . . . And now, among normal people again—women— what am I going to do, Sullivan?"

"I don't know. It—it doesn't bear thinking about."

"I suppose I'll survive."

His glance went over to Medina, and Sullivan knew that he was trying to revive a spark of lust inside himself and was giving it up as useless. He went over and sat beside her, a little apart from Dawson, and took her hand in his. He said, smiling, "We've come a long way."

She nodded, brushing the long hair from her face. "And still a long way to go. But I think now—now they will not come so far from the camp. Not until the chief returns."

It was the first time she had avoided saying "my father." He rolled over on his stomach, trying not to see the sadness in her face. He said lightly, "And when we get there, you'll have a house close to the Garrison. We'll get some American clothes—some dresses . . . Will you like that?"

She turned to him gravely.

"And the other women? The wives of the other officers?"

There was a shadow of a frown on his face. He had been thinking about it himself. He said slowly, forcing a smile, "You will be my wife. I am sure they will all like you. I have many friends in the camp."

"The daughter of a Moro pirate."

"An American officer's wife—like the rest of them. A captive, rescued from the Moros. You will be happy. I promise you that you will be happy."

"And we will go back—together? To America? To the place you told me about?"

"Of course. One day soon now. Another year, perhaps two. Then we will go back together. And there will be no more—no more killing, no more savagery."

"But you are a soldier."

"Soldiering is a good life. Back home, it does not mean so much— fighting."

He said, frowning, "This is something which is hard to under-

[ 151 ]

stand, Medina. The Army is the only life I have ever really known, since I was quite young. It's—it's the major part of my life. It's a good thing and I'm proud of it. Only—only sometimes, in the heat of battle, I'm not proud of myself, can you see what I mean? I believe, deep inside me, that I ought—that any man ought to be competent for something other than fighting. Since I came out here, I'm beginning to wonder if that's all there is to life. Just killing. There was a raid a little while back, you remember? They brought some of the wounded back into the village, and one of them—one of them was a woman. She'd been bayonetted."

"Our women—the women of the Moros often fight with their men. It is very ordinary."

"Yes, I know that. But *bayonetted* . . ." He said urgently, "What is the difference between us if we behave like that, killing women? The first time I saw a Moro hanged—he did not know what he had done or why he was being killed, and the expression on his face . . . I shall never forget it. He just couldn't understand what we were doing to him. I began to ask myself . . . killing . . . killing . . . killing . . . I just don't believe that it's enough. And yet, I'm a soldier. I've been a soldier all my life. Why should I be sickened by death, because that's what I am. Sickened. Sick to the heart with it."

He turned over on his back and saw that Dawson, his long stave tucked under his arm, was standing above him, grinning. Dawson said cheerfully, "You're beginning to see the light, friend. There's hope for you yet."

Sullivan said angrily, "My discontent with the Army is at least prompted by better reasons than yours."

"You mean you've decided that war's a nasty business? That's a startling discovery."

"I mean that what the hell are we doing trying to bring civilization to a people who only want to fight against it? We offer them civilization and we deal out slaughter."

"You don't really believe you're more civilized than they are, do you?" His voice was mocking.

Sullivan said shortly, "You're a fool, Dawson, and you always will be."

"You're just civilized more often, that's all. It's not the same thing, is it? And what sickens you, my friend, is simply your ability to recognize your own competence in your chosen field. You should have been a minister. And why don't we get moving, we've a long way to go."

Sullivan turned to Medina, looking at the slime that had left its streaks across her lovely body. He said gently, "The sun will soon be down. Shall we go on? Can we afford to stay the night here? To rest?"

She looked at him gratefully, knowing that he was thinking of her and Dawson. She said, "This is a good place, I think. We can make a fire."

"A fire? Is it wise?"

"A small one. They will not come so far without the chief. But we must keep watch too."

"All right then."

He stood up abruptly and went to find wood. Dawson pulled his touch-wick lighter from his pocket and unwrapped the rag that had kept it dry. He blew on the wick until it was smoldering redly, and then lit a small bundle of dry grass, and soon a fire was burning brightly.

Medina, looking at them, took off her bodice and held it in front of the flames, and Dawson went further away, muttering to himself, and came back in a moment with his good humor recovered. He said sarcastically, "You ought to know, Medina—I've been looking at you myself for a long time." Gesturing at his crotch, he said, "If it wasn't for this . . ."

"That'll do," Sullivan said sharply. Dawson squinted at him, grinning. He said, "Don't worry. Desire goes too, you know. Leaves you cold and calculating. All I'm calculating now is how soon we can get back to base. And what I'm going to do then. Anybody hungry?"

He produced a filthy rag and unwrapped some strips of dried fish, then went to the edge of the water and washed them, bringing them back and handing them round. They chewed silently on them for a while, and later, when the sun had gone down, kicked at the embers of the fire and then lay on the grass and slept.

Dawson had found himself a place deep under a cluster of ferns, to keep first watch. Sullivan and Medina lay down together, and again he put his shirt over her, slipping his hand down inside her bodice and finding the warmth of her breast. When he began to caress her, letting his palm go over the flat taut skin of her stomach, she turned away from him and whispered, "No, Shay—not now."

He found her thighs with his hand and pressed himself to her, and she said again, whispering urgently, "Not now—when we are married. Please, Shay. For me—if you love me."

Puzzled, disturbed, not understanding the new needs that she was experiencing, he drew a little away from her, and soon, restless, he slept. He woke once in the night and saw that she was wide awake and crying softly, and he put his arm over her shoulder and pulled her close to him, kissing her very gently and not touching her body because he wanted her to know that anything she wanted was all right with him, even if he did not completely understand her. She put her arm round him, too, and in a little while they were both asleep.

They reached the dirt road that led to the tiny, isolated village of Likup when the sun was moving down to the horizon again. Bedraggled, footsore, in rags, stinking with the slime of the swamp, they struggled along in the shade of the palm trees that ran down the edge of the track. Their bodies were streaked with blood and with dirt, and a woman who passed turned and stared at them, standing there silently with a jar of oil on her head. A child ran to them from a hut by the side of the road, and stood solemnly watching them, his feet wide apart and his hands behind his back. His small, plump undernourished stomach stuck out darkly through the gap in his gray flannel shirt; his big brown eyes were gravely melancholy. They paid him no heed and walked slowly into the village.

There was a blockhouse there, Sullivan knew, deserted now but still roofed, and a tiny mission where a Filipino priest ministered to the meager needs of a few hill folk who scratched a living out of the soil with their stick implements. They knocked the boarded-up door of the blockhouse down with the butts of their rifles, and when they went inside, it was dark and cool and silent. A little group of children gathered at the entrance to stare at them, and Sullivan called one of the bigger boys over and told him, in halting Spanish, to go to the Mission and see if the good Father could give them some food. Medina spoke to him in rapid Tagalog, and the boy turned on his heels and went running off, and in a little while, after they had waited, staring at the floor and being too exhausted to talk, a young Filipino priest came over and gave them some bread and a bowl of fish stew, sitting on an upturned box and watching them as they ate ravenously with their fingers. Medina talked with the priest for a while, and once Sullivan saw Dawson look at her sharply, understanding what she was saying but not commenting on it. And then the priest turned to Sullivan and said, smiling, in Spanish, "It is your wish to marry this girl."

It was a flat statement, not a question. Knowing that Dawson was carefully not looking at him, carefully not interfering, he said, "That is what I would like."

The priest said, "If you will wait three weeks, I can marry you in my little church. But I am told—the lady says you wish to be married now. I am afraid that this is not possible."

He was smiling easily, a young man new to the cloth and pleased that his services were in demand.

Sullivan said slowly, "It might be better to wait until we get to Jolo."

He looked at Medina hopefully, aware that his feelings were clear on his face and hating himself for it. Dawson said softly, "Thought you'd try and wriggle out of it."

Sullivan flushed deeply. Looking at the priest, he said steadily, "There must be some way you can marry us, Father. Now, without waiting."

The priest spread his hands wide.

"But how can I?" He was peering at Medina in puzzlement. "If you are both Christian . . ."

In the silence that followed, Dawson said, grinning, "I myself am a Moslem. The lady comes from a Moro village. The good Captain is a solid Presbyterian from Virginia. And if he waits to get back to the barracks, the Commanding Officer is going to forbid the wedding. So you'd better do what you can."

Medina was looking at him, her eyes wide and steady and solemn.

Sullivan said, "This is a mixed marriage, Father. There must be something you can do."

"If the lady is a Moro . . . It is not unusual. As you know, many American soldiers marry our local women. I can ask my colleague to perform the ceremony. In Tagalog. Then, later, if you wish, you can have a Christian ceremony too. This is quite usual. If it is what you want."

"Is this what you want, Medina?"

She did not take her eyes from him.

"I only want to be married to you. To be with you always."

"To be married here? Like this?"

She nodded gravely.

"This is what I want. So that we will be together."

It was a long time before he could bring himself to speak. He was trying to convince himself that his love for her was strong enough to survive the blow to his pride, to overcome the further depression of his quality down to the savage level. He said slowly, "This is what we want, Father. Please call your colleague." He said harshly, "Marry us now. Any way you can."

Later, when he lay on his cot in the barracks, he could not erase the memory of the awful ceremony.

Dawson, his face twisted in a sardonic smile, had been standing to one side, watching. Two Visayan women who had been summoned were the witnesses, and a local pundita, a priest who looked more like a witch doctor, had been called in for the wedding ritual. A group of young men had been hastily gathered and had been seated on the floor with their gongs, waiting for the ceremony to begin. As for the young Filipino priest, he had stood benignly by, his plump soft hands clasped over his stomach, beaming at this token of the religious tolerance which the Americans were preaching, wondering how the rigorous code of the late Spanish priests would have dealt with the problem.

The pundita took Sullivan's hand in his, pressing the two thumbs together, and then laid his thumb on Medina's forehead, asking her if she desired this man for her husband. One of the women made a mixture of betel nut and waved it in the air, and then threw it on the ground at Medina's feet. After a reasonable length of time, to prove her modesty, Medina bent down, without showing unseemly haste, and picked it up so that later, in the privacy of her bedchamber, she could chew it and so assure an immediate pregnancy. The young men beat their gongs, and the Filipino priest came over and shook his hand, and when the problem of paying the pundita arose, Dawson stepped forward and gave him one of the rifles.

They left the blockhouse then, and Sullivan saw with disgust that Medina was still clutching the betel nut in her hand. Angrily, he snatched it from her. He said furiously, "For God's sake throw that filthy stuff away."

He tossed it into a ditch at the side of the gravel road and strode on beside her, saying nothing, listening to the sound of Dawson's stick on the track behind him and the crippled scuffling of his worn-out boots. When he looked at her face he saw that she was crying to herself, not making any noise, but letting the tears run down her face where the thorns of the jungle had left their marks. He bit his lip and said nothing. Then he took her arm and said, very quietly, "It will be all right when we get to Jolo. I promise you."

He squeezed her arm and tried to smile at her, and when she stared ahead of her and did not smile back, he dropped her arm and walked sullenly beside her down the long dry road towards Jolo.

When nightfall came, they found shelter in a deserted barn that had once held hay; the fresh scent of it was rich in the cool air. Dawson, looking at Medina and smiling, said, "It's been a long day—a long march. We'll be there tomorrow. I don't think we need keep watch any more, but—well, I'll be outside somewhere. You both get some sleep."

Sullivan nodded miserably. He went inside the barn with Medina, and he found some remnants of hay in the loft and made it into a bed, and he pushed a long bar of wood under the latch of the door, and then he took off his clothes and spread them out to air.

Angry with himself but knowing that he needed her more than anything in the world, he took her bodily in his arms and carried her over to the crude bed he had made. He pulled off her bodice and her skirt, and ran his hands over her body until he felt the urgent tension rising in her, and then he lay down beside her and made long and violent love to her until he felt that every muscle in her body was fused into his. When they had finished, feeling the warmth and the comfort and the peace within him, he kissed her on the mouth and said, "You mustn't cry any more, Medina. Never again."

"I love you, Shay."

"I love you too. More than you'll ever really understand."

"I think, sometimes, that—that this is all you really want."

"It's part of it, Medina. A great part of it. There's warmth in your blood and it's warmth that I need. Is that so wrong?"

"But it is not all? I am really your wife? Not like a Moro girl your servant has brought you?"

Smiling now, he said, "I married a fine Spanish lady. And I love her very much. I've even locked Dawson out to prove it to you."

Her teeth were bright in the darkness.

"Poor Dawson." Suddenly serious, she said, "What will he do now?"

"I don't know. I will try and find work for him."

"If you can, it will be nice."

Nice? It was an incongruous word. There was a stirring of terror as he thought of her almost contemptuous composure on that dreadful day when they had so violently mutilated Dawson. "If I told him it was you," she had said, "he would have done this thing to you instead. It is best like this."

As if to satisfy himself with that part of her which alone he could understand, he put out his hand and touched her body. She turned her calm face toward him, knowing that he was seeking her help but not knowing why.

"Love me again, Shay," she said. "Now."

Forcing his pain to the back of his mind, he pulled her to him and buried his face in her breast.

[ 158 ]

Later, when he lay wide awake on his back and let the cold night breeze find the wet patches on his body where her lips had been, he knew that she was binding herself to him for ever, telling him, in the only way she could find to make it clear, that she would serve him always, not only as his wife but as his odalisque as well.

The whitewashed buildings of Jolo were clean and fresh and bustling with activity when they reached the town in the cool of the morning. It did not seem to him that so much time had passed by since he had left it on the boar hunt that was to change his life and make him an outcast, and it was hard to believe that so much had happened in the interim.

The sentry at the gates, lolling against the old stone walls, pinched out his cheroot and stared at them curiously as they approached. In answer to his shout, the Sergeant of the Guard came running out. Dawson, nervous now, said quietly, "You won't forget, old boy? About me, I mean?"

"Don't worry. There's nothing I have to say about your past."

"Good. They might—well, I don't know . . ."

The Sergeant was a veteran from the Fourteenth Regiment. Sullivan said briefly, "I'm Captain Sullivan, Twenty-third Infantry."

The Sergeant's grizzled face was creased in smiles.

"Yes, I know, Captain. We all thought you was dead. Glad to see you back."

"I'll have to see the Colonel, is he in?"

"Sure thing, Captain. He's in his office, you know where that is." The Sergeant hesitated, and then said, "What about this woman, Captain? She with you?" Grinning, he added, "Looks like you found yourself a nice piece of—"

"This lady is my wife, Sergeant."

The Sergeant blinked at him, tried hard not to stare at Medina, and then said stolidly, "Yes, sir. And the other—the other gentleman?"

"Mr. Dawson. He escaped with me from a Moro village."

"Yes, sir."

They went on in, the three of them, into the big stone Headquarters building, where the bougainvillaea sprayed a pattern of crimson against the white walls, and where the oleander bushes heavily scented the hot, dusty air. Sullivan took one look round him, across the Plaza de la Marina to where the barracks were, then knocked at the Colonel's door.

They went inside together.

# 10.

In the big, whitewashed room where the Colonel had his office, the journalist Reed, thin and slow-moving and fidgeting with his notebooks, was trying to assert the authority of his position. He said stubbornly, "I was sent here, Colonel, to get the facts. Not to whitewash the Army."

The Colonel's lean face was set and ill-tempered. He said angrily, pulling his lower lip in and feeling the edge of it with his teeth, "We want no whitewashing, Mr. Reed. What the Army is doing here, the Army will stand by."

"Just as long as it remains an army and not an undisciplined rabble."

Two of the younger officers exchanged glances, watching the visible process by which the Colonel forced his anger into recess and laid his patience out neatly in its place. The Colonel pulled a file from his drawer, and standing up with one foot on his chair read:

The *Examiner's* representative charges favoritism shown some newspapers Manila; claims account landing Wheaton force, San Fabian, delayed fifteen hours because substitute censor attending matinee, thereby missing afternoon edition . . . Secretary of War

[ 161 ]

desires your careful consideration, even to change of officer in charge of office if allegations true . . . Signed, Corbin.

He threw the file on the desk petulantly, gesticulating with his broad hand thrust out into Reed's face.

"I have to find out if one of my officers was attending a concert! You think I'm going to do that? Because the New York *Examiner* could not match Lloyd Wheaton's landing with the time of their afternoon editions!"

"As long as we get the facts when we want them, Colonel. The people have a right to know what's happening here."

"The people have a right to a true account of the difficulties the Army is facing. Did you ever think of it like that, Reed?"

"They want the picture, Colonel. All I can paint is what I see."

The Colonel picked up the file again and leafed through it quickly, flipping the pages angrily. He quoted: "'ill-treatment of natives . . .' 'drunkenness among American troops . . .' 'molly-coddling of Spanish prisoners . . .' I'm getting sick to death of these reports. It's too much—too much arrogance."

Reed said mildly, "But it's true, Colonel, that you wanted to hand the arms captured from the rebels back to the Spanish? Isn't it?"

The Colonel flushed. He said stiffly, "General MacArthur suggested that since they were legally the property of the Spanish Government—"

"Even though we captured them by force of arms?"

The Colonel, who did not like being interrupted, said coldly, "We?"

Reed would not be abashed. He said smoothly, "You took them from the guerrillas by force of arms."

"They are still the legal property of the Spanish Government. General MacArthur was prepared to accede to their demand for their return. This is an army, not a band of robbers, Reed."

"Quite. And if the public outcry at home had not prevented it, you would have rearmed the enemy you had just defeated."

"So? A dozen old cannons. You see a fearsome danger here, Mr. Reed? If we behave like civilized human beings . . . Why don't you

[ 162 ]

admit it? You journalists built up the Spanish monster in order to make some heroes you could wave your noisy little flags over when we defeated them. Isn't that so?"

"Are you suggesting, Colonel, that Admiral Dewey, for example, is really not the hero we all believe him to be?"

The Colonel looked at Reed with a great deal of distaste. He said wearily, "You know damn well what I mean. And if you deliberately misrepresent what I say to you, I'll have you deported. Don't try and fool around with me, Reed."

The journalist polished his glasses on a silk handkerchief, his eyes blinking myopically. He said slowly, knowing when he was beaten, "And the question of drunkenness? You must admit, Colonel, it's pretty bad."

"No worse than in any other group of American boys. There's a great deal of—of time-wasting. Of sitting around waiting for something to happen. I do not think they get themselves too drunk too often."

"One man shot himself last night, I believe?"

"Yes, that's correct. It's on the bulletin."

"While he was drunk."

The Colonel felt the pressing of the anger in his chest. He said quietly, "I believe he was."

"And another man was killed last week when a drunken trooper fired his rifle at him."

"There's no more than the expected amount of drunkenness—"

"But a drunk with a gun is a little more dangerous, eh, Colonel?"

"Don't interrupt me when I'm speaking, Reed," the Colonel said coldly. "There is no more drunkenness than would normally be expected. I have already reported to the Adjutant-General to that effect, and I am perfectly prepared to stand on what I have said. Now, if you'll excuse me—"

Reed said, "What about Captain Shay Sullivan?"

The Colonel was in the act of sitting back at his desk, to intimate visibly that the conference was over. He stopped and looked up at Reed in puzzlement.

"Captain Sullivan? What about him?"

"I have certain sources of information which are closed to the Army. I hear he was training the men in Jokiri's hideout."

The Colonel stood up and banged his fist on the table.

"That's a lie!" he exploded. As Reed stared at him coolly, he said, "I beg your pardon, Mr. Reed. What I mean is, of course, that you have been misinformed. Captain Sullivan is one of our best officers, a man of courage and integrity. I'm quite sure that his behavior as a captive has been exemplary."

"You're sure about that, Colonel?"

"I know the officers under my command. Captain Sullivan is one of the best of them."

Reed persisted, "But if you should be wrong?"

"If an accusation is made against Captain Sullivan," the Colonel said patiently, "or against any other officer, then there will be an inquiry."

"And, if necessary, charges will be pressed against him?"

"I do not intend," the Colonel said formally, "to roast one of my best officers to provide a spectacle for the press."

"May I quote you on that, Colonel?"

"You may say that any charge against a U.S. Army officer automatically calls for the fullest inquiry. I'd be glad to know where you get your information from, Mr. Reed."

"The sea-Moros, in the market. They'll talk to me, where they won't talk to you."

"I'd find that rather upsetting, Mr. Reed. It would suggest that they think you are on their side."

"It suggests to me that the *Examiner* is completely impartial."

"Impartial? This is not a war of questionable objectives, Mr. Reed. The Army is bringing peace to a country which has been under the oppression of America's enemies. If you find it necessary to think in terms of impartiality in our skirmishes with the guerrillas, I'm afraid I must doubt either your intelligence or your honesty. And now, if you will excuse me . . ."

Reed had no intention of leaving yet. He said smoothly, ignoring the insult, driving his point home, "My impartial information suggests two things, Colonel. Firstly, that Sullivan was captured for the specific purpose of training the Moros in the use of American arms. And secondly, that he has taken the daughter of Sulu's most notorious pirate as his mistress. Have you any comments that I may quote?"

"None at all, Mr. Reed," the Colonel said frigidly. "Any comment I might have would not be allowed to find its way even into *your* newspaper. You may go, Mr. Reed."

There was a faint smile on the journalist's thin face. He inclined his head, picked up his straw hat, and left. When he had gone, the Colonel turned to his aide, Major Bowman. He said slowly, "The trouble is, there's a grain of truth in what he says. Certainly it's unfortunate that Sullivan should have chosen this particular woman for his—for his wife."

"He came straight from the Moro camp—a matter of two or three days," Bowman said, puzzled. "Where in hell did he find the time to marry her? We should have asked him."

"Well, that will all come out at the Court of Inquiry."

Bowman, worried, turned to him.

"You think that's necessary, Colonel? It automatically puts the Army in a bad light."

"On the contrary, Bowman. If only for his own protection, Sullivan has the right to defend himself against the kind of charges the Press is going to make."

"That man Reed would cut his grandmother's throat for a story."

"Yes, I know. All the more reason we should use a great deal of caution in dealing with him. What worries me is the question of—of this woman. His introduction was clear enough; 'my wife,' he said."

"She's Moro, obviously. Only got to look at the clothes she was wearing."

"I can't really believe that Sullivan wouldn't have thought fit to say she was—she was Jokiri's daughter. He said 'a Spanish girl captured by them,' didn't he?"

"That's what he said."

"I don't like it. I don't like it at all."

"Of course, we can discount entirely the suggestion that he was training them."

"Yes, I'm sure we can."

[ 165 ]

"Did you see those scars on his legs?"

"Astonishing he didn't have to have them amputated. Interesting to know how they healed so quickly. Some native medicine or other, I suppose. We'll get him to have a talk with the medics, too. Where is he now?"

"He went down to the market," Bowman said. "To buy some clothes for his wife. I must say, it's puzzling. Where the devil did he marry her?"

The Colonel put his files away and looked at the clock on the adobe wall. He said, "I think we'd better go and have some lunch. I want a long talk with Sullivan this afternoon. He can be of great help to us now. He knows exactly where Jokiri's fortified village is, and he knows a great deal about the Moro datos who are with him, and therefore he must have some idea of his strength."

"Will he be fit enough to go on the punitive expedition, Colonel? I'd like to have him with me."

"I think it's essential. Certainly. You realize that Jokiri is the last Moro bandit holding out against us?"

"Well," Bowman said, smiling, "I'd rather say he's dragged all the others into his net."

The Colonel nodded ruefully.

"Yes, I'm afraid you're right. But now—now we should have a good chance to get him. See that Sullivan comes to my office soon after lunch, will you?"

They went down to the Mess and ate.

As soon as the doctor had finished with him, Sullivan had talked with the Paymaster and drawn some money, and then he had gone with Medina to the market to buy clothes. She was still sad and quiet, but when he took her to one of the Tagalog women who had been making dresses for the wives of the American garrison, she cheered up a little, fingering the cloth and looking at the patterns excitedly.

For the first time he saw that she was aware of, and ashamed of, her Moro clothes. He took Dawson along with him, and left them there, the two of them, after giving Dawson some money and telling him to get cleaned up to a degree of respectability compatible with the plans he had for him. He had thought deeply about Dawson, and had come to the conclusion that he could safely recommend him to Desting for a job with the Scouts. He had heard at once of the plans being made in the Garrison for the apprehension of Jokiri. Since he had been gone, reinforcements had arrived from the other islands, and there were very many new faces in the little Jolo Garrison. A major operation was under way. The Macabebe Scouts were out in the Sulu hills now, under the command of the cheerful and energetic young Lieutenant Desting whose great-great-grandfather had been a French Admiral, fighting with George Washington against Cornwallis. The drive had already begun, and Headquarters was pretty confident that Jokiri was still in the south-western part of the island. Sullivan had told them about the journey to Tapu that Jokiri had made, and they had nodded solemnly and agreed that it was possible.

He went back to the Garrison now, because the Colonel was waiting to see him, leaving Dawson and Medina together with instructions to find a place to live in the town until he could make the proper arrangements with the billeting officer at the camp. He had said, "It will only be a temporary sort of house, you know. The Engineers put up cabins for us."

She had smiled, and nodded at him, looking admiringly at the neat Moro-style huts that the troopers had built for themselves, pulling her bodice tight about her as the men looked her up and down and grinned. Sullivan had felt embarrassed by them and had said to her uncomfortably, "It will be better when you wear American clothes."

The Colonel was waiting for him, surrounded by a group of junior officers, most of whom were new to him. The younger ones got to their feet as he came in, and the Colonel indicated the others with a careless wave of his hand.

"Major Bowman, Lieutenant Desting you already know, Lieutenant Hobbs, Lieutenant Morrison—Captain Sullivan, gentlemen."

He spread a bright new map of Sulu on the table and they gathered round it, spreading it smooth with their hands, looking at the thin lines that had been drawn across it in colored inks. The

Colonel said, stubbing his fingers on the base of Tumangtangis, "Here—this is where we've decided you must have been. It took you two days and a half to cross the swamp, here—a matter of a couple of hours from the camp to the swamp. There's a neck of dry land here that runs like a causeway up to the base of the volcano; it's heavily overgrown with jungle and is really part of the forest itself. It would explain a lot of things if he's in there."

Lieutenant Desting drew the back of his hand across the map. He said, "My scouts have penetrated this area, here. But we never went over that—that neck of land, because once you reach the mountain you can't go anywhere except *up* it; and we've never believed that Jokiri would allow himself to be bottled up like that. Without a back door, so to speak. He's too good a tactician."

Sullivan said slowly, "Whenever a patrol has gotten near his camp, he's put up a fight and then retreated—in the direction of the mountain, to keep them from crossing the swamp."

Desting nodded vigorously. "Exactly. He probably gets high up on the volcano, figuring we can't follow him with our artillery. And at night he can always break contact and double back on his tracks. Right through our lines."

An orderly came in and served them coffee, a thin, elderly Filipino in a long white coat and bare feet. The Colonel said, "Our problem seems to be to get enough men across this line here, so that he can't break through under cover of darkness. And then to get our batteries up to where he'll have to fight us if he can't sneak away during the night. How many men does he have, Sullivan?"

"Hard to say, sir. I'd imagine in the neighborhood of two or three hundred, all told."

He was aware of a painful silence round him. Lieutenant Hobbs said at last, very carefully, "My latest information places his force at over eight hundred Moros, two hundred Papuans, and a group of three hundred assorted Visayans, Monteses, and Negritos."

"Well," Sullivan said awkwardly, "it's possible. The village itself would not hold more than two or three hundred men. The others must be camped elsewhere."

"How many cannon?" the Colonel asked.

"I personally only saw three, Colonel. Three brass cannon of

Moro manufacture, and a broken Gatling gun that came into the compound, when was it, two weeks ago."

"After their raid on Maymbung Armory," Morrison said. "They also stole eleven rifles and thirteen thousand rounds of ammunition."

Looking at Morrison, feeling the enmity there, feeling also the need to defend himself, Sullivan said heavily, "It wasn't easy for me to move about. After all, I was a prisoner."

"Of course," the Colonel said promptly. "That's perfectly well understood. Now, what about rifles? If and when we trap him, we've got to hold him at arm's length. If he's got enough rifles, then he might like to fight us like that. It's only in hand-to-hand combat at close quarters that we need have any cause for worry."

Morrison said gently, looking at his pencil, "Two volunteer soldiers who were captured last month, Colonel, escaped with some very useful information. Their estimate is that at the compound they were held in, which we overran two weeks ago, there were more than three hundred rifles, eleven small cannon, a number of Mausers, two barrels of explosive, two Gatling guns, and fourteen Colt automatics."

He was carefully not looking at Sullivan as he spoke. The Colonel felt the awkwardness and said shortly, "Yes, I—I saw their report."

He went over to the window and stood looking for a moment out into the hot sunlight, and when he turned round he spoke abruptly.

"Sullivan—one of the journalists here, a man named Reed, had some extraordinary story that he picked up in the bazaar. He said he'd been told you were, well, training the men at the camp. The Moros. Of course, a great deal of information can be picked up in the market, and most of it is wrong. Some of it, I feel sure, is fed to the press because these people know that a good story is always worth a few cigarettes or a handful of pesos. But I'd like your denial, for the record. Unfortunately, the relationship between the military and the fourth estate is a little strained just now."

In the silence that followed, Sullivan, standing straight and stiff, said slowly, "I talked to them once, Colonel, about the Civil War. It could hardly be called training. I just had a—a talk with them."

Frowning, the Colonel stared at him.

"A military talk? That could easily be misconstrued, couldn't it, as giving military advice? It's enough to give Reed the privilege of being told there's a basis of truth in his charges, just what I wanted to avoid. What could possibly have prevailed upon you to do a thing like that?"

"I was—I felt it necessary to gain their confidence, Colonel."

"So you made friends with them?"

"To a certain extent, yes."

The other officers were examining their nails, fiddling with their pencils, looking carefully at the ceiling. The Colonel said, "One thing's never been established. There were eight of you on that pig hunt, and seven of you were killed. Decapitated. You were the only man who was captured. Why?"

Sullivan knew that it was now or never. He took a deep breath and said, surprising himself with the calmness of his voice, "I was told, Colonel, that they wanted me to train them in American tactics. I had no intention of doing that, of course, but to gain time I did once talk to them about the Civil War. I felt that if I could gain their confidence, I could find an opportunity to escape. Then, with the help of the lady I later married, I did, in fact, break out of the camp."

He saw the Colonel exchange an anxious glance with Major Bowman. Bowman, taking his cue, said slowly, "Yes, we were rather worried about that, Captain. We assumed very readily that—well, that a Filipino priest, perhaps, had married you. But now, we rather wonder where and when this marriage took place. There's also the question of exactly who she is. You told us that she was a Spanish captive, and we assumed . . . Well, now this man Reed tells us that she's Jokiri's daughter. I think you should put the record straight, Captain. I must say, she doesn't look very Spanish."

"I married her, Major," Sullivan said stubbornly, "in a Tagalog ceremony shortly after our escape. She is a Spanish woman who has lived with the Moros and has had their—their habits and customs forced on her. It is my intention to marry her in a Christian ceremony at the earliest opportunity. With the Colonel's consent, of course."

The others were staring at him. The Colonel said, peering at him, "Then she's not this pirate's daughter? I can tell Reed his information on that point at least was quite wrong."

"She is his adopted daughter, Colonel."

The silence was heavy in the stuffy room. He was conscious that Morrison had put down his pencil and was sitting back in his chair, looking at him through half-closed eyes. The Colonel said with sudden anger, "But—goddammit, you had to pick the one woman in the camp who could . . . In Heaven's name, Sullivan, where's your common sense? Don't you see the spot that puts you on?"

Sullivan said obstinately, "She's a Spanish lady, sir, a captive as I was. I made her my wife."

"Dammit, you'll have to drop that tone altogether, Captain. There's only one possible thing to do. I'll tell Reed that you escaped with this—this woman's help, and she can go back to her people as soon as—as soon as possible. A Tagalog ceremony, of course, means nothing, so there's no question of annulment."

Turning to Bowman, he said, "I suppose there'd be trouble if we arrested her? To use as a—as an enticement for Jokiri?"

Sullivan felt his anger rising. Before he could say anything, Bowman, glancing at him quickly, said, "It might not be politic, Colonel. The press could make quite a story out of that too."

"Yes, I suppose so. Pity."

The Colonel strode up and down the room for a moment, puffing furiously on his cigar, his rough hand stroking the silk of his beard. He said at last, "Good God in Heaven, I'm on your side, Sullivan! But dammit, you're doing your best to make things difficult for me. Married to a native woman . . ."

"A Spanish lady, sir."

"Is there so much difference?" said the Colonel dryly. "The press is going to roast you alive. If I could only say there were no truth at all in the report. But how can I? Secwar will demand an investigation—and, to tell you frankly, Sullivan, I'm sick to death of Secwar's demands for investigations. What the devil's he going to make of this? Can you tell me that? An American officer lecturing a bunch of savages on Civil War strategy, married to their chief's

[ 171 ]

daughter, while his fellow-officers are dying like flies in their attempts to suppress them? What'll he make of that, Sullivan?"

"I don't know, sir."

"Well I do!" The red was creeping over the Colonel's face. He said angrily, "They'll roast you alive, even if I don't. There's only one possible thing I can do, Captain. You must realize that."

"Yes, sir."

"There'll be a Court of Inquiry. If it's found that your behavior has been in any way reprehensible, then charges will be preferred against you for court-martial." He added gravely, "I hope it won't come to that."

"Thank you, Colonel."

"You'll confine yourself to quarters. Hand your arms in to the Provost Guard."

"There's one thing, Colonel. My wife—"

"That's all, Captain."

"But if I could make the necessary arrangements, sir."

"You're dismissed, Captain. And I don't want to see that woman in the Garrison. Report to your quarters."

Sullivan saluted, swung on his heel, and strode out of the room. In the silence he left behind him, Morrison said softly, "I'd never have believed an officer could do a thing like that. Wait till the press hears about it."

The Colonel said sourly, "The press already knows about it. Now —I want to know about the provisions for the Artillery. Where's the line of supply for the men at Silankan?"

Morrison knew when to withdraw. He said, "By sea, Colonel. One small prahu and four canoes, with two rafts if we need them."

"Your men, Desting?"

Desting said, looking back from the closed door, "We don't need a thing, sir. Plenty of ammunition, plenty of fodder. And all the rice we can eat. By now, ten of my boys will be here," tapping at the map. "Tomorrow morning, I'll join them, and we'll move up another two thousand feet. Then we'll be in position. I think we've got him this time."

The Colonel was deep in thought. He said absently, "Yes, maybe you're right. What an extraordinary thing, about Sullivan. Can't think how he could be so foolish."

Desting said carefully, "Doesn't sound so very serious, Colonel. Not really."

"No," the Colonel said glumly. "If the press hadn't got hold of that juicy little tidbit, we could have let him off with a reprimand. As it is . . . Well, let's take another look at those supply lines to Datu."

They pored over their maps. Morrison stood a little apart from the others, fingering his ear thoughtfully.

His house was a small thatched hut which the Engineers had built soon after the Sulu Islands had been taken over, one of more than sixty which had been quickly thrown up to accommodate the Headquarters staff, and it lay just within the walled compound that was patrolled for the nightly protection of the regiment's officers.

There were three rooms; two bedrooms and a long hall that served as a Mess, a study, a recreation room, and anything else that was needed; and outside close by there was a kitchen built separately where the Filipino servant lived, cooked the meals, and slept.

Desting, the young Lieutenant from the Scouts, shared the quarters with him, and he could hear him now, pacing up and down his room beyond the thin bamboo walls, waiting for one of his night messengers to come in with a report.

He lay on his cot and smoked, staring up at the circle of light that the oil lamp cast on the stretched canvas of the ceiling, watching the gentle movement of it where a rat or a bird was moving invisibly about, scuttling around and looking for insects. In the corner above the bed, a lizard was curled across the angle, watching the jerky motions of a fly, waiting for it to land and be killed. He looked at his watch; it was eleven o'clock.

He got up and took off his shirt and undervest, and rubbed water from the basin over his chest, and when he heard the servant, Obando, knock respectfully at the door, he went over and opened it, standing there with a towel in his hand and the yellow light from the big lamp on the verandah streaming across his body. Obando was grinning at him.

"Captain," the Filipino said softly, "Captain—you want woman? I got."

He resisted the impulse to slam the door; shaking his head wearily, he said, "Not tonight, Obando. Not tonight."

He broke off, staring into the darkness, then opened the door wider and let Medina slip quickly inside. He said bitterly, closing the door, "You have to come here like this? Like a . . . Is this all I can give you?"

She went to him and put her arms round his neck, kissing him on the mouth, holding him tight. She breathed in his ear, her voice low and gentle and sad, "I couldn't wait for you, Shay. I came to the barracks and heard. They told me—what had happened. I am sorry for you."

"It doesn't matter. Not for me. I'd promised you so much. You were expecting so much."

"I was expecting only your love."

"And now my servant has to bring you to me in the middle of the night, like a—"

"I told him I wanted to see you. I told him you would be pleased. You are pleased because I came, are you not? Are you happy?"

Her hand on the back of his head, she was looking into his eyes, trying to fathom the loneliness there. Smiling, he said gently, "I am always happy when I am with you, Medina. I love you so much."

"And I love you."

"So very much."

"And all this that has happened—it doesn't make you angry with me? That I must not come to you in the camp?"

"It was inevitable, Medina. I should have known. I should have known that I would have to choose between—between them and you. I just didn't think enough."

She was strangely silent, looking at him with anxiety in her eyes. He said, "It's an easy choice, Medina. I've had enough of the Army. After all this is over, I'll get my discharge, we'll go back home. To America."

"You think that there it will be better? It will not be the same?"

He scarcely hesitated. "It will be better. Much better."

"I do not want you to give up your Army. I know that it is very important to you."

"So are you, Medina, so are you. And if I can't have both, I know which I want."

She was glancing across to the thin partition of the bamboo that divided the two bedrooms. Seeing her, he said, breaking away and smiling at her, "One friend, at least. Wait."

He went close to the other room and called out, "Desting? Do you have a minute?"

They heard him go out into the Mess, and then he was standing at the door, looking at them, a slight young man with blond hair and an easy smile, his face darkened by the sun, his clothes torn and rumpled. He said easily, "Well, I'll be going out in a few minutes. Just waiting for someone."

Sullivan said clearly, "I want you to meet my wife, Desting."

Desting came forward, his hand outstretched. With old-fashioned courtesy, he said, "Happy to make your acquaintance, Ma'am. I hope—I hope this will all straighten itself out, soon. And I'm sure it will."

She was grateful for his friendship. Looking at Sullivan, he said, "You're a very lucky man. I hope you'll both be very happy. And don't worry about tomorrow." Grinning, he added, "I'm on the Court of Inquiry. And the Colonel's on your side. It's a storm in a teacup, that's all. Just to keep these erudite idiots of the press happy, that's all it is."

"You're a good fellow, Desting."

"Yes, I know. If there's anything I can do . . . There's a bottle of brandy in my cupboard if you'd like to do some celebrating."

Sullivan shook his head.

"When this is all finished we'll celebrate. All of us."

"Sure."

Desting held out his hand again. "Glad to have met you, Ma'am. If there's anything I can do . . . I have a lot of friends in town . . . among—"

He was going to say, "—among your own people," and he checked himself in time. She dropped his hand and turned away, then turned quickly, but not quickly enough, back to him. She said, "You are very kind, Mr. Desting."

Watching her, Sullivan felt a sense of dignity there. She held herself proudly, her head high, forcing herself to ignore what, he knew, she had understood. He said easily, clapping Desting on the back, "He's a good friend, Medina. We'll have some good times together."

The Lieutenant nodded, his flash of embarrassment gone. He said cheerfully, "I'll have to go soon. See you tomorrow?"

Sullivan nodded.

When he had gone, Medina said slowly, looking down at her bare feet, "He has friends among my Moros."

"He didn't mean that, Medina."

"Then what did he mean?"

"Let's not quarrel. This is our wedding night, remember?"

"Yes. I remember, Shay."

There was a moment of anger in him; he knew she was thinking of the betel nut. She sensed his sudden drawing back, and she said, looking at him steadily, holding herself apart from him, "You know that in the Moslem way, all you must do is say, three times, '*I divorce you.*' It is enough. Then you will be free again."

His composure had come back to him quickly. He put his arms round her, holding her tight, feeling the warmth of her close to him.

"You don't really think I want to do that, do you? That I will ever want to do that? When this is all over, it will be different, you'll see. Very different. I'm in love with you, Medina. More than that, I love you."

"And yet you can hate me for what I am. For what I have done to you."

"No. That is not true."

"Hate is very close to love. But it hurts more quickly."

"My love will never hurt you. Never."

"It may hurt you."

"No." He said urgently, "There's only one thing in my life, my darling. Beyond the confines of our love, nothing else exists, nothing. I don't care, as long as we are together. Will you—will you stay with me tonight?"

"This is why I came to you. To love you. To love with you."

"You realize that you must go before the morning? I'm sorry, but—"

"I know that too. Your servant told me."

He hated himself for what he was doing to her. Pulling her down onto the cot, he said urgently, "I'll make it up to you, my darling. When this is all over, we'll go away—together. We'll be together all our lives. Just the two of us—no one else."

He pulled at the ivory buttons of her bodice, tearing it open when he could not undo them quickly enough, pressing his face to her breast and feeling the smooth warmth of her, listening to her accelerating heartbeat, knowing that she was in the Lethean desert that lies between acute sadness and the delirium of ravishment; knowing too that he could lose his own anguish in the turbulence of her love, pressing his loins to hers and knowing that only in the symphysis of their bodies could he find relief from the oppression that was heavy on him. Her long smooth legs encircled him and drew him tight within her embrace, and beyond the enclave of their flesh there was nothing but hatred and fear and apprehension; but within it, there was only ecstasy.

Later that night, one of the Scouts came in with a message that Lieutenant Desting was wanted at once. The young Lieutenant climbed into his civilian clothes, stuck a sword into his belt, took his little pony from the stables, and thundered out into the darkness.

When he came back, it was five o'clock in the morning, but he insisted on having the Colonel woken up. The Colonel came down to see him, pulling a bathrobe round his gaunt frame, his hair sticking ludicrously out from the top of his sleep-lined head. He said grumpily, "I suppose it's important, Desting?"

"Yes, Colonel. I've just had a long talk with one of the Moro datos—a man whose brother Jokiri had tortured and killed. He says that Jokiri is mounting an offensive against Jolo."

There was a moment of astonishment.

"Against Jolo? He wouldn't dare!"

"I think he would, Colonel."

Standing at the door to his quarters, the Colonel turned and said abruptly, "You'd better come inside. Wake up the cook and tell him to make you some breakfast while I get dressed."

He went up to his room on the second floor, and when he came down again, dressed in his blue uniform, Desting was just finishing a plate of fried eggs. He got up hastily. The Colonel said, "Sit down, sit down. Now. How good is your information?"

"The best. A man I've used before, often. He says Jokiri is coming to Jolo for the express purpose of recovering his daughter."

"His daughter? Who the devil is his daughter?"

"Er—Captain Sullivan was telling us that he'd married Jokiri's daughter."

"Oh, yes, of course. Goddammit, Desting, hasn't Sullivan done enough damage?"

"Well, the information is that Jokiri has sworn to get his daughter back again and to kill Captain Sullivan. So he's mounting an attack on Jolo."

"I see. The Army is to become involved in a personal vendetta." The Colonel went over to the maps on the wall and stared morosely at the plan of the town. He said slowly, "There are two thousand men stationed here, four thousand more within immediate call. We're fortified and well defended. How can he dare to attack us?"

Desting said deferentially, "Well, you know how they are, Colonel. They don't care much about the odds against them."

"No, they don't. Well, we'll have to meet them out in the open. How soon before he'll be ready to move in on us?"

"I don't know that yet, but I'll know by tomorrow. They move like lightning."

"If we can get him on the lower slopes of Bud Datu or Agad . . ." Frowning, the Colonel went on, "You'd better not have too much to say about this, Desting. You're a friend of Sullivan's, aren't you?"

"Yes, I am. I've always thought very highly of him."

"If that—if Reed gets hold of the reason for Jokiri's attack . . ."

"Yes, I understand that. But I'm afraid he'll get it anyway. Jokiri's making quite a point of it. The market's fairly buzzing with the news."

The Colonel sighed.

"Well, we'll do what we can for him. But this is not going to help. Now get out of here. Tell the Adjutant I want to see him."

"Yes, sir."

When the Adjutant came in, hastily dressed and wondering what the early call meant, the Colonel arranged a conference of the Garrison officers to map the strategy to meet Jokiri's impudent assault. They knew that it was a desperate, insane, and hopeless bid on the part of the Moro chief; that he could never hope to take so firmly defended a place as the American Headquarters. But they also knew that he could smash his ferocious way to the center of the town and kill every man, woman, and child there, before reinforcements from the mainland would surely drive him out again. They were under no illusion on the question of Jokiri's savage competence or of his murderous determination.

The Engineers began filling sandbags.

# 11.

COLONEL DEVERS WAS NOT A MAN TO WASTE TIME. THE MORNING'S dispatches to Washington contained a carefully worded, guarded reference to the threat that Jokiri was posing over the town. A copy was sent to General MacArthur on Manila, and the Colonel set about strengthening the defenses of Jolo with an alacrity which astonished the townsfolk and kept the troopers busy from dawn to dusk.

The labor battalions came in from the hills, where they had been building access roads and pillboxes for the occasional convenience of the clergy, and began to throw up revetments of sandbags and lumber. The two batteries of the Sixth Artillery and the three batteries of the Third Artillery who were over on Mindanao were shipped back in large prahus, and companies A and B of the Battalion of Engineers were brought into Jolo to supervise the rapid construction of temporary bridges across the rivers Tubig, Hasaan, and Suba' Ligayan. Colonel Devers was a firm believer in the precious arts of deceit; while the arrangements for the defense of Jolo were openly discussed and carried out in full view of the populace, secret plans were made behind closed doors to meet Jokiri on the lower slopes of Bud Datu, which lay across the route he would be forced to take with his main forces. The Colonel had no intention of letting Jolo become a battleground if he could avoid it.

He knew that the Moros' chief asset was their extreme mobility. They could move, as Desting had said, like lightning. He knew too that the Moro leaders would know he was well aware of this and would assume that he would, therefore, hold a static defensive position and force them into the kind of stability which would leave them most vulnerable. This, he figured, would be the reasoning of their chief, for whose military competence he had (dictated by past circumstance) the highest possible regard. This being so, he decided to meet Jokiri out in the open, where he would be least expected, and to drive him into a carefully laid trap on the side of the mountain.

A total of seven batteries, drawn from the Third and Sixth Artillery, were to be sent under cover of night high up on Datu to await the closing of the trap; and then, he hoped, Jokiri's men could be pounded to pieces at maximum range. The Infantry would hold their positions below him to prevent a breakthrough to the bintas, the rafts, and the prahus which he would undoubtedly have hidden away close to the deep water where the swamps met the sea. Two companies of Infantry would be detailed to search the shoreline, to find the vessels, and to destroy them. Desting's Macabebe Scouts would be split into small groups and would instantly report the arrival and the grouping of Moro boats.

When the plans had been drawn, the Colonel studied the thick file of them, his head sunk in his hands, worrying about supplies to the Batteries up on Datu, worrying about the vulnerability of the Scouts, worrying about the difficult and dangerous night movements. But he said to Desting, "Given any kind of luck at all, Desting, we've got him."

Desting said cheerfully, "I think so, Colonel. First mistake he's ever made, really."

"Yes? What's that?"

"Allowing his personal hatreds to affect his military judgment. He ought to know that he shouldn't boast about what he's going to do. He ought to know we'd take up the challenge, one way or the other. He's throwing away his greatest asset: surprise."

"He thinks we're soft. He thinks he doesn't need the element of surprise any more."

"It's more than that, Colonel. Even the sea-Moros are terrified of the slaughter he's planning. That points to only one thing—a hatred so violent that it's blinding him."

"If he gets even a few men into the town . . . Are we sure that he'll be with his main body?"

"Yes, we're sure."

"I hope you're right, Desting. If he tries to hold us at bay on Bud Datu while he makes a sneak attack on the town with a small force of juramentados . . ."

Desting scratched at the fair down on his chin that was slowly becoming a beard of sorts. He said thoughtfully, "I don't want to be stubborn, Colonel—I think he'll stay with the main party. If he sent juramentados in to get Captain Sullivan, then I don't think he'd expect them to do more than slice him to pieces. It's my guess that it wouldn't satisfy the kind of hatred he's suffering from. He'll want to watch him die, slowly. A juramentado's bolo would be too quick."

The Colonel got up from his desk and wandered round the room, looking out the window at the bright red flowers the Filipino gardener had just put in. He said awkwardly, "I've put you on the Court of Inquiry, Desting, because I want to make sure that the facts which come to light are—are not biased in any way. You understand me? I'm being forced by the press into action which perhaps I wouldn't normally take. But the Adjutant-General has been having a bad time in Washington. They say there's no discipline in the Army any more and that the men are getting out of hand. He'll expect pretty drastic action if Captain Sullivan shows cause for a court-martial. I want you to make sure that this won't mitigate against him. He's a good man and he's under a great deal of stress."

"I'll remember that, Colonel."

"Off the record, watch out for Morrison. He's an envious man."

"Yes, sir."

"That's off the record."

"I understand."

The Colonel looked at Desting with a touch of affection. He said clearly, "Yes, I believe you do, Desting. There's one more thing. I know you were expecting promotion—I'm afraid I've had to recommend Morrison instead. I told him so this morning."

Desting, who was nobody's fool, waited just the right amount before he said, smiling, willing to pay the price to help his friend, "I understand that too, Colonel. Only—I wonder if he can be trusted."

"Trusted?"

"He's the kind of man who'd accept a bribe and then welsh on it."

Flushing, the Colonel said sharply, "A bribe, Desting?"

"Well . . ."

In the silence, the Colonel turned away heavily, wondering if he had said too much. He knew that he was making the same mistake as Jokiri—letting his emotions run away with his common sense. He found he was hating the thought of a talk with Morrison, hating the thought of those small, probing eyes and that sardonic, coldly self-seeking mind. Turning back to Desting, feeling a sudden affection for him, he said, "Are you satisfied with the arrangements for the Scouts?"

"Yes, sir. Perfectly."

"Good. Then I want to see the Artillery Officers. But first, send Morrison in to me."


The Court of Inquiry assembled at three o'clock in the afternoon. It consisted of Major Bowman, Headquarters' Staff, sour, sweating in the heat, and completely impartial; of Lieutenant Morrison, Sixth U.S. Artillery, precise, ambitious, and ruthless; and of Lieutenant Desting, late of the Provost Guard and now heading the Macabebe Scouts, young, impetuous, and bright-eyed in cheerful innocence. A Filipino clerk was taking down the evidence, and there was a small group of off-duty officers, mostly friends of Sullivan, who had come to show him that they were on his side.

The journalist Reed sat by himself on a bench at the back of the room. Major Bowman's efforts to keep him out had ended in complete failure. Reed had said, wiping his glasses and squinting at him, "You have no authority, Major, you know that. The public has a right to know—"

"This is not a court-martial, Reed. It's an inquiry into the facts, no more. And I have the authority, as you'll find out if you bother to read your textbooks."

"I've read all I need to read, Major. In cases affecting the national security . . . Is this one of those cases?"

"You know damn well it's not."

"Then you can't keep me out. If you do, I shall make a point of suggesting in my dispatch that we were denied access to the relevant information in the case of Captain Sullivan's alleged disloyalty."

Bowman was trembling. He said coldly, "I've a damn good mind to have you thrown off the island."

Reed said coolly, "If you do that, let me stay long enough to get the information I want from one of the spectators."

The Major turned on his heels and stalked into the inquiry room. Reed, smiling to himself, followed him in and took a seat at the back of the room. Bowman was still quivering with anger when Sullivan came in and sat down in front of the table at the chair which had been set for him.

"This is not a court-martial," Major Bowman said. "It is a Court of Inquiry to establish the facts surrounding the allegations which have been made against you, Captain Sullivan. You can call on any witness you wish to be heard, and you may examine any witness called by this Court, is that clear?"

Sullivan, looking round the bare room, felt the heavy oppression. He was glad that young Desting was there. Morrison was looking at him with a gleam of acute distaste in his small brown eyes. He wondered what was bothering the Major.

Bowman said, "If you wish your evidence to be given on oath, then, of course, it will carry more weight in this Court. If you do not wish to do so—"

Sullivan said quickly, "On oath, sir. I have nothing to hide."

"Good . . . that simplifies matters considerably."

Bowman had not been long with Headquarters. He had come from Mindanao recently to convalesce after a bout of fever that had gone to his liver and left him a very sick man. He hated the formality and the petty clerking of Headquarters. He said briefly, "Swear him in, somebody."

The clerk, his face emotionless, came forward and held out a Bible, and Sullivan laid his hand on it and recited the oath. As the clerk returned to his desk, Lieutenant Morrison said, "Before we begin, am I not right in thinking that you have recently been married, Captain Sullivan?"

Surprised, Sullivan said, "Yes, the day before yesterday."

"In church?"

Sullivan said shortly, "No. In a Tagalog ceremony. None the less, I consider it binding."

Morrison said smoothly, "Wouldn't that suggest that you'd prefer a Koran to swear on, Captain? I'm quite sure we could find one."

Sullivan felt the temper rising to suffuse his face. His mouth set, he said coldly, "I have taken the oath correctly, in accordance with the demands of my religion."

Morrison affected surprise. He said politely, "Oh? Well, that's all right then. Now, would you like to tell us, in your own words, just how you came to be the sole survivor of the massacre at Sunda Canyon, when all the other officers in your party were murdered?"

He could feel the dismay that settled over the court. A few hours ago, someone had spoken to him in the corridor, saying, "It's only a formality, for Heaven's sake. What are you worrying about?"

It had seemed dark and dismal there, with the shutters keeping out the hot afternoon sun and a Filipino servant on his knees washing the stone floor with a foul-smelling mixture of coal oil and sea water which was supposed to keep the insects away. Now, in the shaded courtroom, he was aware of a hostility all round him, coming from Morrison's immediate and sardonic insolence and Reed's mild expectancy in the background. He did not like Reed; he wished Withers were still here. He said slowly, "When we were attacked at the canyon, it seemed to me that deliberate attempts were made to capture me alive, and although we—"

Morrison interrupted, "Only you? You were the only one?"

"Yes, I was. The others were killed quite quickly."

"Your fellow officers."

"I was knocked unconscious and carried to a hideout in the jungle, tied to a bamboo pole. I learned there that Jokiri, the Moro chief, was planning to use me to train his men in the use of American weapons. I made it quite clear that I would do no such thing."

"From whom did you learn this?" Bowman asked.

"From a man named Dawson," Sullivan said. "Another captive who had been there for some time."

Morrison leaned forward in his chair. He said maliciously, "Another renegade, I believe. I understand that Dawson is a deserter from the British Army in Malay."

Sullivan blinked at him, wondering why the Major did not object. He said slowly, "Dawson's position among the Moros was quite clear to me. He had been hamstrung to prevent his escape."

"But they did not take any such measures with you?"

Morrison's question shot out at him almost before he had finished speaking. Sullivan felt the color coming to his face again. Before he could reply, Morrison went on, "Are we to understand that they didn't think it necessary in your case?"

"I don't know what they thought," Sullivan said angrily. "It was not possible for me to escape until I had acquainted myself a little better with the—with the position of the camp."

In the silence that followed, Desting said, "But, of course, there was never any question of your actually training them. I mean, a chat on the Civil War to establish, very necessarily, your apparent friendliness with them could hardly have affected the course of their operations against us, could it?"

"No. It could not."

Morrison said smoothly, "That, of course, is up to this Court to decide. Now, where were we? Oh yes—did you ever do any fighting while you were there?"

Sullivan wondered where he had gotten his information from. He looked over his shoulder and saw that Reed was writing in his notebook. He turned back and said slowly, "There was an attack on the camp by the Dyaks. I defended myself."

Morrison shot back at him: "With what?"

"A campilan."

"Your own?"

"Yes."

"Which the Moros had given to you previously?"

"Yes."

"It had, I believe, a tuft of red hair at the hilt?"

Major Bowman was shuffling his papers impatiently. He said, "Does it really matter, Morrison, whether it was decorated with red hair or green hair or any other kind of hair? Is it material?"

Morrison was smiling quietly. He said softly, "Quite material, Major." Turning to Sullivan again, "A tuft of red hair on a campilan is the badge of a chief, is it not? A minor chief?"

Desting burst out angrily, "Oh rubbish."

"Lieutenant Desting," said the Major reproachfully.

"What I mean, sir—," Desting said, covering up his confusion, "what I mean is, they simply gave Captain Sullivan a weapon as a tribute to his fighting ability. It's the natural gesture of a soldier to his enemies."

"You think so?" Morrison asked. "Well, be that as it may, we have established the fact that they presented Captain Sullivan with a chief's badge of office and a weapon which he could, had he so chosen, use to escape."

"And did, in fact," Desting said triumphantly, "so use."

"Nearly two months later. Yes, of course. But it seems to me that during the course of this attack you spoke of—the Dyak attack on the Moros which, so I understand, effectively destroyed the camp— surely then you could have found an opportunity to get away? Could you not? Unless you were otherwise engaged."

Major Bowman swung round on Morrison again. He said petulantly, "If you've something on your mind, Morrison, I wish you'd come out and say it, instead of beating around the bush like this. Don't know where you get your information, and anyway, I'm not sure that this is the place to air your local knowledge. Now, what are you driving at?"

"It's quite simple, Major," Morrison said calmly. "As I understand it, at the time of the attack Captain Sullivan was protecting one of the Moro women from danger."

Glancing again at Reed, Sullivan saw that the journalist was hunched forward on his bench, waiting for his reply. He thought: *All right, you bastard, I'll give you something to color your dis-*

*patches with.* He said clearly, "The Moro woman you speak of is a Spanish lady who was captured by the Moros. She is now my wife."

Goading him, Morrison said, "Jokiri's adopted daughter."

"Yes."

In the silence, Morrison said mildly, "Of course, we can discount entirely the recent market gossip that she is also Jokiri's mistress."

He felt a violent trembling come over him. It was almost impossible to resist the urge to throw himself on Morrison and hammer his fists into the plump, sardonic face. Desting, white-faced, was staring at Morrison in horror. The Major, open-mouthed, was staring at Sullivan. Sullivan said steadily, "You can discount it altogether."

"Good Heavens," the Major said, shocked. "Really, that was hardly a proper remark to make, Morrison. It's quite unworthy of you."

"I was careful," Morrison said smugly, "to make it quite clear that I did not believe the rumor myself. I am only repeating what is now going around the market and inviting Captain Sullivan to deny it."

"Whether he denies it or not," the Major said coldly, "it has no bearing whatsoever on this Court's function. Clerk, have that remark struck off the record."

"I'm sorry," Morrison said mildly, "I really was not intending to discredit Captain Sullivan. As you suggest, we are not here to inquire into his morals, but only into the question of his loyalty."

The inquiry dragged on. The emptiness inside him grew cold as the room itself grew colder. He told them, almost verbatim, how he had talked to the Moro datos about Bull Run; how they had solemnly presented him with his campilan; how Dawson had warned him that any premature escape could only lead to disaster; and once Morrison interrupted to ask, "This man Dawson. You knew he was a deserter from the British Army, did you not? And had been with the Moros for more than two years?"

"I knew that."

"And yet you still, I understand, recommended him to Lieutenant Desting here for a position with the Scouts against the people with whom he has been fighting."

"I thought his knowledge would be useful."

"Since we are talking in analogies of previous American campaigns," Morrison said coldly, "I cannot help thinking of Benedict Arnold."

The moment of violent hatred had gone quickly. In its place, a slow-burning depression had settled over him. He thought of his home in Virginia, with the whitewashed walls, soiled with the damp and badly in need of repair, carrying the portraits of the long line of soldiers in his family. He thought of his mother, a fragile, stiff-backed lady who sat on the wide verandah and stared out at a ravished estate that would never seem like home to her again; of the saber over the doors in the great hall; of the faded uniforms still stored in trunks in the dusty attic; of the forelock-touching Negroes who passed by the house and bowed their respectful heads just as they had done in the old days. He said to himself: *Mother, I want you to meet my wife—her name is Medina. The Moros captured her from the Dyaks, and I took her from the Moros. Her skin is dark, but it's only sunburn, and I love her dearly.* He heard Morrison saying, from a long way away: ". . . and since, by your own admission, you fought against the Dyaks with your Moro weapons, surely you could have turned those weapons on the Moros themselves?"

The anger and the pain were flooding over him. He said wearily, "What do you think I should have done? Stolen into their huts in the night and cut their throats while they slept? Is this what you think I should have done?"

Morrison said quietly, "It is exactly what I think you might have done. Or was the idea of killing your girl friend's father too obnoxious to you?"

Before the Major could reprimand him again, he added quickly, "Are we to assume that your affection for this—this woman precluded any attack against her people?"

"You can assume whatever you like."

He knew that Desting was trying not to look at him, that Morrison's eyes were aflame with personal triumph, that the Major was trying to put the distaste from his mind and remain as impartial as he had determined, at the outset, that he would be. He knew that Reed had risen silently and was leaving the room, and he knew that with the gesture all his hopes of relief had gone too, gone for ever.

He put his hands over his face, dropping his head down and resting his elbows on the table, and when someone asked him a question he did not answer. He was wondering what Medina was doing now, at this moment, wondering why the happiness he had promised her was so stubbornly avoiding them, wondering if his love for her was foredoomed to failure.

Dimly, he heard the Major saying—and he detected a note of sadness in his tired voice—". . . recommended for court-martial . . . confined under open arrest to your quarters . . . for the convenience of the Commanding Officer . . ."

And then he buried his face in his hands and wept.

A sympathetic Sergeant of the Provost Guard took him by the arm and led him from the building, and when they reached his house, the Sergeant said unhappily, "I'm afraid you'll have to hand in your weapons, Captain."

"Yes. Yes, I know that."

He gave him his pistol and his saber. The Sergeant looked at the barong which was in its scabbard, hanging on the wall, and said nothing. Sullivan said tightly, indicating it with a jerk of his head, "You want this too?"

The Sergeant smiled. "Only regulation weapons, sir. And if there's anything you want, sir—I could get a bottle of whisky."

"No. Thank you."

The Sergeant was a good-natured man who had done well in the Army even though he didn't like it very much. He said hesitantly, "Don't worry too much about it, Captain. It happens to the best of us."

"Does it, Sergeant?"

"Well, it'll be different at the court-martial, sir. That Lieutenant Morrison . . ."

"Yes. I know."

"If there's anything I could do, sir."

"Well—if you could find Mr. Dawson for me, tell him I can't—

tell him what's happened. Ask him to make sure my wife is all right. Perhaps he could come and see me."

"All right, Captain. Leave it to me. I'll bring him over here before sundown."

When the Sergeant had gone, he took off his boots and his shirt, and lay down on his cot, smoking a cheroot and looking up at the lizard that lay in wait for a fly on the ceiling, watching as it flicked out a cold gray tongue to catch his prey in one smooth movement of mobile, greedy flesh. Outside, he heard the bell at the Mission tolling the six o'clock mass. He wondered what Medina was doing, and if she knew of the mounting operations against Jokiri.

He shuddered. The picture was clear in his mind and would not be blacked out by the effort of will. She was lying there on the hard earth of Jokiri's house, behind the curtain where he slept, and Jokiri was running a yellow hand over her smooth full breasts, pressing them, scratching at the nipples with his hard nails, moving his hand slowly down to her white, white groin, feeling the shaved Moslem smoothness of her, pressing his wiry, muscular body into hers and groaning with the ecstasy of it. She clutched at him, clawing at his back and panting, feeling the life bursting within her. She lay back then, breathing heavily, and in a little while she came over to his hut and scratched at the thatch of the back wall, and when he opened it for her she came to him and said fiercely, "Take me again . . . again . . . again . . ." clawing at him as she had clawed at Jokiri. Only his body was white and clean, and sweet, and Jokiri's was yellow and sweaty and sour-smelling, and the taste of him was still on her. And Jokiri was in the hills, summoning his warriors together, swearing vengeance on the man who had taken his concubine from him, sharpening his barong to a razor-edge, waiting in smoldering, patient hatred to carve him slowly to death with little cuts across the body that drew the life out in agonizing slowness. And Medina was in the native quarter, wondering why he did not come to her, wondering why they had confined him to the camp for making love to her, and soon Jokiri would come and take her again, carrying her off in triumph like a slave, because she had been defiled and the seed of an infidel was in her.

He forced the sordid image of it away from him, and took his pen and paper and sat down to write a letter to his mother. He sat for a long time staring out the window, searching for innocent phrases, wondering, indeed, what he had to tell her. He said aloud, savoring the words, "*Dear mother . . . I will be home soon. I have been cashiered.*"

He put his papers away and went into Desting's room and took the bottle of brandy he knew was there, and went back to his own room and settled down to get drunk.

It was no way out of his dilemma, and he knew it. But he thought: *What the hell, who cares, anyway? The Army's finished with you, Shay Sullivan. You'll go back home with a dishonorable discharge and a native woman for a wife. Native? She's Spanish, Sullivan, a fine Spanish lady. Yes? And in the market there's a rumor that she sleeps with her adopted father. Well, you can easily put a stop to that, Shay Sullivan. Take her away with you, take her body, it's all you really want. Obando will bring her to you, grinning as he always does, and you can make love to her and forget about everything, and in the morning she can sneak out of the compound before it's light, hoping that the sentry at the gate won't stop her, won't take her under the bushes as the price of his silence, yes, Sullivan, that's what they do, take them under the bushes and hope the Sergeant of the Guard doesn't come by, and if he does, that's what the Sergeant will do too. And if she goes back to the sug and finds herself a tiny room over an odious fish-stall, then let her weep, Sullivan, because there's nothing you can do for her any more, you're a cashiered Army officer with the taint of treason on you.*

*But a bottle of brandy will help. Not help, really, only lessen the pain and make it bearable. It's still there, the pain, but you don't feel it so much.*

*We'll go home together, and take up where we left off. Of course, we can't go home to Virginia, but America's a big country. New York, perhaps, or the West. Or we could wander about like Dawson, only there'd be two of us, and we'd be together and we'd forget about Jokiri and the secret love-making, forget about the long years with the Moslems who shave their bodies, and there she is in her room, weeping, weeping because the Sergeant has told her—a good fellow, the Sergeant—I'm sorry, Ma'am, but your husband has* been put under open arrest for marrying you, you see what you've done to him? They'll try him tomorrow for treason, maybe they'll hang him on the nice new gallows, and you can watch him die, Ma'am, it's quite a spectacle.

So forget her, Sullivan, forget she's your wife and the woman you love, and let her weep, who cares? This is what she's done to you, Captain Sullivan. But what have you done to her?

Go to sleep, Shay.

Go to hell, Shay.

The moment of loneliness stayed with him, as though time were standing still.

# 12.

GENERAL KOBBE HIMSELF CAME OVER FROM MINDANAO TO MOUNT the operation against Jokiri.

Kobbe was a skilled and resourceful officer. He knew that the days of trench warfare had gone, perhaps never to come back again. He knew that the only way to fight guerrillas was with guerrilla tactics. It was foolish to rely upon the old-fashioned precept: *let them hurl themselves against our Gatling guns and our Colt automatics. Let the artillery pound them to pieces and then go in with the infantry to mop up.* Here it was different. Not only would the enemy carefully refrain from throwing himself on the guns, he would dart nimbly from the dense wet shadows of the forest, make his rapid, murderous kill, and be gone before the guns could be levered into position to hit him. He would steal through the jungle in the darkness, cut a few throats, take a few heads, make off with a few guns, and disappear before the frenzied guard, perhaps with his dying breath, could shout hoarsely that the guerrillas were coming.

The Moros had no political axe to grind. They were not fighting for their independence. They were fighting because this was the only life they knew, and it mattered precious little to them whether they were fighting Spaniard or Visayan, Dyak or American. They fought as a matter of principle, of habit, of age-old custom. They fought because the Americans had shiny new weapons which could be stolen, and because they were foreigners, and because it was natural for a Moro to kill anyone else who was not a Moro. They used their custom-sharpened tactics of murderously silent strikes followed by darkness and emptiness, and they used them with consistent and terror-filled competence.

But Kobbe, talking to the Colonel, had said with satisfaction, "You know, Devers, I think you've got this Jokiri. He's made a mistake. He can't hit us where we don't expect him and then run back to his damned cover in the jungle. He's got to hit us where Sullivan is, and he's got to keep on hitting. It's as simple as that. They've never had to fight us like this before, and this time . . . This time, I think you've got him. We know *what* his objective is, we know *where* his objective is. If we waylay him on his way to the objective . . . Dammit, it's the first time in history that we've had this knowledge. It's the one advantage we have, and it's the first time we've had it."

"I believe so, General," Devers had said. "The only thing is, Jokiri's no fool. He must know our thinking. He must know we'll seize on that. I'm wondering how he'll try to turn it to his advantage."

"Well, the market's buzzing with excitement. Surely you can pick up some information there? After all, he doesn't seem to mind that we know he's coming."

"On the contrary, he's boasting about it. Young Desting's boys, the Scouts—they're down there every minute of the day. The trouble this time is not shortage of information; there's a surfeit of it."

"And of course, they know we're expecting him."

"I'm afraid so. They have their intelligence too."

"Keep a strong enough force in Jolo to fool him into thinking we're going to wait for him here."

"Exactly what we planned, General."

"Good."

The two officers went over to the Mess, leaving the planners standing over their maps in the Headquarters office. Pouring himself a large glass of whisky, Kobbe said, "It's not easy to bring democracy to a people who don't want it."

"And at the same time," Devers said, "to put an end to the senseless slaughter of American boys."

"The easiest way to do that would be to withdraw. Get back to the States, all of us."

Devers sank back into the red plush armchair that someone had looted from a burned-out Spanish house. He said sourly, "Randolph Hearst would never allow it."

"Yes. That's true enough, isn't it? Has it ever occurred to you, Devers, that the Army turns a man into a robot? A machine? It denies him the use of the brain that God gave him. We do as we're told, whether we like it or not."

"Unless we begin to feel that it doesn't matter any more—the Army, I mean."

"Is that how you feel, Devers?"

"No. Not me. I was thinking of Sullivan."

"Oh. That's a very bad business."

"I think that, whether he knows it or not, Sullivan's finally revolted against the Army. There was a time when he—well, not so long ago he was the best officer we had. Now look at him. He's dangling, without support, not quite sure where he belongs, but only sure that it's not in the Army."

"Shows you what a woman can do for you."

"No, General. It's not that. I'm quite sure in my own mind of what his trouble is. He's been exposed too much to the—well, the unpleasant side of our work. He's sick of killing. He's seen too much of it. He's had to do too much of it himself, at close quarters. And he's beginning to ask himself questions he's not mentally equipped to answer. Again, that's what the Army does to a man. He's made the discovery that his strongest talents lie in the arts of killing, and it's sickened him because he's been too close to the end results of that talent."

Kobbe lit a cigar and blew a thick cloud of gray smoke up to the ceiling, leaning back and putting his hands behind his head, stretching his long, booted legs out in front of him. He said, "You're

[ 196 ]

saying that every soldier behind a gun, sooner or later, is going to ask himself about God."

"No. The soldier behind the gun doesn't really see what he's doing. There's nothing personal in it. He shoots a man, and he never sees him again. Sullivan has had to carve into these people and watch them bleed their lives away, and that's quite a different story. Modern weapons have made us all killers by—by nonchalance. If we had to go back to hand-to-hand combat for very long, there wouldn't be a goddam soldier left in the United States."

"We've become too moral."

"Exactly. We go to church and pray for peace, like the solid citizens we are, and our consciences are clean because we don't see the bodies of the men we kill. Sullivan has seen them, too many of them. And that's his trouble."

"All of which doesn't alter the fact that if we could trust him, he'd be invaluable to us in this operation. You think we can? That we can trust him?"

"No. I'm damned sure that we can't. I don't doubt his loyalty as long as he's clear in his own mind as to where that loyalty is. But he doesn't know. And that makes it too dangerous."

"We're back to the woman."

"I'm afraid so."

"Is it true, that she's Spanish?"

Devers shrugged. "They say so. Last time I saw her, she'd got hold of some Spanish clothes. Or American. I suppose she's trying to persuade herself as much as she's trying to persuade us. I'm afraid they didn't sit very well on her. I don't think it matters very much. She's a woman he picked up in a Moro village, and she's the daughter—or worse—of our worst enemy."

"What's that supposed to mean?" Kobbe was looking at him shrewdly.

Devers went on: "This rumor that's going around. They say that she was Jokiri's mistress. Now that Sullivan's stolen her away from him, the secret's out."

"Go on."

Worrying about it, Devers said carefully, "What started off as a personal quarrel between two men over the same woman has been built up into a major battle between two armies."

"So?"

Devers said heavily, "I'm very fond of Sullivan. I'm sorry for what happened to him. But it means . . . at the court-martial, I'm afraid it's bound to go against him. I may have to see that it does."

Kobbe stood up and sent the orderly for his hat and sword. He said shortly, "That's your problem, Devers. Do what you think is best."

"Yes, sir."

"You're happy with the arrangements for the drive?"

"Yes, this time I don't think he'll escape. I think we've got him. And there's not an officer in the Mess who isn't all keyed up for it."

"Good. Well, I'll be on my way."

The excitement had spread to the men too. They picked it up from their officers, and those who had come down from the other islands where they had been fighting the lesser tribes of the North were wondering what it would be like to fight against pirates. The local boys, who knew all about the Moros, who had fought them before, who carried bolo scars on their arms, they were having a grand old time sitting round the fires and telling unbelievable stories that grew less believable in the telling.

But they knew that once the battle started, the ancient venoms that lie in man, whether he be Moro or American, Moslem or solid Presbyterian, whether he pride himself on his democratic culture or on his fighting prowess, would surge to the front of his mind and make him once more the fighting animal that he had always been since the earliest days of his history.

In the depths of the forest, the Moros too were gathering. The village beyond the swamp had been abandoned to the natives who had once lived there, and the warriors had split up into smaller groups which were carefully concealed among the shrubs that came down to the water's edge. Six small brass cannon had been gathered beyond Lakasan, where the volcanic mass of Tukay rose steeply to the sky. They were being moved at night, darkly, carried by carabao cart along the trails that led through the jungle. A depot had been set up in the village of Sululu, where more than a score of Moro smiths were fashioning blades from scrap iron, from carriage springs and long bolts, from the steel rims of military carts, from anything that would provide good metal. They heated them to a glowing crimson over charcoal fires, and they hammered them patiently into the beautiful shapes that their craftsmanship demanded. Sometimes, when there was an insufficiency of steel, they would take the coarse iron which their ancestors had always mined and, heating it with bellows-fanned flames, pack it with charcoal in heavy clay boxes until it had absorbed enough carbon to become steel. And finally, they would hone the edges on smooth rock, drawing the hard bright surface in slow strokes regulated by custom and ritual, until a hair could be cut in two with a light stroke across it. And then the wooden handles would be firmly riveted into place, rubbed smooth with the palm of the hand, and heavily ornamented with stones, or shell, or mother-of-pearl, or ivory, or with pigeon-blood rubies and star sapphires.

They had pride in the weapons, and a good bolo was not only deadly; it was an object of exquisite artistry as well.

On the other side of the island, near the point of Tandu Panu'm, the bintas were coming in stealthily from the smaller islands, loaded with Moros from the other clans who owed allegiance to Jokiri. They landed in silence, speaking in low voices, cupping their hands over their American cigarettes, pulling their canoes up over the sand and hiding them in the bushes, then slipping quickly through the forest to their prearranged rendezvous where guides were waiting to take them to the secret gathering-points.

In the market, a dozen shopkeepers found that they had new delivery boys to take the supplies for the Garrison into the guarded confines of the barracks. Some of them were what the Americans called "friendly Moros," who had sworn to obey the puppet Sultan and desist in their attacks. Some of them were sea-Moros who were regarded as being harmless. Some of them were Igorrots, and some Monteses. But all of them were quiet and peaceful and obedient and respectful; and they were also observant.

At night these men would run through the woods and report on the day's activities to small, wiry Moros who, in turn would run through the early hours of the morning to report to their own head-quarters.

Once, Jokiri himself came into town, alone, unescorted, dressed like a peasant. He handed his farmer's cane-cutting knife, called a sundang, to the guard at the gates of the barracks, and went inside to pick up the empty sacks that had held grain for the Colonel's horse. On his way out, he bowed respectfully to the sentry, collected his weapon, gestured with a grin to his mouth in the customary request for a cigarette, and as the good-natured guard fumbled in his pockets (they had told him: "Try and maintain friendly relations with the natives") he lifted his sundang and brought it down swiftly on the top of the trooper's head, slitting the wide-brimmed slouch hat down the center, splitting the skull like a coconut from the crown to the neck, and then picking up the rifle and cutting away the heavy bandolier. By the time the first hoarse shout sounded, Jokiri was out of sight and no one had seen the murder.

It was merely a matter of principle. An American soldier. Kill him.


Beyond the slopes of the mountain, there was not a crest on which a Moro was not concealed. Nothing moved on the trails below but that the knowledge of it reached Jokiri. The carabao carts that came and went, the patrols that moved along the paths, the riders carrying messages to the outposts, the returning details that were being called into Jolo—nothing moved in secret any more. The breastworks that were being hastily flung up to reinforce the walls of the town, the trenches dug to the outlying blockhouses, the stores of ammuntion that moved to the smaller forts—none of this escaped Jokiri's notice. And in the market of the town itself, there were a hundred spies reporting to him.

Both sides, it seemed, made their plans openly. Both had their secrets, but there was talk and gossip and rumor, the like of which had never been heard before. And underneath it all, the spies were carefully watching.

For Desting, it became a matter of intense application to sort out the true from the untrue. Worried, he went to see Sullivan in his room. He said, "I don't believe it, Shay. Everything I know about this man makes it absolutely impossible. The stories—he's going to hit us here, in Jolo. I refuse to believe it. It's against every principle of Moro strategy. What do you say?"

He sat down on the edge of the bed and listened while Sullivan told him all he knew about Jokiri, smoking in silence, his youthful face composed and thoughtful. Listening, computing, deciding. He said at last, "I suppose you know we're planning to meet him on Datu?"

Sullivan nodded wearily. "If he comes that way."

"He must."

"I wish they'd let me out to fight. Surely they must know I'm the most useful man they have right now."

"I know. It's that damned journalist. He's waiting for the Colonel to spring you. There'd be an unholy row, and the Colonel knows it. But don't worry, you'll be well represented at the court-martial. The outcome of that, at least, is assured. Absolutely assured. You've nothing to worry about."

"That's what they told me at the inquiry."

"Take my word for it. The Colonel's not going to make a spectacle for the press. This is as far as he's prepared to go, a token arrest."

"I hope you're right."

"I am, believe me. It's a matter of a few days more."

"Till the battle's over. Till one of us is dead."

Desting looked up, surprised. "You don't really believe he'll get here, do you? Jokiri?"

"He might. Have you seen Medina? Or Dawson?"

"Dawson's keeping as clear of us as he can. I wanted to take him on as a Scout, but Morrison put a stop to that. I don't know how he found out that Dawson's a deserter from the British Army."

"I still think he'd be mighty useful."

"So do I. But the Colonel wouldn't hear of it. After all, if we start hiring British deserters . . . Think what the press could make of *that*."

"The Hearst War."

"I know. Nothing we can do about it."

"What about Medina? I wish to hell she'd come and see me—openly."

"I'm trying to fix it. They—they won't allow her into the barracks, you know."

Sullivan said savagely, "She's my wife! The wife of a United States Officer! They've got no right—"

"She's also the adopted daughter of Jokiri."

Sullivan said slowly, "There've been a lot of—of ugly rumors about her."

"No one really believes them. At least, your friends don't."

Sullivan stood up and went to the window, looking out onto the hard-packed earth of the parade ground. The cheerful Sergeant passed outside and made a point of saluting him. In the long, oppressed silence, Sullivan turned and said, "I wouldn't tell this to anyone else. The rumors are true."

Desting, expecting something like this, said evenly, "It's a thing you can't possibly be sure about. It's conjecture. Nothing more."

"I know. I know that it's true."

"Did—did she tell you so?"

"No. She won't discuss it. But I know."

"Now you're being stubborn, Shay. I've talked to her, in the market. She's a fine lady."

"I wish I could be with her."

Lowering his voice, Desting said, "If you'll be very careful about it, I'll try and get her in here again tonight. Won't be easy, but—well, I'll try. But if they find out, I'll be a buck private tomorrow."

"You're a good fellow, Desting. I'll be careful."

He felt a tremor run through his loins at the thought of her. The palms of his hands were itching as though they had just cupped her breast. Desting said, "Tonight. Some time tonight."

"I'll be waiting."

But she did not come that night.

Instead, in the early morning, when the sun was still cool and yellow, before the dust had begun to rise and hang in the still air, Dawson came in to see him. Desting was with him.

He knew at once that something was radically wrong. There was a feeling of conspiracy in their attitude. As soon as they were seated,

Desting said quickly, "We've got some news—something you ought to know about."

Dawson said, "She's gone. She left town during the night."

"What?"

Dawson spread his hands, hopelessly. He said quickly, "I tried to stop her, in Heaven's name I tried. But she wouldn't listen. I'm afraid—I'm afraid she's gone back to Jokiri."

He felt the leaden weight in his stomach. A sickness came over him and he thought he was going to vomit. He sat down heavily on the cot, his hands pressed to his face, hearing Dawson's urgent, nervous voice.

"She came to my room—I've got a room down there, you know. She came to my room and asked me if I knew about the attack Jokiri was going to make on Jolo—if I knew the reason for it. Of course, I told her—well, it's all over the market place. I thought she was worried you'd be killed, so I told her that you were perfectly safe, that he'd never get into the barracks. But he knows about the troops we're sending after him, and he's going to send a small party in to get you while the main battle is going on. He'll tie our forces down on the mountain and send a raiding party into the town to get you."

Sullivan looked up and saw Desting nodding his head. Running a hand through his blond hair he said ruefully, "I suppose it was too much to expect that we'd fool him. We've been making very open preparations to defend Jolo, but keeping the actual operation fairly secret. But they learned about it from the sea-Moros. She knew that we were planning to meet Jokiri on Mount Datu. She knew we'd trap him somehow or other and she's—well, she thinks that it's a question of your life or Jokiri's. She thinks that she can persuade him to call off the attack."

"She changed her clothes," Dawson said. "Got into her Moro dress and went off in the middle of the night. She told me it was the only way—that she had to go. She said—well, she said she loves you and this is the only way your life can be saved."

The words sounded foreign in Dawson's throat. Trying to hide his embarrassment, he said, "She told me to tell you that she loves

[ 203 ]

you very much. She said that if—if she goes back to her father, perhaps he will not kill you."

Sullivan covered his face with his hands, pressing his fingertips tight to his temples, trying to force back the ugly image that was fighting for recognition. He said brokenly, his voice sounding dull and hollow, "She's gone back to his bed."

"No."

Desting's negative was an angry explosion. He said again, "No. It's not that at all. I saw the way she looked at you that night. She loves you, Shay, you've got to realize that. And this is the only way she can save you. At least, she thinks it's the only way."

"If you were right," Sullivan said wearily, "if you were right, she must know that he'll kill her. And knowing that, she'd never go back."

Dawson interrupted him angrily, "Are you mad? That's the way she feels about you, you damned fool! She knows that Jokiri will kill her, or worse, and yet it's the only way she can find to save your skin. She's gone to plead with her father. For you."

Sullivan said viciously, "To plead with her lover? I don't believe it."

He turned to the wall and struck at it with his fist, hammering repeatedly on it, listening to the sound of the crackling bamboo under his blows, feeling the tears come unashamedly to his eyes. There was silence behind him, and he knew that Desting and Dawson were watching him curiously, feeling his shame, feeling the sadness that was smothering him.

He said haltingly, "Is it—does the Colonel know this?"

Desting hesitated. He said slowly, "I'll have to tell him. You know that."

"Yes, I realize that. When an officer's wife goes over to the enemy . . ."

Desting took him by the shoulder and shook him impatiently.

"For God's sake," he said, "pull yourself together! She's gone to try and save your life, I tell you! It's the only reason."

"You know her so well, Desting?"

"Well enough. I know her people better than you do, a great deal better."

He stopped and bit his lip. Sullivan said bitterly, "Her people. It comes out of your own mouth."

"You know what I mean. Ask Dawson."

"The man who first told me that Jokiri was her lover."

"And the man who knows them best of all. Go on, ask him."

Sullivan turned away. Dawson said slowly, bringing emphasis with his patience, "It's hard to try and get into her mind. But I know this; when she said she loved you, she meant it. She was trying not to cry. And as for that other business—I could easily have been wrong, you know. Now, I believe I was wrong."

"You told me once I didn't lie very easily."

"All right, and I don't either. But she loves you, that's no lie. What's the matter, you want Jokiri to kill her before you'll believe it? You know as well as I do the things that he can do to her."

He did not know what to believe. In the hopelessness and the oppression, he heard Desting say, "She can't know where Jokiri is, but she's gone to try and find him. She'll beg for your life, and if he doesn't kill her—"

He said brokenly, "And if you're right . . . What am I going to do, Desting?"

He had not given up his doubts. But there was an urgent need that stifled his reasoning, a need to search for any grain of comfort that would ease the pain. He remembered how she had begged for his love, begged for the physical emotion of it, pressing her body close against his. He said again, "What can I do? What can I do to help her?"

Desting said sadly, "There's nothing you can do, nothing. You can only hope that she won't find him in time."

It was the cunning of the trapped animal that made him ask, "In time?"

"Jokiri's already approaching the volcano. The heavy guns are waiting for him up on Datu and the Infantry's behind him. He knows about the Infantry but he doesn't know about the Artillery."

The animal cunning again. "Whereabouts on Datu?"

Dawson, his eyes gleaming, was watching him closely now. But Desting said, "In the pass between the two volcanoes. He's got to cross the dry land that separates the sources of the two rivers. That's

[ 205 ]

where we hit him. There's only one way he can go then: up. It's his custom, and it's common sense too. That's where the Artillery's waiting. We'll have him trapped."

Carefully keeping his eyes from Dawson, Sullivan said, "Then she'll find him in time. It's less than six or seven miles."

Desting shook his head.

"The town's ringed with troops. All movement out of Jolo stopped at daybreak this morning. They're not letting anyone through. She'll have to get past the guards—there are patrols. It's not just a straight walk there. My guess is she'll have to hide out until it gets dark again."

"Unless she reaches him before daylight."

Dawson said carefully, "She doesn't know exactly where he is. Your information is better than hers."

Desting shot him a puzzled glance and then dismissed it. He said frankly, "My Scouts just came in. That's how we know where he is. A column of nearly a thousand Moros. They'll hide out on the slopes until dark; that's when they plan to move in on us. But we won't wait, we'll hit him at daybreak. He's been moving all night, while our main forces have been sleeping. This time, we've got him."

Neither of them said anything about the court-martial. He knew why; if he'd had any chance before, now it had become a major disaster. There was not a single officer in the camp who would side with him now. Even Desting could turn.

They left then, and outside in the corridor Dawson said quickly, "I meant to leave him some cigarettes. I'll join you outside."

He went back and pressed a pack of cigarettes into Sullivan's hand. He said very quietly, "I'll be at the empty blockhouse on the Matanda track—waiting."

Sullivan looked at him and said nothing. When they had been gone for half an hour, an orderly brought him his breakfast. The orderly was a young recruit fresh out from the States, one of the replacements the *Aztec* had brought a week ago, a tall, raw-boned boy from Texas with a shock of tousled flaxen hair. He waited until the Texan had gone back to the cookhouse, and then looked out quickly into the compound, saw that it was deserted, and strode out into the bright sunlight. On the parade ground, a trooper looked at him curiously, but said nothing. He walked on, reached the gate, nodded at the sentry, and went outside into the town.

It was midday when he reached the blockhouse where Dawson was waiting, grinning at him, slapping him on the back. The Englishman said, "Well, I gathered you were thinking of getting away. Was it hard?"

Sullivan shook his head. He said somberly, "It's the end of my military career. I've broken open arrest."

"I knew you'd have to get out. Only possible thing to do. If we can stop her from reaching Jokiri—well, they'll have your guts one way or the other, but like this, at least—well, if I may borrow one of your somber sentiments, at least honor will be saved."

"You needn't laugh at it."

Dawson raised an expressive eyebrow.

"I'm not laughing, my dear fellow. There's even a faint tinge of admiration at the back of my mind. You'd still have got away with a clean bill of health at the court-martial, maybe, but you'd have had difficulty facing your fellow-officers for the rest of your life. Like this, you'll get a jail term and dishonorable discharge, but they'll know that you chose that deliberately. Makes a difference."

Changing the subject, Sullivan said brusquely, "I hope you brought the things we'll need."

Dawson's face wreathed happily.

"Two rifles, two canteens, a pair of binoculars, a barong, some food. Just like old times. The place is lousy with patrols. And you know that it's alive with Moros too. In theory, they're keeping an eye on the military. But they're bound to recognize us, at least anyone from the camp will. So, my friend, we'd better watch out. I suggest we wait till dark and make a token effort to find her."

"They'll start fighting any minute now."

Sighing, Dawson said, "A token effort. I thought you wouldn't agree."

"So let's move out."

They slung their rifles over their shoulders and set off across the track to the woods that lay beyond.

The ground sloped gradually upward as they moved south. The triple peaks of Datu, Agad, and Pula half-circled them ahead, and they could feel the cool breeze from the sea at their backs. They came out of the forest and crossed a wide, deserted field where sugar cane had once grown, marveling at the stillness, wondering how many secret eyes were watching them as they moved steadily onward. Sullivan was in front, pushing on impatiently, and Dawson, leaning heavily on his cane, hobbled along behind, panting with the effort and with the dry heat of the day. Once they stopped, and Dawson sank heavily to the hard red rock, breathing painfully, and pulled a flask of whisky from his pocket, drinking deeply and offering it to Sullivan. Sullivan shook his head. He said impatiently, "Let's move on."

There was a terrible determination driving him. The rough volcanic rock was hot and hard under their feet, and they stumbled over dry rivulets and staggered across wide gullies, but he knew nothing, felt nothing, except the urgent need to go forward. He fell once and rolled down a steep, thorn-covered bank, but he pulled himself to his feet and went on without stopping, pulling the sharp needles from his flesh as he went, not knowing the pain of them. He was blinding himself to all else save the need to reach the objective, to find his wife and bring her by force of arms, back to the life he had decreed for her. Above and behind it, there was a new thought crowding for space in his mind. He knew that he must kill Jokiri. He knew that he must kill him in personal combat, and that then he must take his wife and carry her back to some sort of rehabilitation. He knew that he must assert the authority of the American over the Moro, that he must claim what was rightfully his, and that the deep-scarring question of his military future was nothing at all compared with this overwhelming and implacable need.

He tried to secure in his mind the image of her as she had appeared for the first time in American clothes, the long, sober print dress falling to her ankles, and her slight figure confined by the unaccustomed bodice, with the Moro jabul lying on the floor, discarded with her recent past, and soon, but for this, to be forgotten. He froze the image of her hesitancy by the injection of his own cold refusal to recognize that in her mind too there were doubts and fears, and a refusal to believe that her complete rejection by the Americans at the Garrison could wound her, could force her into saying once again, as she had said to him so long ago: "I am not a Spaniard; I am a Moro." He wondered, for the first time, about the depth of the wounds they had caused her.

He had said to her, smiling, "You'll have to stay in town for a while until I can find proper quarters. They build us nice little huts." He had seen the admiration in her eyes as she had looked at them, and he had not sensed that she was aware of the restraint he felt, of the belief he had felt that there might be some difficulty. They had called her "the woman with you," as though she were one of the girls who were sneaked into the barracks at night and out again clandestinely before daylight, with a drink for one of the troopers on sentry duty, or perhaps a hurried fumbling in the dark, on the way out, an urgent, hasty love-making to a grinning private with his boots on under the shade of the bushes in exchange for his looking the other way. He said aloud, "She's my wife, Dawson. My wife."

Dawson looked at him and nodded, saying nothing. His face was paler now, and Sullivan wondered if a cripple could keep up this pace much longer.

They sat on an outcrop of rock, and swept the bare hills with the glasses. On the top of a ridge, more than a mile away, he could see the figure of a man, dressed in bright green with a scarlet turban, and it seemed to him that, with the long-range vision of the natives, the man was staring at him, watching, perhaps, the glint of sunlight on the lenses. He handed the binoculars to Dawson, saying, "Over there—on the ridge."

"I know," Dawson said. "They're all around us. They have been, all day."

"Have you seen any of our people?"

Dawson was holding the glasses to his eyes, looking out to the peak of Datu. He said, holding them out, "Over on the west ridge. Artillery."

Sullivan lay down on the hot rock and watched. There were ten or twenty troopers there, hauling a gun up onto a steep bluff with block and tackle. He could see the sweat glistening on their faces, see the dust rising from their clothes as they struggled and stumbled to get the thousand pounds of hot metal into position overlooking the crater, and an officer was standing to one side, pointing the way for them. He waited, watching carefully, until one of the troopers threw out a rope and started lashing the wheels into place on the uneven, heavily sloping ground, binding the tackle to the trunk of a shriveled tree. He said softly, "They're in the crater—the Moros. Does that make sense?"

Dawson was squinting into the distance, shading his eyes from the sun. A dark cloud was gathering on the horizon, heavy with rain, and the air was suddenly humid and oppressing. He said slowly, "Well, it's as good a place to hide as any, but he won't have a back door. He won't be able to get back out again. Unless he can cut them to pieces at long range . . ."

Sullivan got to his feet quickly. He said briefly, "Let's get over there."

Sighing, Dawson leaned on his stick and followed Sullivan down the long slope that led from the eminence they were resting on. A creek ran across their path, and they scouted round for a way to ford it, finding a crossing a little to their left, across a pebble-trilled swath that led to a rice field. Even the women who planted the rice had gone. They stopped in the middle of the paddy, the water up to their knees, and Dawson pointed out the track that led across their front from the north.

"That way," he said. "That's the way she must have come."

Sullivan was silent. He knew that they were too late. The load in his mind was heavy, pressing against his consciousness, stinging him with the barbs of hopelessness, leaving him a lonely shell of a man struggling in the mire of despair with the soiled plane of military respectability far beyond his reach now. There was nothing left for him, he knew, except death or disgrace, or both.

Reading his thoughts, Dawson said gently, "Whatever happens, you'll have her back. You can go away—Malay, perhaps, or China. It's not hard to start a new life if it's different enough. I know. I've done it. Come to that, I'll have to do it again. At least, you'll have her."

When Sullivan still did not answer him, he said awkwardly, groping for the words with unaccustomed inarticulation, "She really meant it, you know, when she said she loved you. I know her—I know her better than you do. I spent a long time with her. She would have said nothing at all unless—unless she felt you might doubt her. She wanted to make sure you didn't, that you knew what she was doing. She's been with them long enough to have acquired the same sort of—of understanding that they have. You needn't say a word to them; they know what you are thinking. For us, it's different. But she knows. She knows how you feel. This must have cost her as much as it's costing you. Believe me, I know what I'm talking about."

"For God's sake," Sullivan said savagely. "For God's sake shut up!"

Dawson bit his lip and said nothing. Sullivan was conscious more than ever of the broken way in which he dragged his useless leg behind him, trying to keep up, and in a little while he said quietly, "Don't mind me, Dawson. There's a lot on my mind."

"I know. You're wondering if she's there—if she'll be fighting with them."

"Will she?"

"Maybe. The women do, you know. In a major battle like this, it's almost certain that most of their women will be fighting too. If Jokiri takes her back, then she'll be among them."

"That's what I thought."

"Well, it's a kind of perverse reasoning, I suppose, but—if she were sure of herself, she wouldn't go to such lengths to prove it. I've only seen her fighting once before, when a small group of Dyaks—it could have been an old hatred of them for what they did to her, or it could have been self-preservation. It was a long time ago. She can use a rifle, but—well, I don't know, I just don't know. But I tell you this, if she's got a rifle in her hands when you see her, it will mean only one thing—that she's trying to prove to herself that she's one of them. And that in turn means that she's not at all sure of herself. And that also means that you'll be able to free her once and for all of the old—the old habit. After all, she was a Spaniard. It will come back to her. In time."

"The wife of a fugitive."

"With the man she loves."

"Perhaps. We'll see."

"You know you can count on me. For any help."

"Yes. Yes, I know that."

They clambered out of the rice paddy and onto hard ground. The water dripping from their clothes and forming into dirty puddles at their feet, they stood for a moment staring at the distant rim of the volcano, looking for signs of life there. Dawson murmured, "We're too low. We'll have to take the next ridge."

And then a shot rang out, loud and clear and unbelievably close by. They threw themselves to the ground instinctively, and in a moment the air was cut to ribbons above their heads as bullets whined about them. The deep bass of a cannon sounded, and someone far away screamed. There was the far-off rattle of controlled rifle-fire, and the sporadic answer of assorted weapons from higher up on the volcano, and Sullivan shouted, *"Up to the top!"*

It was a command, as though he were leading a charge. His rifle slung low in his left hand, his right gripped tight round the haft of his naked barong, he ran fast up the slope, bent double, not waiting for the crippled man behind him, thinking only of the urgency of his hatred. When he breasted the rise and flung himself over the crest, a Moro leaped out at him from a clump of grass and slashed out at him with a campilan. He knew, then, that they had walked into the flank of Jokiri's position, and in a moment he was fighting for his life with a desperation born not of fear but of hatred. There were six or seven of them there, Moros and Papuans, and he threw away his rifle and charged at them with his blade, swinging it round him in a savage ecstasy, not caring if Dawson had come up to him or not.

When he felt the barong slice deeply into human flesh, all the old exultation came back to him, and he knew now that he was a savage like the rest of them.

It did not matter any more. The control had gone, and he was fighting only to kill. The lust for blood was overpowering.

# 13.

In the forthcoming battle, four medals of honor were to be won that day.

Six troops of the Sixth U.S. Cavalry from Brigadier-General Schwann's First Division had come in from the north, making the perilous crossing to the island in a broken-down tugboat called the *Medea*. But the terrain proved to be unsuitable for the horses. The oily waters of the swamp left filthy, slimy slugs clinging to their withers and sucking at their blood so that they were wild with pain and fright. The tough grasses of the higher slopes, where corn-stalks had dried out in the hot sun, were rutted with irrigation ditches into which they stumbled and broke their legs. And higher up, the hard lava rock was pitted with tiny sores and littered with shale that crumbled as they struggled over it. Finally it was decided that the animals would be taken back to the beach and tethered under guard, while the troopers proceeded on foot.

The Infantry was not so lucky. Almost half the Fourteenth Regiment, twenty-two officers and seven hundred and four men, had been deployed in a long line running northeast to southwest with its left flank on a bluff that rose four hundred feet straight up into the hot blue of the sky, and its right flank touching the edge of the jungle that covered the lower slopes of Tumangtangis. Three companies of the Twentieth Regiment, more than five hundred strong, were similarly deployed with their right, or northern, flank tight against a stream that tumbled down from Bud Agad, and their left, or southern, flank carefully concealed in the long grasses less than a mile from the right flank of the Fourteenth. Into this mile-wide gap it had been expected that the long column of Jokiri's force would wind its silent way in ignorance of the fact that two human gates would swing carefully shut behind them as soon as they entered the broad pass between the two mountains. And even if Jokiri were to discover their presence, past experience had taught both Colonel Devers and General Kobbe that he would head for the heights of the volcano ahead of him as soon as he realized that the force behind him was too strong to attack. What they hoped he would not know was that the Artillery was in ambush high up on the mountain, effectively barring his progress with their mountain guns.

Seven batteries, from the Third and the Sixth, would be waiting for him. With block and tackle, sweating heavily even in the cool of the night, fighting for time and knowing they'd never make it before daylight, they had groaned and cursed and blasphemed the guns into position, hauling them bodily, sometimes, watching apprehensively as they swung free on the ends of ropes and wondering if the ropes would hold. Someone had said, "Get 'em over the rim before it's light and then we won't have to worry; we'll have all day to find us some real nice cover."

It was the first time they had heard, some of them, that they would be fighting within the crater of the volcano itself.

They were mostly older men, in their middle thirties, though there was a scattering of youngsters too. A lot of the older ones wore moustaches, heavily drooping over their upper lips, stained with the yellow of chewing tobacco, and some of the young ones were trying to raise beards so that they would not stand out so obviously as greenhorns—and also because it was a nuisance to have to shave three or four times a week. Their campaign hats were dusty gray, covered with the fine red powder that seemed to rise up around them every time they moved. They wore blue trousers and darker blue shirts, and some of them wore jackets as well, for the night had been cold. They carried their canteens of water (some of them had been heavily spiked with whisky) on the right side, and their filled haversacks on the left.

Below them, far below, the outlying Scouts of the Infantry had received the flash of heliograph from the mountain that meant the Batteries had reached the rim itself and were crossing over into the uneasy shelter of the cone. It was not a moment too soon, although the sun had been up a bare half hour and was, in fact, still out of sight to those on the plain below. Then Desting's personal Scout, a Macabebe called Antonio, had come galloping in on his tiny, wiry, Filipino mare, to where the young officer, camouflaged and carefully concealed, was crouching in the shade of the brush, carrying the news that a force of more than seven hundred Moros was snaking silently through the forest a little less than three miles behind them. The men, hearing the whispered Spanish close by, watching the urgent hand-signals by which Antonio indicated the length of the column, seemed to crouch lower in the long grass, burying themselves more deeply out of sight, feeling an affinity with the earth, which, in its mausoleum analogy, would have worried them had they stopped to think about it. Someone grinned and whispered, touching the left side of his neck: "Here—keep ya b'ynet here—on guard. That's where the bolo hits."

Antonio picked up a message, stopped to get a cigarette off a soldier (they themselves were not allowed to smoke and looked at him enviously as he lit up) and then leaped lithely onto his fragile-seeming mount and, with his officer, was gone.

A little while later Lieutenant Desting came back, on foot, his finger to his mouth, crouching deep in the grass, and made hand-signals to the Captain who held the farthermost position on the flank. As they tried to merge even more fluidly into the earth, they saw, hearing nothing, that a party of eight Moros, heavily armed, their weapons sheathed, was moving quickly past them, less than a hundred yards away; they did not dare to breathe as they watched. When they were gone, the young Captain, whose name was Roberts, looked around for the Lieutenant. Not seeing him, he stared at the green shrubbery where he had been, and then the shrubbery moved and it was Desting, rising silently as a Moro out of the ground, moving like an Apache in the native sandals that he always wore in the bush. Captain Roberts wondered how an American could move like that, and there was distaste in his wondering because he had been trained at the Point where the proper course of war had been plotted in a gentlemanly manner a long time ago and had left no room for the trails of Scouts who moved and thought and lived like natives. He knew that he was being harsh, and he smiled to hide his puzzlement. Desting said, very softly, so that his voice was quieter even than the sound of the breeze that came through the valley from the beach, "Their outriders—another on the other side. You'll see the main party in a minute. Only hope they won't be too close to the Fourteenth."

The Captain said hoarsely, trying to emulate the soft sound of Desting's voice and not succeeding, "Who's over there?"

"Leidekker—Major Leidekker. He's backed his men up a bit to make room for them."

"And he doesn't know we're here? Jokiri?"

The Captain felt a thrill running through his stomach, as though he personally had outwitted the pirate. Desting grinned at him.

"He knows. But he doesn't know how strong we are. He thinks it's the same old game—that we're trying to trap him like we've always tried before; a company of Infantry to drive him out into the open. Right now he believes that he can fight his way through us if he has to. Same old game."

"You think we'll get him?"

"Shhh . . . Shhh . . ."

As they crouched down and peered through the grasses, they could see the bright line of color that Roberts knew was their turbans; yellows and greens and reds and purples, with bright splashings of gold and silver, a river of brilliant color that bobbed along in absolute silence a couple of hundred yards away. Desting nodded in satisfaction. He knew that while he was with them there would be silence, because the men respected his ability and tried to emulate it. On the other side, with the troopers under Leidekker, he was not so sure. Placing his mouth close to Roberts' ear, he breathed, "They're a long way from the Fourteenth. That's good."

[ 216 ]

Roberts nodded, staring in fascination at the snaking fantasy of color, wondering why they didn't adopt a more protective coloring, wondering, for that matter, why the Army didn't do the same thing; their own dusty blues stood out like demanding targets against the reds and greens and grays of the soil. Looking at the Moros, he could not repress a shudder; there were so *many* of them. He felt Desting's hand on his arm, signaling for urgent silence, and then he saw a tall Papuan in war paint, his brilliantly painted wooden shield across his black shoulder, slipping past him within a dozen yards, clutching a bundle of spears in one hand and a Springfield in the other, moving in silent leaps over the ground, catching up. He could not even hear the pad-fall of his feet. When he had gone, the Captain muttered, "They move like foxes."

He was thinking of the first fox he had ever seen, a red and silver bundle of fur and muscle that had been trapped among his uncle's chickens and caged for the kids to come and look at. He had stared at it, fascinated by the way it moved as it stepped daintily up and down the hard-packed earth of the run, its feet falling with absolute silence as it moved. Not believing, he had bent down to listen, and not even then had the pads made any sound at all. That night, the fox had burrowed deep under the stakes that had been set four or five feet into the ground and had gotten away, and his chagrined uncle had said, ruefully, "They varmints—cain't ever trap 'em for long." He wondered if the fox Jokiri would burrow his way out too.

The Papuan had gone, and all was silence. Desting, watching, was chewing on a piece of coconut, and Roberts saw that he carried no haversack and therefore no rations. He wondered what a Scout's life was like, moving in and out of the Garrison at odd hours of the day and night, gone sometimes for a week or more at a time, speaking in snatches of Tagalog or Spanish or one of the other thousand and one dialects, knowing a little about everything and living in undisciplined, splendid danger. He wondered if he would like to be a Scout, and when he thought about it, he knew that nothing was preferable to the comfortable, easy life of the Mess, with clean sheets to sleep in, good food to eat, and your name in the papers back home if you shared a friendly bottle of whisky with the local journalist. Looking at Desting now, amused by the twigs and foliage that covered his clothes from head to foot, he said quietly, trying to make friends, "I wonder what your famous ancestor would think of you now?"

Everyone knew about Desting's great-great-grandfather, D'Estaing. At the Point they had studied every move he had made against Cornwallis.

Desting grinned and said happily, "He was an Admiral. All he ever understood was how to move ships. Out here, he'd be a dead duck."

He looked at Roberts, knowing the Captain wanted to be friendly, knowing that it was the first sign of fear, knowing that there were some people who only felt safe when there were others of their kind close to them, knowing that the Captain was a good soldier who would be lost without the company of men around him; that he would fight bravely and with stupid gallantry against any kind of odds—provided he were not alone. He wondered how he would like to be like that, and he knew that for him the only life was the one he was leading; he never felt safe except when he had no one to rely on but himself. Musing, he thought, *It's always someone else who lets you down.*

He stood up then, very slowly, being careful to keep within the long shadow of the bamboo clump that stood to the east of him, watching the long, long line of Moros that never seemed to end, pressing himself close to the shiny yellow poles and merging his camouflage into them expertly, watching and gauging the number of them, nodding with satisfaction as he saw them bear to one side and head for the gap between the mountains. He looked up at the rim of the crater, frowning, then stopped and silently took Roberts' binoculars from his hand. He watched the skyline for a moment, and then muttered, "Idiots. Idiots."

"What is it?"

Desting said slowly, "I saw a flash of light up there. Some bloody fool from the Artillery hasn't got into the crater yet. Can't see a damn thing now, but . . . That's all we need; one bloody fool up there to show himself." He added inconsequentially, "And one of your men is smoking."

Roberts looked around. Seeing nothing, he hissed sharply, "Put that cigarette out, soldier!"

Further down the line, an astonished trooper pinched out the cheroot he had carefully, secretly, lit, grimacing at the man next to him and wondering how his careful maneuver had been seen. As he tucked it back into his pocket, the other trooper touched his nose and jerked his head towards Desting, and the soldier nodded his head, understanding that if Desting could smell it, then so could the Moros.

They were gone now, the long line of them, headed like bright children on their way to a picnic, some of them carrying flowers tucked into their headdresses; one of them had even stopped to pick a scarlet orchid and fasten it behind his ear. Desting said gently, smiling, "They're in the trap. Give them half an hour, then start your wing moving around. I'm going over to see Leidekker."

"Won't they have a rear-guard?"

"I'm more worried about that idiot on the volcano. If Jokiri sees him—all this trouble is for nothing."

Staring up at the mountain, Roberts said, "I don't see a thing. Could you be wrong?"

"Maybe. Could have been the sun on an abandoned empty can —I don't think so. It was a long way from the crater. Could have been a bat-hunter, perhaps. The Artillery were supposed to be over the rim by sunup. I knew they'd never make it in time. Not easy to shift those guns up there."

Antonio came creeping in, snaking through the grass in silence, and when Desting swung round on him, there was another whispered consultation; Leidekker wanted to know when he could start moving across the valley. Roberts realized that the Scout had crossed through the middle of the line of Moros to get there so quickly, and he shuddered at the thought of anyone, even a Macabebe, trying to beat them at their own, invisible, silent game. Before they went, still trying to be friendly, he said, "Anything you want, Desting? I've got some liquor in my canteen."

Desting shook his head. He said, "I'll take a hunk of your bacon if you've got some. And I'll be very grateful for it."

Roberts reached into his haversack and pulled out a cloth-wrapped piece of gammon. Desting stopped him when he was about to slice it in two, and instead carved himself a small piece of the fat with his hunting-knife, and slipped it into his mouth, then handed the rest of it back with a nod and a quick smile. Roberts was about to offer it to Antonio, but he realized in time that Antonio was a Moslem and would be offended. He wrapped the bacon again carefully and put it back into the haversack, and by the time he had found his cigarettes instead, which he could not smoke now anyway, Antonio had gone.

Desting said, "In half an hour. The Moros will be above you, but out of sight. Only, just in case, keep well under cover. When you join up with Leidekker, one of my Scouts will bring me word. I'll report to the Colonel, and it's open fighting from then on in."

Roberts nodded. He wondered how so much responsibility could fall on so young a man, still fair and golden with the beauty of youth.

Then Desting was gone and the Captain looked at his watch and settled down to wait.

High up on the volcano, a detail of eleven men of K Battery had been ordered to drag one of the guns over a long thin outcrop of rock that led to a cave within the lip of the crater itself. They had ropes, and pulleys, and the strength of their arms, and it was a task they attacked with the kind of relish a simple man derives from attempting the impossible. But Sergeant Kowalski, a grizzled old man who had fought in Cuba and Puerto Rico and who had been with the China Relief Expedition, had boasted: "Any place a mule kin go, I kin get they guns." One of the junior officers had taken him up on this, saying, "See that cave up there, Kowalski?"

"I got eyes, Lootenant."

"Think you can get a gun over there? We'd cover the approach to the cone from the west, and make it impossible for anyone to get out alive. Think you can do it?"

Spitting a stream of black tobacco juice onto the sizzling red rock, taking off his campaign hat and scratching at the bald white patch on his head with long black fingernails, the Sergeant had said scornfully, "Lootenant, you been in this Army long as me, you know all you gotta say, 'Kowalski, hitch that gun of yours on the top of Tumangtangis,' I haul ass up there with it personally. I guarantee it."

The Lieutenant, who still thought of the Army as a disciplined body of respectful troopers led by far-seeing and highly intelligent officers, had said stiffly, "All right, Sergeant, get it over there."

He had turned away sharply, leaving the Sergeant to scratch and wonder how the hell he could move a thousand-pound gun with another thousand pounds of ammunition up a sheer wall fifty feet high without a tree or boulder, or anything else that would do as an anchor, within a thousand yards of them. But Kowalski was not a man to be dismayed by the impossible. He knew that all you had to do was have a crack at it, and nine times out of ten that wonderful God of the simple man came to your rescue and showed you a way out of the difficulty.

He got a detail of men together, "borrowed" a long pole from the unwary Corporal in command of another detail, and began forcing the gun up the lower slope of the incline to a point where it might be feasible to reach it with a rope from the top, anchored by the sheer weights of three or four brawny troopers. What would happen when the full weight of the gun devolved upon them, he did not really worry about; he knew that one of them would come up with an idea, even if he couldn't himself. He took a long swig from his canteen, and set to work.

The gun rolled on its wheels for the first fifty feet, and then three of them hitched themselves to it like mules and pulled, while three more pushed from behind and the youngest of them, a scrawny trooper from Delaware named Gillespie, slid the long pole under the off-side wheel and levered it up and along. When they had reached the limits of their progress in this fashion, they wedged a small boulder tight into a crevasse in the rock, wedged the pole in firmly beside it, and eased the full weight of the gun gently against it while they took off their shirts and wiped the sweat off their chests. Gillespie climbed nimbly up the sheer height of the cliff, finding hazardous foot- and hand-holds in the tiny cracks where the bats hid out during the day. When he reached the top, he lowered his rope, and three of the others, Troopers Helstead,

Fox, and Cohen, clambered hand over hand up it, the lightest going first and the heaviest last, so that by the time Cohen, who weighed more than two hundred and thirty pounds, had reached the top, the others were there to support him. They found a deep crack in the lava, and hunted around for rocks to use as wedges, and when they were ready they rammed the loose end of their tackle deep into the crack, hammered rocks in on top of and around it, and dropped the other end with the pulley on it over the edge. The rope slithered down the steep side of the cliff, and Kowalski put a hitch on the barrel and called out to them to take up the slack. They pulled it taut, and then lowered their second rope, which Kowalski tied to the two wheels of the carriage so that it would go up "arse uppards," as he called it, to protect the breech from any damage that could be done by the hard outcrop of lava at the top which his expert eye saw it would have to surmount.

His work done, with the ropes tight and straining, he called to them to put their weight on the second rope while he and the others hauled on the first.

The heavy gun stirred slightly, came free of the pole that was supporting it, and swung round in a tight half-circle. The weight of it was formidable. Kowalski yelled, and three of them flung themselves at the barrel, twisting it round by brute force, hoping there were no officers in sight to see the mess they were making of it, knowing that the strength of their arms would soon put things right again. The gun swung clear, and as Cohen's great weight came on the rope at the top, slowly righted itself. Inch by inch, the swinging mass of metal and wood eased itself up the steep face, dangling in mid-air, creaking ominously, with Kowalski and his sweating, half-naked men doubled up on the rope below, kicking their heels against the hard red earth, forcing the projection of their wiry muscles into the ropes, and with Cohen and Gillespie hauling at the top for all they were worth, and with Fox and Helstead standing by with rocks to force quickly into the dry, sun-baked crevasse should one of the wedges come loose. Slowly, the gun tee-tered its way upwards, and when it was less than a yard from the top, the pulley slipped its pin and the gun twisted unexpectedly round and came crashing down.

The men below saw it coming, felt the sudden easement of their rope, and they leaped clear with shouts of alarm. The gun landed on its left wheel, splintered to fragments, and spewed its remains in jagged pieces around them. Kowalski was hit in the stomach by a broken spoke that had catapulted out of the wheel like an arrow, and as he fell, winded and only semiconscious with the gasping pain of it, he saw the huge bulk of Cohen at the end of a rope high above him against the hot sky, his arms outspread and his feet flying as he fell, still tangled in the rope that had flung a malicious tentacle round his ankle. He heard the terrible squelch as flesh hit rock, and then the earth rolled over on him and he lost consciousness.

When he came to, a moment later, Gillespie, who had slipped quickly down the bluff, was helping him to his feet, and one of the other men was bending over a trooper whose head had been gashed open by a flying fragment. Clutching at his stomach, feeling the warm blood in his mouth, Kowalski gasped blankly, "Wha' —wha' happened?"

Gillespie had a slim arm around him, pulling him up. He said, "The tackle—it came adrift—pulley broke."

Kowalski wiped a smear of blood from his mouth, touched a hand to his paunch to feel for the broken rib, wincing as he found it, then straightened up and went over to the bloody mass that was Cohen. He had been killed instantly by the fall, and his broken limbs were twisted under him in ridiculous fashion that was somehow astonishing rather than gruesome. The men gathered round, staring at the body, then moved over to the trooper whose head had been cut open. He was unconscious but still breathing. The young Lieutenant who had ordered the gun moved came running over, and an orderly of the Hospital Corps came running up with his bag of medicine. Three of the men had been hurt by flying pieces of the wrecked gun, but only two of them seriously—Kowalski and the trooper with the gashed head; his name was Wennman. The officer stared at them a minute, white-faced because he felt that it was his fault about Cohen, who was a good soldier lost unnecessarily. Then he ordered up a detail to take Kowalski and Wennman down to the Command Post where a hospital tent had been set up. Kowalski, still smarting from the pain and from his failure, said, "Naw—I'm fine, Lootenant. Git Wennman back's all you gotta do."

The Lieutenant insisted. He said sharply, aware of the criticism that would devolve upon him later, "That's an order, Sergeant." Knowing that the fault was his, he added, "You'll be moving through enemy territory."

"They Moros?" Kowalski tried to spit, remembered he had lost his wad of tobacco, and started hunting for it. "Don't you worry none about they Moros, Lootenant."

"Two stretcher-bearers, yourself, and take three men with you. Watch out how you move. They may be all around us by now."

Kowalski found his wet wad in the red sand, wiped at it disconsolately for a moment or two, and then put it back into his mouth; tobacco was in short supply. He brushed the back of his hand across his mouth, trying to hide the smear of blood; he swallowed the warmness that was under his tongue, and set off down the steep slope of the volcano.

An hour later, he had to sit down and rest, and when he felt the dizziness come over him he forced himself to start moving again, ignoring the warning of the hospital orderlies who told him he ought to be carried, him with a busted rib. They had not gone a hundred paces further, when a fusillade of ragged shots rang out on both sides of them. It was the Moro flank that had closed in around them as they had rested.

In three minutes, every one of the seven men lay dead. A dato stood up in the clump of boulders they had been approaching, and shouted a guttural order; two Moros slipped from the grasses at the side and took their rifles, and as the talibong man slipped in among them to take their heads, a volley of controlled fire from a detail of Desting's Scouts who had reached a point near the rim of the crater came cracking through the hot silence that was all around them. The Moros, surprised, dropped their bolos and seized their rifles. An officer of H Battery, under orders to fire at any target of opportunity, fired prematurely at long range into the grasses where Desting's men were hidden, killing two of them and wounding one other. The Moros, caught between the two fires, slipped quickly back among the boulders and began an orderly fusillade towards the Artillery while two of them scuttled like jack-rabbits to the rear to find a way out of the trap they had walked into. Both of them fell, struck by Scouts' bullets.

The long bright line of Jokiri's men, caught in the instant of leaving the shelter of the bamboos and the stunted thorn-trees at the edge of the highest forest, stopped in its tracks, waited in orderly fashion for the signal from their leader, and then were suddenly gone, melting their brilliant colors unexpectedly into cover where, a moment before, there had been no cover of any sort.

Behind them, the long, widespread line that was the junction of the Fourteenth and the Twentieth, twelve hundred trained and disciplined men, moved forward and came out of the forest, first in straggling groups that had lost contact in the darkness of the jungle, and then others who made the scatterings a line again as the officers ran quickly from point to point urging their men into formation. Having heard the shooting and the Artillery's salvo, they were running now, moving forward and upward steadily, running a hundred paces and then walking a hundred, the lucky ones who had gone too fast through the jungle taking a breather while the slower ones caught up, and at last, as Colonel Devers himself, his saber glistening in the sun, came out of the shadows and ran to a high point of black rock from which he could see all of his lower force, the whole long barrier took shape. They were almost shoulder to shoulder, their rifles at the ready, their bayonets gleaming, each individual one of them moving as an integral part of a deadly and menacing machine. It came up from the south like an avenging god whose sole intent was destruction.

To the east, only the Macabebe scouts were holding the gap that lay between Colonel Devers' right flank and the patch of tortured sandstone that Kowalski's gun would have covered. It was into this gap, with the quick awareness born of long experience in the arts of cunning, that the Moros began to wheel. It was an open battle-ground of sandstone, where the redder, harder rock of the lava was split by an ancient fissure which, in the course of centuries, had slowly filled with windswept sand. Grasses had taken root there, and then bamboo and thorn. There was a scrub of cactus and the gray-green leaves of unnamed plants that found their moisture only from the damp of the night and were therefore as arid and harsh and cruel as the battle itself was to be.

Into this gap the Moros poured, their rifles slung and their bolos waved high, for they knew that the soldiers behind them would follow tight on their heels, and that then the guns which they had heard above them would be silenced, unable to fire with their own comrades so close.

And it was into this gap that Sullivan and Dawson had stumbled in their search for Medina; for Mrs. Sullivan, wife of an American officer under detention pending court-martial, and now, the wife of a deserter.

But the Infantry did not follow.

Colonel Devers, too, was a man of cunning. And so was General Kobbe. They had not reached their rank, nor their responsibility, by accident. Kobbe had said, back at base, speaking distinctly because he liked to be clearly understood the first time and no nonsense, "They'll try and get you to close quarters, Devers. You've got to keep them at arm's length. Once they get among our men with their bolos . . . This is not a casual skirmish with a small group of hit-and-run pirates. It's likely to be a full-scale battle."

Devers had said smoothly, tapping the back of his hand on the map, "And I want the Artillery to have a field day. The Infantry's job will be merely to block their retreat. If all goes well, for once in our lives we'll have him out in the open. The Infantry will take whatever cover it can and shoot at whatever targets it can find. But primarily, this is an Artillery battle. A bombardment."

Kobbe had nodded approvingly. Devers was an Infantryman, and it was good to see the rivalry between the branches of the service put so firmly in the background. Under Devers' cool competence, even the Cavalry, who always wanted to charge everything in columns of platoons, had willingly sent their horses back to the beach with hardly a murmur; except, of course, from the old veterans of the Civil War who still could not forget their youthful glories under Philip Sheridan, nor the ten thousand horses the Union had assembled into the most formidable force of Cavalry in United States history.

Now, Devers stood high and competent and alone on his pinnacle of granite, watching the long line move forward. Higher still above him, so far above as to be no more than a pinpoint against the bright afternoon sky, Lieutenant Desting sat panting on his horse, the tiny pony that he had incredibly brought on its pointed, sure-footed hoofs to this barren height, patting its foaming side where the sweat was still building up on its pain-heaving flank, watching the scene below him as though it were on a sand-table set out in the lecture hall for the instruction of junior officers.

Two hundred yards away from him, three men of Company F, Signal Corps, sat close by the tripod of their heliograph; one of his own Scouts who had placed them there was standing still and silent beside them. They were waiting for his signal, and they were sighted on the valley below.

Desting held his neckerchief high in his hand. A solitary bullet hit the rock far below him and whined in ricochet over his head, but he did not move. The Scout who was with the heliograph men raised his rifle and fired, almost casually, and then another shot went past Desting, close enough for him to hear, and the Scout fired twice again in rapid succession. In the silence that followed, Desting waited. When he was quite sure that the flank of the column beyond sight of the Colonel had reached the final point in its march forward, he brought his hand down and the helio began clicking. He heard the distant sound of Devers' shrill whistle, and somewhere a bugle sounded. And then the long line of Infantry ground to a halt and took on a new form as the men dropped to their bellies and lay in the firing position. He heard the muted sound of distant orders shouted, and little groups of men stood up and ran forward to straighten the line or to get better cover.

The helio ceased its clicking, and the three men scuttled back to the cover of the crater. Only then did Desting climb down from his horse, patting its wet neck. He held a handful of broken coconut meat under its mouth and waited till it lipped the pieces wetly away from him, and then he led the animal gently to the shadows cast by the boulders close by. The Scout who had been with the signalers jumped down lightly and came running over, crouching down with his broad felt hat that a soldier had given him, filling it with water from his canteen and watching the pony drink thirstily, patting its flank because he knew that this was what the American officer liked him to do.

There was silence all around. Somewhere between the waiting Infantry and the waiting Artillery, seven or eight hundred Moros, brightly dressed in red silks, yellow cottons, and purple velvets, with green pantaloons and orange shirts, with bright blue cummerbunds and golden sashes, with scarlet flowers in their hair—seven or eight hundred painted fighting men were waiting too, fingering the razor edges of their weapons, touching the hot barrels of their rifles, and waiting for the fierce, ecstatic, violent pleasures of the battle to begin.

Forty or fifty of them were women. They were the younger ones, mostly, between the ages of sixteen and thirty. Some of them carried spare bandoliers of ammunition for the men's rifles; some of them carried food; some of them carried bolos and were waiting, as feverishly as the men, for the sadistic satisfaction of blood. And some of them were there simply because, in time of trouble, it was their place to be with their men.

Among these was Medina.

She sat in a clump of yellow grass that waved gently above her head, her eyes cast down. Jokiri was beside her, hidden, waiting for his runners to come in and tell him where the enemy had taken their positions. His hand was on her arm in a gesture of unaccustomed and surprising affection, and when one of the Papuans who had been her bodyguard and was now a runner came slinking on his belly to whisper that he had seen the two men, the Englishman Dawson and the American officer Sullivan, and that they were high on the crater close to where the guns were, he said nothing for a long time. The Papuan waited patiently, picking at a sore on his leg. At last Jokiri told him to pass the word along to the datos that they would head for the crater where the guns were and make a frontal attack on them. When the runner had gone, he said to Medina, speaking very low in the guttural dialect he used with her, "They have brought him here so that I will not attack Jolo."

She said very softly, "Unless he has escaped to find me."

Jokiri turned his tiny, cruel, porcine eyes on her, frowning, wondering about the breach that had appeared between them. He thought for a long time over what she had said. Then in a silence heavy with hatred: "I do not think he is so clever."

"He escaped once before, remember."

"Yes. Because you helped him. Because you were tired of me."

She said steadily, pleading, "I beg you again—do not kill him. If there is any feeling for me left in your heart . . ."

"In my heart? I have no heart. My heart has been killed. I have only knowledge and hatred. Hatred for what has been done, and knowledge of what I must do."

"Then take my life instead."

"I do not need you dead. You will serve me as you have always served me. You will know that the strength of the seed that flows into you is the strength of my seed, and not the weak passion of this Christian. I will not spare his life, and I will not take yours."

She did not answer, and mistaking her silence, he leaned forward and pressed his hand deep into the fold of her jabul where it lay between the soft insides of her thighs. It was the first time that he had touched her since she had come back, trembling before his anger, to plead for the life of her lover. She felt the hard pressure of his hand as it brushed the cloth aside and the calloused tips of his fingers explored her body. She felt the pressure of his hand but it stirred no answering emotion, either of love or of hate; it was almost a formal caress, made dispassionately, and she could not tell whether it was done to indicate that the soiling of her had been forgiven in the urgency of his need for her, or whether it was merely to re-establish ownership of a chattel. Pressing his hand tight into her, fondling her, his eyes gleaming with hatred, he said, "I will give you, first, his genitals. You will press the blood out of them until they are dry."

Her head was low, and he could not see that she was crying.

In the silence, the two opposing armies waited.

# 14.

SULLIVAN TOO, WAS WAITING.

The body of a small, elderly Moro, bloody and silent in death, still lay close beside him, the red blood splashing the green and golden stripes of his pantaloons. His bright blue turban lay incongruously, down beside him, showing the sweat-dirt on its white lining. He moved away from it in disgust, stooping to wipe the blade of his barong on a tuft of grass. He said, "Where are they, Dawson? Our people?"

Dawson, crouched in the scrub beside him, his rifle ready, said, "Up on the top there—the Artillery. There's a couple of hundred Moros down there in the grass. God knows where the Infantry is."

"Behind the Moros, my guess. Give me the glasses."

He took the binoculars from Dawson and lay down on his belly on the hard rock, feeling the small sharp stones bite into his flesh. He focused them on the patch of grass that Dawson was pointing to, and in a little while he could make out the bright colors that he knew must be Jokiri's men. He marveled at their ability to hide. He moved over to one side, walking carefully, prepared to see one of them rise up at him again, cursing the scrub that could hide them, but not him, then lay down again and studied the lie of the land. But now he could see nothing, and he wondered if it had been an illusion. He rolled over on his back, watching Dawson hobble over to crouch beside him. He said wearily, "And now? The next step?"

"You tell me," Dawson said, grinning. "This is your personal fight. We came here to find your wife. So we found a couple of hundred warriors. And there'll be more of them, take my word for it."

"Someone will start shooting again soon. What the bloody hell's the Artillery doing?"

"Waiting, like all good soldiers. Waiting for orders."

"I suppose so. If Jokiri himself is down there—you suppose he might be?"

Dawson shrugged. "How the hell should I know? He's your father-in-law, not mine."

Sullivan was too tired to snap back at him, and Dawson said peevishly, "Hell, I'm getting as bad-tempered . . . Why don't we fire a couple of rounds into them just for the hell of it?"

Sullivan said stubbornly, "I want Jokiri. No good going off at half-cock. I can wait as long as they can."

"It won't be for long. As soon as Jokiri has decided what he wants to do, he'll do it. Take my word for it."

Knowing that a kind of careless coma was creeping over him, he looked up at the bright hot sky and said slowly, "We're right in the middle of God knows how many of them. Doesn't it scare the guts out of you?"

"I gave up being scared a long time ago. I tell you . . ."

Sullivan had seen the fright in Dawson's eyes when the Moro jumped them. He said, "When all this is over, I'm going back to the Garrison to take what's coming to me."

"You don't have to. I told you before, you can count on my help. Easy enough to get a boat on the other side of the island. We could go to Borneo—take a look at the pearl-beds. There's money to be made over there. More than money—there's forgetfulness. I put my country out of mind a long, long time ago. You could do the same. It's easy enough."

"I'm going back."

[ 231 ]

"To prison?"

"It won't be for long."

"Dishonorable discharge."

"I know. It doesn't matter."

He knew that it did matter. How was it possible, even at his age, to cut the umbilical cord, to separate the two distinct lives that had grown further apart with every passing year but were still bound together so firmly? He said aloud, "Until my mother dies—as long as she's still alive I have a duty to my family."

"Deserters are two a penny in your Army. Didn't you know? Take a look at the figures."

"They are rare in my family."

"My family."

"I think it's important."

"Just tell me why, Sullivan, and I'll listen."

"I don't know why."

"Honor, tradition, the decent thing to do—is that all it is? You'll rot in a filthy jail because it's better to die in prison than live like a free man?"

"I would not be free of my conscience."

He knew he was being stuffy again, and he waited for the outburst. Instead, Dawson said slowly, "In my more sober moments I might envy you. If I thought it would do me any good. But it won't, so you can go to hell with your pride. Me, I'll take a sword, a bottle of Scotch and a woman. It's all a man really needs out here." He said bitterly, "A woman . . ."

Sullivan looked at him curiously. "Did you have—were you—had you a wife in the camp? With the Moros? I often wondered."

Dawson recovered his good humor, though he spoke sarcastically. "Hell, no. Wasn't for want of opportunity. They tried to make me take a wife, once. But I didn't need one. They all thought it would be nice to have a white husband, so it was easy enough to get what I wanted. Moro, Tagalog, Montese, Visayan, Dyak—hell, I've screwed them all. Even those flat-nosed Papuan bitches. You don't get fussy after a while. Anything that's warm will do. And take it from me, those Papuans may not be much to look at, but

[ 232 ]

brother, spread 'em out on the ground . . . And now, that's all gone. For ever. A eunuch."

Sullivan said nothing. Feeling the silence, Dawson said, "Want a drink? Some whisky in my canteen."

"No. Not now."

He rolled over onto his stomach again and focused the binoculars on the Moros. Watching steadily, he said, "They're moving up. Up towards the crater."

Dawson held out his hand for the glasses, and when Sullivan gave them to him he watched for a while and said slowly, "They're creeping forward. I believe they're going to try and reach the top. They must know the Artillery's up there. Didn't they hear that gun go off?"

"They must have."

"Hell, they'll be wiped out before they get within rifleshot."

"You'd think so. There's a hundred yards—more—no cover."

"Unless there's a huge number of them. Have you ever seen them charge straight into guns?"

"No," Dawson said. "They will, though. If the heat's on hot enough. Look at it like this. The Infantry is supposed to be behind them—"

"It will be."

"Well, then, damn near two regiments behind them, the only way they can make the Infantry useless is to get up close to the guns so that the boys below can't fire."

"If they try that, Devers will take his men in for hand-to-hand combat."

"The one thing he ought to avoid."

Sullivan put the binoculars down and looked at Dawson. He said slowly, "I'm beginning to reason like a Moro; that's exactly what I was thinking. I tried to draw Medina close—close to us. Instead, they've drawn me closer to *them*."

Dawson was grinning again. He said jocularly, "Well, don't let that worry you. Moro, American or Englishman, we're all bloody savages, so why should you be surprised? A weapon in the hand and the lust for murder in our hearts. You think you're civilized because you wear a hat?"

[ 233 ]

Jokiri himself was the first man out of the shelter of the grasses. With five of his datos he reached the edge of the lava and halted, staring at the position on the skyline above him. He knew the guns were there, and he briefly wished he could find out how many of them there were. But he knew that he could not send a runner over the two or three hundred paces of open country and expect to get him back with the information he needed. So, by the instinctive rule of logic, he reckoned only on a number that his force could handle, knowing that if there were five guns or five hundred, he would still be able to take care of them. It was not in his philosophy to count the odds and they meant nothing to him. Why then, should he bother his mind with so abstract and academic a problem?

Earlier in the day the news had been brought to him; the Englishman and Captain Sullivan had left Jolo and were making their way up to the top of the mountain where the guns were. Jokiri, his face expressionless, had sent two runners to find their tracks. One of them had returned, saying that he had seen signs of them close by—a clear trail in the sandy path that led to the crater itself before it had petered out on the rock. The other runner, Jokiri was told, had moved in too close; the Captain had killed him.

Jokiri called his datos around him and told them of his plan to mount a frontal attack on the guns of the Artillery. One of them, older and wiser than the others, had shaken his head, fearing for the heavy odds against them, and Jokiri had listened to him patiently, for this was his custom; and then he had taken a vote from all of them, for this was his custom too and one of the reasons for which they respected him so highly.

They had voted for attack without further delay as soon as the warriors who had been sent to the western flank were in position. Pointing to the sky, Jokiri had said, "When the sun is there—we attack."

They had nodded their heads at his wisdom. They knew that, while in the coming night they could escape from the trap that had been laid for them by slipping silently through the lines of the Infantry behind them, yet this was not what their chief wanted. He wanted a fight, and he wanted to capture the American who had raped his daughter and gone off with her into the city. And they knew, or feared, that under the friendly cover of the darkness, perhaps the American might escape too. Jokiri had said to them clearly, "This man must not be killed. I want him."

They had nodded their approval. Only the priests were silent. Only the priests knew that a personal vendetta was risking the whole of the Moro army. For the priests were still smarting under Jokiri's insults. Sitting there cross-legged under the tall grasses, one of them had said slowly, raising a didactic finger, "When this girl was taken by the Englishman, she should have been killed. The Englishman too. It was not enough to deprive him of his manhood."

Someone answered him, an old priest who was bent and shriveled and full of wisdom. "And when she came back, there was no doubt. She told us. She said 'I have lain with this man because I love him.' Can she love an infidel?"

"She should have been killed. There will be much trouble for our people."

"Allah is wise and merciful, but this—this he cannot forgive."

"It is not only that she is his daughter. I believe other things."

There was silence now, because all of them had the same thought. The old man said at last, "So it has been said. She has spread wide her legs for the American, and Jokiri will not have her killed. It is because she spreads her legs also for him."

The silence was heavy and oppressing, because the evil things they had discussed could only lead to disaster. And now, almost as though he could read their thoughts, Jokiri made a terrible, sardonic, and wicked gesture, throwing their secular authority into their teeth. It was a calculated and deliberate gesture of defiance.

It meant so much to them, the virginity of a woman. So much that, when one of their Moslem girls married, the parents and the priests and the headman of the village, dressed in their finest robes, all gathered outside the hut where the marriage, immediately after the ceremony, was consummated; and in a little while, it was the custom for the bride's mother to go into the hut and bring out the blood-stained jabul which would show to the priests and to the approving villagers that the girl was a virgin. It had been the custom for thousands of years. But lately, since the foreigners had brought

[ 235 ]

their strange ways and their loose concepts to the Islands, many of the girls had lost their virginity long before their marriage, and a new custom, silently sanctioned by tacit understanding, had found its way into the villages. A chicken was slain as part of the wedding ritual, and in cases of necessity, its blood was sprinkled over the marriage gown, and no prestige was lost. This too had been the custom for a long, long time.

And now, waiting for the warriors to gather on the flank, knowing that the ancient enmity between priest and ruler must now be resolved for all time, Jokiri had made his studied, careful insult to the priests. With the tense expectancy of the battle driving the heat through his veins, he had pulled Medina into the shadows of the bushes, and there had stripped off the jabul with which she had clothed herself, and he had lain with her long and savagely, forcing himself deep inside her until all the sorrow for her had been drawn out of him with the fierce spasm of his passion for her. Then, he had taken his knife, and with the sharp point of it he had cut open his own arm, letting his blood flow onto her skirt. He had dressed her in his own gold sash, and had carried the blood-stained jabul to where the priests, glancing at him wonderingly over their shoulders, were waiting.

He had thrown the skirt down at their feet, scornfully, mocking their shocked silence. His tiny eyes gleaming, he had said, "She is my woman. This blood you see is her blood. She is mine."

He had not even bothered to hide the cut on his arm, letting them see it, wanting them to see it, making them believe; *She is a virgin because I say she is a virgin. This is the proof you will accept. I will not have it otherwise. This is her blood that you see. She is mine.*

When he had gone back to Medina and had lifted her to her feet (he could not see her tears), and had sent her to join the other women because the battle was soon to begin, the priests gathered together and almost without prompting from each other had begun a ritual incantation that would put a curse on Jokiri until he died, that would stay with him even beyond his death and would deny him entrance to his own particular paradise.

The incantation was slow and soft and subdued. But Jokiri heard it. Knowing what it was, he listened for a while and grunted his scorn. Then he shouted the order for the advance to begin.

Five hundred Moros rose out of the scrub like bright dolls in a nursery playground. Two hundred ran back to attack the long line of the Infantry and draw them forward under their own guns. The rest ran to the flanks, heading for the other side of the crater and the rear of the guns. The air was filled with their shrieks. Below, the Infantry began their methodical volleys under the calm control of Colonel Devers; above, the guns of the Artillery began their relentless pounding; and the ground in between them was a living, chaotic thing, a savage bowl of hatred that blazed into life and death under the hot bright sun, bursting with terror and with anguish and with pain.

Somewhere on the edge of the killing-ground, running from the shelter of the red boulders, bent double and filled with hatred, Sullivan shouted, *"To me!"*

He ran blindly forward into the melee.

It was like the bursting of a painful ulcer that has slowly been building up its poison until the flesh can no longer contain it. Had he been an introspective man, he would have known that the tensions inside him, which had really begun when, in that fight against Pangiran, he had felt sickened by his own prowess with a native weapon, had been slowly increasing their pressure ever since. The strange, uneasy marriage which had been forced upon him (though he would not admit it, even to himself) had served merely to make painfully clear to him that his emotions were those of a savage, because in his relationship with Medina the compelling need for her was an animal one. He could call it love or by any name he chose, but the relief he felt in her arms was bodily, and he could not gauge the degree by which the power of his spiritual affinity with her, growing now within him, was slowly superseding his purely physical need for her. And with the growth of this love, he came to know that Desting and Dawson had been right; what she was doing, she was doing for him. There was nothing left for him to do but break the hold Jokiri had on her by breaking Jokiri himself.

He knew that he had, with his escape, stepped over the tolerant limits within which an officer was expected to confine himself, that he could no longer look to the Army as his home, his life, and his *raison d'etre*. And it was his realization that the sole purpose of that Army was to turn him into the efficient fighting machine that he had become which so sickened him now. He knew there was no escape from it. And now that he had, physically, made an escape, he knew that it was nothing more than a temporary freeing of the bonds that were there for life, whether he wanted them or not; that they would claim him again, but, because he had once tried to lose them, would now be constricting rather than nurturing. He would become a cashiered officer, one of the breed, only a short step higher in the scale than the deserters like Dawson.

For the first time in his life, he felt alone. Not alone in the sense that no one was with him; but in a deeper fashion that left him hanging, as it were, between God and the animals, not knowing whether he should reach for the one or allow himself to be pulled down to the other.

His purpose now was twofold. He knew that he had to kill Jokiri, and he knew that he had to reclaim his wife. It did not matter to him how difficult it might be to accomplish this dual objective; like Jokiri, he could not count the odds. He knew only what he had to do, and he set about doing it, blindly.

He ran without thinking, towards the heat of the battle, only dimly aware that on the wide sweep of the battlefield the Moros, huge numbers of them, it seemed, were yelling savagely and racing upwards into the bursting mouths of the cannon. He caught a glimpse of his friend Desting, leaping over the edge of the crater's lip and racing towards them, and he wondered what he was doing. He saw the angry flashes as the guns exploded, and he saw shattered yellow limbs lying around him.

In the confusion he saw that he had joined the enemy and was racing with them towards the guns, and he wondered why he was not hit. Once, he found himself shoulder to shoulder with a surprised Moro, but neither of them made a move towards the other, and in a moment they separated. Then the violence of a bursting shell threw him off his feet and he rolled back down the hill a little way, then staggered to his feet again, feeling the shock of the explosion still within him.

He stumbled on again, and into the confused orbit of his senses a crimson flash of hair showed starkly bright in the chaos. He thought for an instant of coma that it was blood on the hair of his wife, and then reasoning came to him and it was a tuft at the handle of a campilan that was coming at him; a Moro was down on his knees, swinging at his legs. Without thinking, he shot him, watching the spreading blood, and then Dawson, hobbling and using his rifle as a crutch, was close beside him. There was confusion and absolute chaos, and wherever he looked there were shrieking warriors, many of them lying in their own blood on the hot dry slope of the volcano. He felt his hair grasped from behind and he swung round to drive his rifle-butt into a Moro's face. He saw Dawson stagger and fall, then swing wildly with a barong, pulling the blade of it across a yellow, wiry chest. In a little while, he heard a scream, and saw Dawson, his face taut with pain, his eyes wild, the saliva streaming down his face. He was on his knees as though he were praying, and both his arms were gone. He held up the bloody stumps of them and he was screaming "Help me, Sullivan—help me—" and then the screaming changed to an incoherent prayer, and Dawson the Moslem was whimpering, "Mother of Jesus—Mother of God—" and as he watched, sickened into immobility, a Moro stood above the mutilated Englishman and drove the point of a kris deep into his throat, and another ran up and began hacking at his head, splitting it open as an axe splits kindling. And then they were all round him and he could feel the clutch of their hands at him, and he fired his rifle until it was empty and then dropped it and wrested a barong from a dead hand and fought with it in a blind fury the like of which he had never before known. He saw a group of troopers running towards him, and he forced his way towards them.

He felt a hand on his shoulder and he threw himself round and slashed out wildly. It was Desting.

He could not pull the blow in time. The fury was on him, overpowering him, driving him beyond the confines of reason and coherence, and when the awareness came upon him he saw with revulsion that he had driven his barong deep into Desting's stomach. There was a moment of horror as the young Lieutenant stood there, his hands clutching at the yellow intestines that spewed themselves out of him, and then they fell, together, locked tight in an embrace. He stumbled to his hands and knees, crouching over him, fumbling for lucidity in the darkness, feeling that someone was pulling him to his feet.

He heard a voice shouting "Hold on, Captain!" And when he opened his eyes to see who it was, one of the troopers was charging towards him, a pistol in each hand, firing as he ran. There were others behind him, and together they pulled him over the lip of the cone and into the crater. He heard someone say, anxiously, "That was a close thing, Captain."

Someone shouted, "They're coming!" and an instant later the Moros were pouring over the crest and into the volcano, more than a hundred of them, tumbling over each other and running towards the broad plateau where the guns were.

A gunner was lying dead across a rifle, and Sullivan pulled it from under him and began firing, watching the Moros try to seize the guns. The explosion of them was loud in his ears; a young lieutenant was standing by calm and cool and giving the order to fire at point blank range. They fell like ants that had been crushed by a huge boot, and still they came, getting closer with every wave.

He heard the Lieutenant calling, "We can't hold, sir—they're coming over," and he saw him draw his saber and wait for them, standing firm and young and proud while he waited. As Sullivan watched, he saw a bullet take him through the center of the chest and throw him, crumpled, to the ground. Before the youth fell, a tiny, leaping, brown-skinned man with shaved eyebrows was on him, slicing at the already dead neck with a kris, not waiting for the tali-bong man to come up for his ritual duty. A Sergeant ran in to take his place, waving a sword in his left hand; his right arm had been cut off at the elbow, and the blood from the stump of it was spraying onto the remnants of his torn clothes. Then, for a moment, the sword was high in the air on one side of him and the bloody stump was high in the other, a good arm and the shattered remnant of one held out like a twisted crucifix; and in this position, all movement went from the Sergeant as he swayed, held for a moment, and then slowly sank to the ground. The tiny red spot at the back of his neck that looked like a bullet-hole took on the feathered form of a blow-gun dart, and as he swayed, on his knees now, his arms lowered and the sword falling from his dying grip, kneeling as though in prayer for his life once more, a bullet from an old-fashioned muzzle-loader, fired at close range, took the top of his head quite off.

There were shouts then, as the Infantry, urgently called forward by Desting when he had seen, before anyone else, that the guns would be overrun, tumbled in scattered, yelling formation over the lip and fell on the Moros with their bayonets. He saw Colonel Devers, bleeding from the chest and the arm and the neck, still in command, clambering over the rocks that stood between him and a group of Moros. He saw him fall as a bolo severed his leg, saw the weapon rise again and come down on the Colonel's skull. Then the soldier who had helped him to safety and whose name, though he did not know it, was Gillespie, fell with a kris in the throat. He saw Desting's head Scout—what was his name? Antonio?—stagger and fall to his face, a spear between his shoulder-blades. The gunner beside him, who was clutching a pistol in his hand, was dead; Sullivan pulled the weapon from his already stiff grasp and emptied it into the swarm of flesh around him, feeling the surge of tumult inside him as they fell back.

A small group of troopers, six or seven of them, with a broadshouldered Captain in their midst, were forcing a way through the tight-packed mass of them to the other side of the crater, where a fall of rocks had made a natural palisade. He fought his way towards them, striking out with a barong now, using a kris as well and still not knowing where he had acquired it.

He could not guess how many men he had killed, and he wondered why he himself had not been hurt; and when he looked at himself in surprise he saw that there was blood everywhere, on his chest, on his legs, on his arms, running down the side of his boots. He did not know how much of it was his. He reached the troopers, and someone shouted his name, but in the confusion he could not see who it was. They threw themselves among the rocks, finding that the cover behind them was littered with the dead and mangled bodies of their own men. A Papuan was bending over one of them, stripping off the boots, and the thickset Captain kicked him in the face and then shot him as he went reeling back. Sullivan saw that it was Morrison, the officer on the Court of Inquiry who had been so needlessly cruel about his wife. He wondered about the promotion.

*Medina, where are you?*

There was time to exchange a glance with Morrison. He tried to see what was behind the Captain's eyes, but he could not; and then Morrison too went down, silently, slowly, crumbling for no apparent reason, and one of the soldiers yelled and as he swung round he saw a tall, plump Montese, looking like a eunuch in his grass skirt, lifting the bloody bolo that had just killed Morrison. He swung at him as the soldier fired, and in the precise second that he saw the Montese drop his weapons and clutch at his stomach, where the bullet struck, he cut him across the shoulder, feeling the barong bite deep into the chest and fasten itself to the ribs so that he could not get it free. He dropped it then and seized a rifle, wondering what had happened to his kris, and began firing again at random, firing into the tight-packed rabble around him.

He heard a shrill whistle and saw the dense body of flesh part as if by magic, and in a moment there was no one in the crater except a score of Artillerymen, leaning on their guns and panting, staring at the empty carcasses of their comrades. He stared blankly for a moment, wondering what had happened, and then the Infantry came pouring over the lip, their bayonets gleaming. Someone shouted, "They're getting away—keep firing!"

A cheer went up from the gunners, and then on the other side the reserve under Major Leidekker was breaking over the edge, turning quickly and firing back the way they had come; a Major whom he did not know was urging the troopers on. He ran to the edge of the breastwork, over the broken, mutilated bodies, slipping in the blood of them, forcing himself to fire steadily with the others, not caring any more for anything but the blind necessity to kill and keep on killing. The Hospital Corps men were already breaking out their bandages, though there were few who had been wounded and left alive.

The last of the Moros had gone, and the firing had stopped. He leaned against a soft, resilient body which he knew was a dead trooper and he closed his eyes, letting the rifle slip from his grasp, knowing that his work was not yet done and that he had failed.

*Medina, where are you?*

He opened his eyes, then, and saw a woman, a Moro, climbing slowly to her feet some fifty yards down the side of the hill. She was clutching at her face, and he knew that she was blinded. Her skin was bloodied, and her naked breasts were long and skinny; there was a cut down the side of her leg which showed clearly through a rent in her jabul as she staggered off, unseeing, and when she dropped her hands and swung round, feeling for the air, he saw that half her face had been blown off. One of the soldiers muttered, "For Christ's sake," and raised his rifle. It was Fox, the young trooper who had lost the gun with Kowalski. His words were an invocation, and Sullivan heard him fire, then saw him cross himself.

*Medina, where are you?*

Leidekker was peering at him myopically, trying to find his features through the blood and dirt on his face. He said hesitantly, "Aren't you Captain Sullivan?"

Sullivan nodded, not looking at him. He stared around the perimeter of the crater and started, without feeling, to count the dead, not knowing why he was doing so. There were more of them than he could count in two minutes, perhaps a hundred and fifty of them, and the slopes of the mountain were littered with many more. Leidekker said stiffly, "I thought you were under open arrest, Sullivan."

He did not answer. He picked up a rifle and climbed mechanically over the rocks that stood between him and the dead bodies out there. He pushed aside a trooper who tried to restrain him—or was it Leidekker?—and walked over to where Desting lay, the camouflage branches that were strapped round his waist almost hiding his young blond body. He found Dawson too, and did not know how a carcass could be so emptied of blood, so yellow and fragile and hollow-seeming. There were many men whom he knew there, men from his own Regiment. Three officers lay together in a mangled heap as though they had died defending each other; all of them were headless. He stood for a moment looking at the body of the Moro woman who had been blinded, and wondered if it had been from a shell or perhaps from one of his own bullets. Her half-naked body was scarred and ugly with age, and her jabul was held by an empty bolo scabbard. He turned over the body of one dato with his foot, hoping it was not Jokiri, and then another and another. Someone shouted at him from the enclave of the crater, but he paid no heed, and in the heavy, brooding silence he walked on, wondering where the Moros had gone, wondering how they had broken through the barrier of the Infantry, through the alternate companies that were holding a line below to prevent a breakthrough.

And then he pulled up short.

It was the sixth sense of the instinctive soldier again. He thought of it with dispassion as he stood listening for a repetition of the sound that had disturbed him. It could have been the stirring of a foot on shale, or a rustle in the scrub—or the sigh of a dying man. And as he stared and waited, his rifle ready, he saw a man rise slowly out of the ground before him, rising up from the miraculous cover of an inch-high shrub that he would have thought could not have concealed a snail. He threw up his gun in an automatic, mechanical gesture, thinking of Desting and holding his fire.

It was Jokiri.

His yellow, royal turban was gone, and his embroidered jacket was torn till it was little more than a rag. The green striped pantaloons were ripped down one leg and a crude bandage had been fastened around the calf; he was barefoot. The campilan scabbard at his belt was empty, and the bandoliers that hung round his wiry chest were empty too; he had no gun.

Sullivan lowered his rifle. For a long time, the two men stood facing each other, neither of them willing to make a move. Then Sullivan dropped his weapons with a clatter to the ground and moved slowly forward.

He did not know, even as he moved, what was in his mind. His clarity of thought had gone, and it seemed for a moment that he was waiting for Jokiri to kill him. And then, as he stepped forward, he became conscious of the golden-bronze form that was at his feet.

[ 244 ]

He did not dare to take his eyes from Jokiri, but then he knew that he must and he lowered them to look at the silent, motionless bundle that had so suddenly obtruded itself upon his view.

It was Medina, and she was dead.

She lay where Jokiri had found her, with his golden sash still wrapped around her. There was a small round hole in her side where a bullet had gone in, and the stain of her blood was on the golden sash. He stared at her in horror for a moment, forgetting everything except the overpowering love he had for her, and which he knew now had been with him since the day when he had seen her tears for the first time.

"For God's sake," he had said, "for God's sake throw that filthy stuff away."

He had watched her tears coming, watched with uneasiness, unable to penetrate the obscurity of the feeling that was wrenching at him and which he now knew was the torment of his love for her. The ulcer had been opened, and the free flow of the pain had left behind it a clarity in which he saw her clearly as the fire that had been held out for him to grasp, the fire which he had let die down until, in its own ashes, it had been smothered in the monstrous injustice of death.

He knelt and touched her body. It was still warm, and the warmth that flowed from it into his hands brought back the pain of his love and the urgent need for her, and he felt the tears coming into his eyes, and then Jokiri was on him, tearing at him with his bare hands, gouging at his eyes, ripping at his throat like an animal.

He rolled over with him and struck out with all his force, hitting with the edge of his hand at the ear as Desting had once taught him to do, rolling over and over on the hard ground and feeling his head being lifted and smashed back against it. He pushed the chief away and stumbled to his feet, and as Jokiri rolled free he lashed out at him with his foot, a savage unreasoning blow that caught him in the throat and sent him rolling down the slope. He threw himself after him then, leaping blindly on him with outstretched arms, feeling the impact of the lava rock as Jokiri rolled clear and let him fall on his face.

There was blood in his eyes when he staggered to his feet, and the Moro was on his back, wrenching him round, trying to break his spine with a knee between his shoulder blades. The strength was gone from him, and he fought blindly, twisting himself round to free the load from his neck, feeling the pain in him, throwing himself back on the ground to break the hold. The chief's sharp teeth were in his throat now, and the pain was excruciating; he could hear the grinding as the teeth met and wrenched at the tendons of his neck. He fancied he could feel the brown betel nut poison of them working in his bloodstream and he seized an ear and twisted it, wrenching it forcibly off and feeling the slime of it in his hands.

His neck was free now, and he doubled his fist and drove it into the chief's face, feeling the nose break, then jabbed his thumb hard into the tiny eye that was gleaming with a premature triumph. There was no sound from him, and he felt an overwhelming desire to make him scream, but he could not. He felt the eyeball burst under his thumb, and still there was no sound. They rolled over and over on the rocks together, and once he tried by sheer weight to break his opponent's back over a boulder, forcing his spine into an arc and bearing down with all the weight of his great height, driving his fists repeatedly into Jokiri's throat. Then his fist met rock, and he knew in his blindness that Jokiri had slipped free. He swung round as the brown arms came at him, throwing himself backward and holding his adversary high over his own supine body. He heard the sound of a shot, and knew, suddenly and unaccountably, that Jokiri was dead and that the blood that was falling into his face and blinding him was Jokiri's blood.

He dropped him then, letting him fall clumsily to the ground. He looked up in alarm at the shadow that fell across him. It was Leidekker, and he was standing there with his feet wide-spaced, blowing the smoke out of the barrel of his automatic. There were three troopers standing beside him, and one of them placed the bayonet of his rifle against the dead chest of the chief and leaned on it slowly, driving it through him and into the ground; he heard the scrape of its point on the lava.

He pulled himself from under the bleeding body and stood up, staring down at the man they had killed for him. He heard himself scream, and was conscious that he was trying to speak rationally but could not: "Why—why did you do that? Why?"

His voice was hoarse and shrill and broken, like the voice of a madman. He threw himself at Leidekker, and the trooper who had driven his bayonet into Jokiri stepped forward quite slowly and pulled him away. Another soldier took him by the shoulders and held him as he struggled, and then he went limp and waited till they released him, and not hearing what Leidekker was saying, he stooped down and picked up the shattered body of his wife in his arms, covering her carefully with the golden sash that he knew had been Jokiri's, holding her tight against his chest in the futile hope that he might perhaps hear the last beatings of her heart, knowing that they were together once more and that now nothing would ever separate them again.

He could not feel the pain in his limbs as he moved slowly towards the crater, past the dead body of his friend Desting whom he had killed, past the dead body of Dawson who was going to steal a boat so that they could all go to Borneo and look for pearls together, past the blinded Moro woman whom the young Catholic soldier, in sadness and in anguish, had shot, past the dead bodies of his men and the silent orderlies who were gathering them together, past the burial details which were already looking for patches of softer earth in which they could start digging. He did not know that Leidekker and the troopers, exchanging worried glances, had fallen into step behind him.

He went to the edge of the crater and stood there for a moment, watching the remnants of the Infantry fall into column behind the young Captain who had brought up the reserve, and when they were ready and started moving out, he followed them, still holding his wife tight in his arms, feeling only the pain of the stillness in her body.

The long column clambered slowly over the crest of the ridge. The pale gold of the sun was striking obliquely at the purple top of the mountain, lighting it with golden splendor. They began the long walk down to the valley, down to the river they called the Tubig Hasa'an. The track twisted and turned far below them, a distant ribbon that wound its dusty way through the forests, across the rice paddies, and over the green haciendas.

It would lead them, eventually, to the broken walls of Jolo.